Exit Strategy

A Robert Fairchild Novel

By Matthew McCleery

Praise for 'The Shipping Man' Series

A gripping novel...Seamlessly woven into the plot are keen insights into the arcane worlds of Wall Street and Marine Transport. In view of the author's second resounding success, his readers will cry out for yet another book to complete the trilogy.
— **Wilbur Ross**, *United States Secretary of Commerce*

The fictional Robert Fairchild is one of the hottest names on Wall Street.
— **Isaac Arnsdorf** and **Mary Childs**, *Bloomberg*

Set at the intersection of finance and the high seas, *The Shipping Man* is essential reading for anyone with shipping stocks in their portfolio, but, for the rest of us, it's simply a great read.
— *Forbes*

It is very hard to marry entertainment with education — especially in the world of finance and shipping, but McCleery succeeds spectacularly in doing so.
— **Mohnish Pabrai**, *Managing Partner, Pabrai Investment Funds*

What else do the rich like? Boats! Rich people, I have been led to believe, enjoy the boating lifestyle. And if you want to read a book about boats, a book that you can read about boats is *The Shipping Man*, by Matthew McCleery. I hesitate to recommend it too strongly, in part because you've probably already read it. *Bloomberg Businessweek* reported that everyone on Wall Street has read it this year, and they've apparently all gone out and either bought cargo ships or, if they already had cargo ships, they hired McCleery to sell them.
— **Matt Levine**, *Bloomberg*

To read more reviews, please visit
shippingmanbooks.wordpress.com.

For the Seafarers

This book is respectfully dedicated to the nearly two million hardworking women and men at sea who keep the 80,000+ vessels in the global fleet moving. Often away from family and always battling the world's last untamed frontier, they are the true heroes of international trade.

Acknowledgments

A special thank you to Jeff Parry, who helped me start this book, and Steve Whelley, who helped me finish it. I am also very grateful to Suzy Barnard for allowing me to use her paintings on the cover of all three books in this series. You can see more of Suzy's fabulous work at www.suzybarnard.com. Thanks to Julia Hull for pulling the book together and Alexa Lawrence for cleaning it up.

Once again, I have been humbled by the help I've received from friends around the world. They encouraged me, inspired me, graciously suffered through early drafts and tried to make sure the details were correct. I'm sure I didn't get everything right in this book, but without them I would've gotten a lot more things wrong. I am grateful for the help I received from: Jim Lawrence, Lars-Peter Madsen, Tony Gurnee, Robert Bugbee, Mike, Michael, Buffy, Rufus, Murphy and Homer McCleery, Michael Tusiani, Morten Arntzen, Harris Loukopoulos, Riaz Khan, John Kulukundis, Stefan Rindfleisch, Hamish Norton, Ioannis Martinos, Scott Borgerson, Brian Ladin, Nicolai Heidenreich, Rick Rockhold, JM Radziwill, Kees Koolhof, Nick Bailey, Manos Kouligkas, Nick Georgiou, Anil Sharma, Evan Sproviero, Michael Parker, Arlie Sterling, Lorraine Parsons, Mary Crooks and Elaine Lanmon.

About the Author

Matthew McCleery is the President of Marine Money. He is also Managing Director of Blue Sea Capital, Inc., where he advises shipowners and investors on ship financing, mergers and acquisitions, and vessel investment transactions. He can be reached at mmccleery@marinemoney.com.

Prologue

It was just after midnight when he first noticed the yellow headlights twinkling in the frigid Norwegian night. With a cigarette glowing in his mouth and an oil-stained rag slung over his shoulder, sixteen-year-old Coco Jacobsen leaned against the solitary red petrol pump and waited.

He watched in silence as a dark blue Rolls-Royce slowly emerged from the darkness like a surfacing sea creature. The image reminded him of the hilarious bedtime stories his dad used to tell him about a kraken named Lars who dreamed of having a career on Broadway. That was before a Christmas gale sent him and his commercial fishing boat on a one-way voyage to the bottom of the icy North Sea.

Coco remained motionless as the massive vehicle pulled off the unlit asphalt highway and onto the gravel of the Esso station where he had been working the graveyard shift ever since his dad died. When the car came to a stop and the throaty rumble fell silent, the only thing Coco could hear was the pinging of the cooling engine and an owl screeching in the distance.

The chauffeur exited the right-hand-drive vehicle, quickly shuffled to the opposite side, and opened the back door. A few seconds later, Coco was stunned to see Hilmar August Reksten, the richest man in Norway and one of the richest in the world at that particular moment in time, unfold from the backseat. The celebrity shipowner was about to change the trajectory of Coco Jacobsen's life — but not before he had relieved himself behind a stand of cedar trees sagging under the weight of heavy snow.

When the tall man reappeared, he walked aggressively toward Coco and stopped when he was just a few feet away. Coco looked him over from head to toe. He was swaddled in a long black cashmere overcoat buttoned to the top. The combination of his upturned collar and the iconic plaid scarf synched tightly around his neck made it appear as if his bald and savagely tanned head was floating atop his body. His mouth was scowling, but his eyes were smiling.

"May I help you, sir?" Coco finally asked the man, who was still silently inspecting him, the plumes of his frosty breath slowly rising into the air.

"I think we can help each other," he replied as he placed a white card into Coco's greasy hand. "Don't lose that."

"What is it?"

"That's the business card of Mr. Arne Johnson," the man said, his voice bouncing. "He is my exclusive shipbroker in Oslo."

"Okay."

"He will hire you to help charter my oil tankers. Learn everything you can about the shipping business, because after one year, you are on your own. You're going to get knocked around a lot, all shipowners do, but you need to have grit to survive in this game."

"Why are you doing this for me, sir?" Coco asked as the man began to walk back to the car, the frozen ground crunching beneath his feet. "You don't even know me."

He turned around to face Coco.

"You just happened to be in the right place at the right time, which is what shipping is all about," he said, smiling with his eyes. "While we were at dinner tonight, my wife told me that I won't ever be my best until I help someone else be their best. She has given me a lot of good advice in my life, so I decided to try it immediately, because I am running out of time."

"I don't know what to say," Coco said and lowered his head respectfully.

"Good. It's almost always better to shut up and listen," the old man replied as he dug into the pocket of his flannel trousers and fished out a thick wad of Kroner notes held together with a sterling-silver money clip.

Coco nodded silently.

"Take this," the man said, pressing the bulging money clip into Coco's rough hand. "Use it for train fare to Oslo and to get a room, and some new clothes," he added as he dropped back into his cavernous backseat. "And get a haircut while you're at it."

Coco stared down in disbelief at the wad of money in his open hand. It was more cash than he had ever seen in his life.

"How can I thank you?" he asked.

The man hesitated as he gave serious thought to the question. "You can thank me by figuring out what your superpowers are and putting them to good use," he said. "That would make me very happy."

"But I don't think I have any superpowers," Coco said, his confidence badly damaged from years of frustrating failure in school.

"You are clearly a hardworking kid, and working hard is the greatest superpower of all," the man replied, smiling.

"I hope that's enough," Coco said, momentarily thinking about his mom and dad.

"And who knows, kid, you might even end up being the chosen one."

"Chosen for *what?*" Coco asked.

"Maybe you are the special person who will somehow manage to bring shipowners together in one room and convince them that if they work together, they have the power to change the world."

"I'll always do my best, sir," Coco said, closing his eyes and lowering his head as if accepting an assignment that he would accomplish or die trying.

"And let me give you a bit of advice," he said as he looked up at Coco. "Always leave the party while you're still having fun, that way you'll have nice memories, and that's worth a lot," the old man said just as the chauffeur slammed the door with a heavy thud.

Chapter 1

Coco Jacobsen squeezed the Wilson tennis ball so hard he could have crushed it. As he prepared to serve for the set, the sixty-five-year-old Norwegian oil tanker tycoon pulled down on the bill of his white cap to block the blinding Bahamian sunshine.

With sweat and sunblock stinging his pale blue eyes, he carefully studied the position of his opponent, a bespectacled and unnaturally muscular eighty-year-old private equity titan from New York named Horace Buttersworth.

It was the finals of the Churchill Cay Member/ Guest Tournament, and Coco was battling his way back from a deep deficit. He had dropped the first set four to six and had been down three to five in the second set before he managed to shift the momentum in his favor.

The sight and sounds of Coco's comeback had been so electrifying that it had attracted the substantial crowd now clustered around the pro shop's lush green lawn one court away. The spectators were getting rowdier with each point and every sip of supercharged Mount Gay and tonic. The suspense was palpable.

Coco was now beating Horace six to five in the seven-point tiebreaker — and it was his serve. If he won the point, he would win the set. If he won the set, he was confident that he would pummel the octogenarian asset manager in the third and take home the giant silver trophy glittering on the folding card table twenty feet away. The pressure was on.

As a self-made shipping magnate who'd made and lost hundreds of millions on the back of black swan events from crude oil contango to coups d'état, Coco almost always scored his biggest wins after everyone had written him off. But today he was tired.

Ships never stopped working, which meant shipowners and their crews never stopped working either. He had been on the phone until midnight negotiating a problematic scrubber installation with a Chinese shipyard and was woken at 4 a.m. when his shipbroker, Peder Hanssen, called from London to tell him the bad news: A Russian oil trader based in Switzerland had backed out of a deal to charter two of his Very Large Crude Carriers (VLCCs) after a crude oil arbitrage opportunity suddenly closed.

That meant half of his thirty supertankers were operating close to breakeven — and the other half were sitting in drydock earning nothing. It was a disaster. He knew the tanker market would turn eventually, it always did, but his highly leveraged fleet was hemorrhaging cash and he was running out of time.

Coco had made countless bets and trades during his fabled forty-five-year career, but nine months earlier he had executed the best one by far: packing up his wife, Alexandra, and their twin nine-year-old boys, Thor and Olav, shuttering his Curzon Street office and Knightsbridge mansion, and exchanging rainy London for a sunny life aboard their eighty-meter yacht, *Kon Tiki*.

The Jacobsen family embarked in Monaco the previous June. They spent the summer gunkholing around the Med before crossing the Atlantic and winter wandering through the West Indies, ultimately settling on the French island of St. Bart's.

But when Alex's younger sister died suddenly, making Alex and Coco the legal guardians of their disabled niece, Maisy, they hoisted the anchors and headed north to Churchill Cay, a 600-acre gated preserve on the island of New Providence. The Bahamas were as close as they could get to Maisy's residential school in Miami without actually being *in* the United States — where Coco was subject to arrest on a warrant stemming from a bogus charge.

When Coco's elderly opponent crouched down on two brace-wrapped knees, the inebriated pro shop posse fell silent. The six-and-a-half-foot Coco knew it was time to unleash his explosive 100-mile-an-hour first serve; it was a low-probability, high-return strategy that mimicked his style of ship owning.

He began a series of OCD-inspired pre-serve rituals. He tugged at the sweat-soaked white shirt clinging to his powerful shoulders. He bounced the tennis ball seven times with his left hand. He took twelve deep breaths and slowly exhaled through his nose.

Once he was fully focused and adequately oxygenated, the towering Scandinavian shipowner mechanically tossed the ball high into the air and brought his racquet back. For one magic moment he resembled the luminous silver figure standing atop the coveted trophy.

But just before he made violent contact with the ball, producing a projectile capable of killing the zillionaire, the silence was brutally shattered.

"Hey, um, so, I'm looking for someone named Coco Jacobsen," shouted a stammering, high-pitched voice. "I think it's actually a *dude*."

The millisecond lapse of focus caused Coco's cannon to misfire, sending the tennis ball soaring high over the black wire fence before bouncing high off a parked golf cart.

"I believe that one was out," Horace chuckled under his breath as he took a few insulting steps toward the net, in preparation for Coco's significantly softer second serve.

Coco tried to remain calm, but when he heard the snarky snicker from the spectators, the combination of insult and injury caused his blood to boil. He squinted his eyes and slowly scanned the crowd, searching for the perpetrator.

"I'm taking a medical time out," the Norwegian declared as he marched off the court.

"By all means, Coco," Horace replied. "But according to the rules you only have three minutes."

Horace was delighted to let Coco willingly squander his all-important momentum while he took the opportunity to sit down, catch his breath, and enjoy a sip of icy water in the shade of a giant blue umbrella.

Coco was seething with rage as he scuffed his feet across a freshly swept clay court to unload on whomever had just cost him the critical serve — and possibly even the tournament. As he drew closer, he immediately identified the likely perpetrator: a pasty-skinned and porky five-foot-six male with a mess of uncombed blond hair.

The boy was wearing white mesh gym shorts, pink flip-flops, and an untucked blue T-shirt that read *Coed Naked Lacrosse*. The kid stood out like a sore thumb among the ritzy retired resort crowd. Coco wondered who had allowed the boy to enter the club.

"Didn't your parents teach you that it's rude to talk when someone is serving for set point?" Coco said as he stormed toward the boy, who now appeared to be giggling as he looked down and texted on his phone. "Tennis is a game of *focus!*" he shouted.

"My grandfather sent me down here from Connecticut to give you this, Mr. Jacobsen," the awkward young man looked up at the giant Norwegian while holding out a thick envelope. It was shrink-wrapped in plastic and marked *Urgent, Sensitive and Highly Confidential* in aggressive red ink.

"Your *grandfather?*"

"Yeah, he sent me and a couple of my fraternity brothers to Atlantis Resort as payment for hand-delivering this thing to you," he said. The boy glanced back at his compadres, who were staring down at their phones. "He said sending us here was cheaper than sending the letter by courier. And he said he can write off our whole trip as a business expense."

"Give me that thing," Coco hissed as he attempted to grab the dossier so he could return to his match.

"Not so fast," the boy said as he stepped outside of Coco's considerable reach.

The rubbernecking crowd fell silent. They were captivated by the bizarre standoff between the disheveled American boy and the mysterious and long-haired Norwegian shipping magnate whose massive yacht had barely squeezed into the seventy-six-slip marina late on Christmas Eve.

"But you said it was for me?" Coco complained.

"It is, but gramps wants me to text him a selfie of me giving it to you," the boy said. "His lawyer needs proof that you received it."

"Yeah, and we want to put it on our Instagram story," one of the friends mumbled without looking up.

"I realize you aren't yet a member, Coco, so I'd like to remind you that phone use is strictly prohibited on club property," Horace called out from his sitting position.

"Looks like you aren't getting the envelope," the smart-ass kid replied.

"Just take the picture," Coco said bitterly, and he struck a pose that showed him taking possession of the document.

"It's been a pleasure doing business with you, sir," the boy said when the transaction had been concluded.

"I hope my sons don't turn out like you," Coco said.

The Norwegian was fuming angry as he put the envelope under his arm and returned to the court to resume the match. As he feared, the encounter had killed his concentration. He immediately shanked the next serve to double fault and then summarily made two unforced errors to lose the annual tournament 4–6, 6–7(6).

"Jah, but I am happy you won the match, Horace," Coco said with a smile as he approached the net to shake hands. "Congratulations."

"Thanks, Coco, but I'm a little surprised to hear you say that," Horace said smugly as their hands came together. "You seemed a bit frustrated out there."

"Letting you win was the least I could do after all the charity that you private equity guys have generously given to the shipping industry," Coco chuckled.

"Very funny, Coco, but a tennis match isn't the only thing you are going to lose." Horace laughed as he raised one black eyebrow and glanced at the envelope under Coco's arm. "I believe your luck has finally run out, Mr. Jacobsen."

Chapter 2

After accepting his lousy second-place ribbon, Coco watched in horror as Horace posed for photos — the investor had the giant tennis trophy clutched in one muscular arm and his emaciated trophy wife in the other.

Once the ceremony was over, Coco proceeded directly to the white wooden chaise that had been left in the middle of the thick lawn and violently threw his tennis bag to the ground.

He ripped open the envelope that the kid had given him, pulled out the two-inch-thick document, and quickly flipped through the forty-five pages, scanning for buzz words. He didn't need to actually read the legalese to get the gist of it: His historically gentlemanly German ship lender, Reeperbahn Landesbank (RLB), had just sold his $750 million loan to a distressed credit fund in New York City called Loan-to-Own Capital (LTO).

Things were getting very ugly, very fast. The wire transfers for the secondary market loan sale had barely cleared, but LTO was already claiming the debt was in default and was threatening to foreclose on his fleet of aging supertankers. He needed answers, and he needed them now.

Like a dog digging for a buried bone, Coco began rifling through the bottom of his tennis bag with both hands in search of his phone. Within seconds the manicured lawn was littered with a debris field of towels, sunblock, aspirin, Marlboros, peppermints, sweatbands, a bunch of Euro notes, bandages, and half a dozen rolls of neon yellow over-grip.

When he finally fished out the device, he poked at the cracked screen until he had dialed the mobile phone number of Gerhard Haffenreffer, the head of ship finance at RLB in Hamburg.

"What the hell, Gerhard!" Coco shouted into his phone as he smacked his white sneakers together to relieve his rage and remove the red clay before he went back aboard the yacht.

"Good afternoon, Coco."

"Not for me it's not."

"I gather you've received the letter from LTO Capital," the German said gravely.

The German banker was fantastically fit and stylishly bald. He was sitting in his elegant nineteenth-century stone office, gazing out across the glassy evening water of the Binnenalster. On the far side of the lake, he could see the twinkling yellow lights of the posh Four Seasons hotel; ironically, that was where he had agreed to arrange the $750 million loan for Coco over a crispy Wiener schnitzel and a chilled Grüner Veltliner the previous summer. Fortunes changed quickly and violently for shipowners and their financiers.

"I sure did!" Coco shouted. "A pimple-popping college kid from Connecticut just served it on me while I was in the finals of a tennis tournament!" Coco shouted. His *grandfather* sent him down here to give it to me, and he took a photo like I'm some kind of circus animal!"

Gerhard didn't feel right playing the role of parent to the remarkable Coco Jacobsen, a shipping rock star who had ascended from being a petrol-pumping eighth-grade dropout to being top dog at the most exclusive, high-stakes table in the world — the supertanker spot market.

"Served it, during tennis," the German mused softly. "Nice pun."

"That little turd cost me the tournament! And he made me look like a criminal in front of my new friends," Coco said. "Just when I'm trying to make a good first impression down here!"

A Danish shipowner friend had sponsored Coco for membership at the exclusive and low-key Churchill Cay Club, where he was permitted to keep *Kon Tiki* in a slip while his membership application was under review. But the membership committee had gone silent for several weeks, and Coco feared it was because his background check had exposed something sordid.

Like many aggressive international shipowners, Coco was the defendant in dozens of legal cases. They ranged from trading with countries like Cuba, Venezuela, and Iran, which were sanctioned by some countries but not others, to oily water separator violations and dozens of different tax disputes.

But the mother of them all was the outstanding warrant for Coco's arrest that had been activated by his eighty-nine-year-old archrival, Didier "Rocky" DuBois, the cantankerous Cajun CEO of American Refining Corporation, one of the most active charterers of the global fleet of nearly 800 supertankers.

Rocky had falsely accused Coco of perpetrating systematic theft of ship's fuel, known in the industry as "bunkers." Like rental cars, ships on charter had to be returned to their owner with the same amount of fuel they had when they were picked up; if a ship's crew frothed up the fuel to overstate its quantity upon delivery to the charterer, a shipowner could pocket millions of dollars in free money when the charterer topped up the tanks before giving the ship back.

When Rocky's lawyers filed the bogus charges in a Houston courthouse and they were made public, the shipping industry's widely read newspaper *Ahoy Matey!* ran the giant frontpage headline *Cappuccino Bunker Caper* above a file photo of Coco laughing as he drank coffee with a bunch of shipping buddies at Theatercaféen inside Oslo's Hotel Continental.

"It must have been very embarrassing to have a kid do that to you in front of the members," Gerhard said.

"Yes, but how could *you* have done this to me?" Coco wailed. "I thought we were friends."

"We *are* friends," Gerhard pleaded.

"No friend would sell my loan to some blood-sucking vampire hedge fund without even telling me," Coco said.

"It wasn't me," the German said.

"Wasn't you? Don't lie to me, man!" Coco laughed like a lunatic.

"I didn't do it."

"I've been one of your best customers for twenty years. I borrowed and repaid billions of dollars from all the banks you've worked at. I've paid you tens of millions in fees. I have helped put your kids through university and probably even paid for that fancy ski chalet in Kitzbühel!" Coco said, the volume of his voice rising with each spoken word.

"I am very appreciative of our relationship," Gerhard said. "I hope my capital has also been helpful to you."

"Money is money," Coco said.

"Only when you have enough of it," Gerhard said softly.

"But come on, the least you can do is be honest with me!" Coco moaned as if he were performing the final scene of a Shakespearean tragedy.

He was now screaming so loud that he received a scathing reprimand from a surly line judge at the ladies' doubles final fifty yards away. Between the raucous behavior, the outstanding warrant, and the flagrant public phone use, Coco knew he might soon have to find a new marina for *Kon Tiki* after his application for membership was rejected.

Despite the Academy Award–quality theatrics that Coco tried to bring to all his business encounters, the truth was he wasn't totally surprised RLB had sold his loan; ever since the Great Financial Crisis ten years earlier, European commercial banks had been shedding shipping debt in an effort to exit the challenging industry. But what surprised him, and irritated him, was that his friend Gerhard hadn't given him the courtesy of a heads-up.

"Of course I would have told you, Coco," Gerhard said, "but I honestly didn't even *know* the loan was being sold. I was just informed yesterday. That's when I was told the transaction had been finalized and you would be receiving the letter from LTO."

"But you are the head of the bank's ship finance department!" Coco protested. "How could you *possibly* not have known?"

"They don't always tell the relationship manager when they decide to exit a transaction prematurely," Gerhard said. "They don't want it to get personal."

"Who is *'they'*?" Coco demanded. "I did that deal with *you!*"

"The ESG people," Gerhard said softly. "They are the ones who pulled the trigger."

"The *who?*" Coco asked. "What the hell are you talking about?"

"The ESG people," he repeated. "It's a newly formed task force within the bank that's in charge of auditing every single one of our borrowers and assessing their strategies for managing the risks associated with environmental, social, and governance issues. If the bank doesn't like what they see, they take action."

"An ESG *task force?* An *audit?*" Coco laughed. "Is this some kind of joke?"

"Not at all," Gerhard said. "ESG originated as activism, and it has now spread to capitalism. All the big financial institutions are doing it."

"But I am in business to make money," Coco said. "So are you."

"The data shows that companies with strong ESG policies actually outperform the ones with weak ones."

"Jah, but this is exactly why I have remained a *private* shipowner," Coco complained as he watched a Hobie Cat captained by two tourists being pummeled by a surf break as it slowly drifted toward a jagged coral reef. "Let the NYSE and NASDAQ companies worry about things like ESG!"

"Not even private shipowners are safe from ESG anymore," Gerhard said. "Within the next few years it will be as compulsory as having audited financial statements. Your ESG profile will be requested by your charterers, your insurance companies, and your lenders before they will do business with you."

"Lenders like *you*," he said with disgust. "I know you Germans are excited about wind and solar and Birkenstocks but —"

"It's not just the Germans," Gerhard interrupted. "In fact, we were one of the last major shipping banks to sign onto the Poseidon Principles."

"Poseidon Principles? You mean the Ernest Borgnine movie?" Coco asked.

"That's the *Poseidon Adventure*," Gerhard said. "The Poseidon Principals is an agreement among banks that requires them to monitor and systemically reduce the quantity of CO_2 emissions produced by the ships in their loan portfolios."

There were a variety of frameworks and agreements that had been put in place to help financial institutions integrate ESG factors into their investment analysis and decision-making, but the Poseidon Principles was special; it was the first time an individual industry had created and implemented a self-imposed system to track and reduce carbon emissions — a notable achievement for an industry some felt was slow to adapt to change."

"But why on earth would you join the Poseidon Principals? That just gives a free ride to the lenders who don't sign it."

"We signed it because we want the CO_2 emissions of our loan portfolio to be aligned with the United Nations' goal of cutting the shipping industry's 2008 greenhouse gas emissions by fifty percent before 2050 — while trying to get to net zero emissions as soon as possible. The industry is currently producing one billion tons of CO_2 every year, so the potential for improvement is thrilling."

"I don't find this thrilling," Coco said.

"Even small reductions can have a big impact," the German said. "A few percent here and there can really make a difference."

"But 2050 isn't for thirty years!" Coco shouted.

"This will be a long transition," Gerhard admitted.

"My ships and I will be scrapped by then."

"*Recycled*," Gerhard said.

"Why didn't you guys just let my loan go full term like we agreed and then refuse to roll it over in five years when it came due?" Coco asked. "That's what the polite people at Norway Bank did."

"It's a long story, Coco," Gerhard said with a sigh, wishing he was one of the people merrily riding bikes around the lake.

"I love stories," Coco said as he leaned back on the chaise and put on his sunglasses. "The only thing better than listening to stories is acting them out on stage in front of an audience."

"Great."

"So why don't you go ahead and tell me the story of why your bank decided to sell my fully performing loan less than one year into a five-year term."

As Coco watched the tourists dive off the Hobie Cat and start swimming for shore, he couldn't help but wonder if the shipping gods were sending him a message: *Abandon ship!*

"There are certain issues of confidentiality that must be respected," Gerhard said as he lit a cigarette and considered whether or not he should be straight with the shipping tycoon or just hustle him off the phone and go meet his friend Stefan for a beer at the Zwick.

"Bullshit," Coco said.

"Okay, Coco, fine," he said and inhaled deeply. "Just between us, we sold your loan because of the World Economic Forum."

"The World Economic Forum? You mean that lovefest in Davos where the rich guys fly in on private jets and promise that they will reduce carbon emissions and wealth disparity?"

"That's the one."

"The Chinese energy minister made me go to that thing a few years ago when they wanted my LNG ships," Coco said. "But what does a conference have to do with the loan on my fleet?"

"As you may have seen in the *Financial Times*, RLB has been the target of student protests recently, which has caused our largest European institutional investors to threaten to sell their holdings if we don't stop funding businesses that produce a large amount of carbon dioxide, like oil and gas companies, coal plants...and shipping companies."

"So?"

"So the bank has stated publicly that it will cut net greenhouse gas emissions to zero by 2025 and has committed to capture more carbon than it produces."

"So?"

"So that's why RLB formed the ESG task force and appointed a chief sustainability officer to run the audit."

"Oh."

"Even the big oil companies have a plan to achieve net zero emissions."

"It's a sad day when even oil companies don't like oil anymore," Coco said.

"The world is changing around us," Gerhard said.

"But I still don't understand what Davos has to do with you guys selling my loan."

"Here's what happened," replied Gerhard. "Our chairman was moderating a panel discussion among leading European institutional investors at the World Economic Forum conference, and..."

"And *what?*"

"And he wanted to announce in his introductory remarks that RLB has started selling off the most polluting loans in our portfolio," Gerhard said softly. "He wanted to give a concrete example, not just talk about it."

"Wait, *I* was the concrete example?"

"Yes, you were."

"Are you saying that going into the market and flogging my loan was part of a public relations stunt?"

"Oh, no, RLB would *never* have marketed your loan for sale," Gerhard said. "That's against the culture of our bank."

"So what happened?"

"We received an unsolicited offer for your loan from LTO. Our chairman agreed to accept it because he thought it would comfort our critics and improve our low valuation. Plus, the bank has allocated several hundred million euros of loss provisions for fossil-fuel-related write-offs, and he was keen to use some of those before he lost them."

"My deal was one of the most ESG-unfriendly loans in the entire shipping portfolio?" said Coco, who couldn't decide whether to laugh or cry.

"Not exactly," Gerhard said sadly.

"Good," Coco said. "Because my wife would *kill* me if that were the case. She is quite concerned about climate issues."

"Your loan was the most ESG-unfriendly loan in the *entire bank*," Gerhard said. "That's why they made an example of you, just like they've done with the other vice industries."

"*Vice industries?!*" Coco objected bitterly. "Are you kidding? Ships carry ninety percent of everything! Ships have facilitated human migration and comparative advantage and lifted more than one billion people out of poverty! Ships provide basic human necessities like food and heat and giant flat-screen TVs from China! My crews deserve a medal of honor for the work they do, not called a 'vice industry' by some overstuffed banker sitting in a fancy office!"

"Let's not forget the pollution risks associated with oil tankers," Gerhard said.

"*Pollution risks?* My ships spill less oil when they discharge two million barrels of crude than an American soccer mom does when she puts the nozzle back after filling up her minivan," Coco said.

"Your corporate governance score wasn't so good either," Gerhard said.

"My score? You have some kind of *report card* on me?" Coco said, momentarily flashing back to his brief and frustrating career as a student.

"I'm sorry, Coco. I really am."

"As you bloody well should be! Whatever happened to relationship banking?"

Gerhard took another drag before seizing on an opportunity to shift the balance of power.

"That's just it," Gerhard said. "Do you remember when we having dinner at the Four Seasons? I told you that I would help you get the $750 million after all the other shipping banks turned you down?"

"You know I never forget an act of loyalty," Coco said, "or *disloyalty*."

"Everyone knows that," Gerhard said.

"You said that RLB was trying to get out of ship finance, but you helped me out by booking my new loan through your wealth management department in Zurich."

"That's right," Gerhard said. "RLB had recently changed its strategy from corporate banking to ultra-high net worth wealth management."

"Lending money to people who don't need it," Coco said. "That's why you made me keep my kids' trust fund on deposit there."

"I pushed very hard to get your deal done, even though my instincts told me it wasn't a good idea for you *or* the bank," Gerhard said.

"I remember," Coco said.

"Then, a few months ago, when you wanted to raise the $150 million of preferred equity from Black Boulder Asset Management in New York to install scrubbers, I convinced my colleagues in Zurich to give their consent even though I thought it was very risky to put that much debt on a fleet of tankers that are more than fifteen years of age."

"What's your point?"

"My point is that when you're in a long-term relationship like ours, sometimes you have to just go along with things even when you don't agree with them," Gerhard said. "That's what a relationship is. Giving the other person the benefit of the doubt. Trusting in their judgement. Having faith. Hoping for the best."

"Hope isn't a strategy," Coco said.

"Hope is the *only* strategy," Gerhard corrected.

"That's sad."

"Coco, did you ever consider the possibility that you have been presented with a spectacular opportunity here?"

"An opportunity?" Coco laughed. "To get eaten by wolves? Gee, Gerhard, thanks a lot."

"An opportunity to make some money," he said. "Serious money. Fast money. Mad money."

"Keep talking."

"I don't know anything about LTO, but you and I both know that some of the guys in New York who buy shipping loans can be inexperienced. They don't know how the shipping game is played."

"Jah, I had a little experience with this in the American junk bond market," Coco said with a laugh.

"Precisely."

"That's an easier way to make money than running tankers," Coco said.

"Indeed," Gerhard said. "I'm not supposed to tell you this, but RLB sold your loan to LTO at a ten percent discount."

"You took a *$75 million* haircut on my loan?!"

"We did," Gerhard replied as he rubbed his recently moisturized cranium. "We got an appraisal on the ships and sold the loan for what we would have recovered had we sold the ships ourselves in this market," he said. "That's common practice among banks."

"That's insulting."

"No, that's your opportunity," Gerhard said.

"Opportunity?"

"Yes, of course," he said. "As you may know, it is customary for the borrower and the distressed loan buyer to work together and share the discount, which means there might be a $37.5 million profit in this for you, assuming you can play nice with LTO Capital and find someone else to refinance the loan."

"I don't suppose *you* could refinance my fleet?" Coco laughed. He was suddenly euphoric about the possibility of netting a quick $37.5 million by coming to a peaceful resolution with LTO.

"Not unless your ships have net zero carbon emissions," Gerhard replied. "Which seems highly unlikely for a fleet of vintage supertankers."

"Thank you just the same," Coco said with a smile. "For a $37.5 million payday I can get creative."

"I know you can," Gerhard said. "And allow me to give you a bit of friendly advice before you hang up."

"I know," Coco said. "Less cholesterol."

"If Viking Tankers, I mean Scrubber Ships, had *any* kind of ESG policy whatsoever that even *mentioned* the 2015 Paris Agreement to stop global warming, there's a good chance my ESG people wouldn't have sold your loan."

"Give me a break," Coco said. "What do environmental, social, and governance even have to do with each other anyway? They are all important, I agree, but they are completely different things."

"Some people will disagree with that," Gerhard said. "Some people think they all revolve around the values of a business and its leaders."

"Okay, but there isn't even an agreed-upon standard of measurement for ESG! We both know that the only thing ESG means is more regulations, more reporting, more consultants, and even less money for the owner. ESG will be another nail in the coffin of the independent shipowner."

"You need to clean up your act."

"No, what I need is for my ships to earn enough to pay operating expenses," Coco said.

"Try to look at this a different way," Gerhard said respectfully. "ESG represents the shipping industry's best chance of long-term profitability and access to competitively priced capital, at least for those owners who can figure it out."

"Jah, but sadly I'm not in that category," Coco said.

"Perhaps Robert Fairchild, your CFO, could help you," Gerhard offered delicately. "He is quite up to speed on this kind of thing."

"*Ex*-CFO," Coco snarled. "After what he did to me, I suggest you never mention that man's name again in my presence."

Chapter 3

It was date night, and Coco Jacobsen believed his bad day was about to get better. After suffering disappointment in both business and sport, he was greatly looking forward to spending time in his wife's loving arms and forgetting his problems if only for a little while.

As Alex freshened up in *Kon Tiki*'s squash-court-size master bathroom, the Norwegian shipping tycoon savored the exquisite pleasure of anticipation. Date night, he realized, wasn't so different from a red-hot tanker market; the waiting was half the fun — and the good times never seemed to last long enough.

Kon Tiki was normally buzzing with activity, but tonight the majestic vessel was quiet, dimly lit and delightfully devoid of life. Coco had hung a hand-written sign, *Closed for Business*, on the white plastic gangway chain, and Alex had arranged for Thor and Olav to have a sleepover party with the third-grade teacher she had imported from Boca Raton to "yacht-school" them.

Coco had even sent the twelve-member crew to the Atlantis Resort and Casino on nearby Paradise Island. He had given his most muscular Ukrainian deckhand a description of the cocky college boy from Connecticut who had served him the loan default notice, just in case their paths should cross at the tiki bar.

The table was set. It was time to feast.

Coco's senses sprang to life as he lay motionless on his back with his ankles crossed, his iPhone powered down, and his hands cupped behind his long, grackle-black hair. He closed his eyes, breathed into his diaphragm, and savored the rare pleasure of being present and peaceful.

The Norwegian shipowner was tuned into every detail of the yacht's luxurious master stateroom: The galaxy of tiny dim lights recessed into the Florentine millwork of the mahogany ceiling. The softness of the high-thread-count German bed-sheets. The smell of French perfume on the pillow-case. He even imagined hearing the haunting strum of "The Pineapple Song" carried on the breeze that was lightly tapping the rigging of sailboats in Churchill Cay Harbour.

"*Yoo-hoo!*" Coco yodeled to his wife. "Date night isn't over yet! Don't forget about me!"

He didn't want to appear too eager, but Alex had been "freshening up" for what seemed like an eternity. He was nervous because he didn't hear a sound coming from the bathroom, not even a trickle of water.

Until his bride went missing about twenty minutes earlier, the evening had been going perfectly to plan. They had been dutifully adhering to a strict sequence of events: Drinking an ice-cold bottle of her favorite Montrachet. Eating the clawless lobsters that Coco and his local fishing guide and spiritual shaman, Ziggy, had liberated from the milky blue waters surrounding Eleuthera.

They had also binge-watched three episodes of *The Sopranos* on Netflix. Ever since Coco had told his wife he thought Ferris Buehler was a dry cargo broker in Bremen, she had been making him watch hundreds of classic American movies and television shows to better understand her sense of humor.

Just as Coco was about to get out of bed to check on his missing spouse, Alex bolted out of the bathroom wearing nothing but the racy outfit he'd gotten her for Valentine's Day. In a blur of tan lines and leopard-print lingerie, she streaked toward him.

She was screaming and wielding a white, tubular object above her head like a tiny battle ax. Before Coco recognized the need to defend himself from an attack by his irate lover, she had smacked him on the head with the tiny homemade weapon.

"I'm going to *kill you!*" Alex shouted in his face before scurrying like a crab to the safety of the far end of the massive bed.

"*Awesome!*" the Norwegian tanker tycoon said, smiling with excitement as he sat up, slowly rubbing the welt rising on his head.

"*Awesome?*" She lunged toward him and whacked him on the arm before retreating again. "How is this awesome?"

"Jah, but we've been married for many years and I had no idea you were into this kind of stuff," he said as he started rubbing his arm. "It's invigorating."

"*Invigorating?*"

Whack!

"It is just very nice to know that we are still getting to know each other in certain ways," he said.

"I'm so pissed at you I could rip your nuts off with my bare hands," she seethed. "Would that be a nice surprise?" *Whack!* "Would that be awesome?" *Whack!* "Would that be invigorating?" *Whack!*

"I think we should agree to a safe word now," he said, "because this might be getting a little too rough for me. How about if you stop when I say the word 'Worldscale'?"

"There is no word that can keep you safe from me right now," she said.

"Wait, are we doing *Fatal Attraction* role-play?" Coco asked eagerly, proud of his growing knowledge of 1980s American cinema. "Do I need to hide my bunny rabbits?"

"You're insane, Coco," she said.

"If I recall the film correctly, I think *you* are supposed to be the one who is insane," Coco said. "But we can talk more about this after we're finished."

"We *are* finished, big guy," she said. "And I mean *FINISHED!*"

"Are you being serious?" Coco asked.

"Serious as your heart condition," she said. "Which, by the way, you are going to have to get repaired at some point."

"Operations are like special surveys," Coco said. "The longer you push them off, the more work you can get done while you're off-hire in the drydock. But what did I *do* to make you so angry?" Coco pleaded. "You seemed so happy when you went into the bathroom."

"You're a jerk is what you did," she said as she slowly approached him.

Alex lifted her club to strike again but instead just held it menacingly over his head and snarled like a junkyard dog. Her blue eyes were darting back and forth, searching for answers.

"I'm sure I did it, whatever it is," he chuckled. "But can you give me some details?"

"You want some details?" she said as she unfurled the paper club and held it up in front of his face with both hands. "How do you like *these* details?"

"Oh, shit," Coco said softly when he saw the letterhead of LTO capital. He thought he had concealed the nastygram inside the latest issue of *Ahoy Matey!*, but he must have forgotten.

"Were you planning to tell me about this?"

"I was waiting for the right moment."

"I don't believe you," she scoffed. "We both know you're the kind of person who thinks it's better to ask for forgiveness instead of permission."

"It usually is," the shipowner replied. "Better odds."

"Well, not this time!" *Whack!*

"Come on, Alex, stop hitting me and come back to bed," Coco said as he tapped his hand on the puffy white duvet. "I've gotten so many letters like that over the years I could wallpaper our bedroom."

"This is going to be *my* bedroom after I divorce you," she said.

"*Divorce me?*" Coco pleaded. "But we agreed to stick together in sickness and health."

"Sickness and health is one thing, honey," she said as she waved the document in the air, "but I never agreed to stick together in stupidity and recklessness."

"But marriage is like a deal," Coco said, "and you know how I feel about people who back trade on deals."

"Even the best deals sometimes need a bit of restructuring, sweetheart," she said.

Chapter 4

"You are totally missing the point here," Coco said, laughing confidently at his wife.

"What *point* are you referring to?" Alex asked.

"This little thing with LTO is actually a blessing in disguise."

"A *blessing in disguise?*" She choked on the words as she sat down on the blue-and-white Greek-patterned upholstered bench at the foot of the bed. "You think this is a *blessing?*"

"Never waste a good crisis," he said.

"Have you lost your mind?"

"Don't you see? We have a chance to make some fast money just like we did with the investors you brought into the Viking Tankers junk bond. Some of these New York loan buyers know absolutely nothing about how the shipping game is played. That means I have the advantage," Coco added.

"Holy crap!" she said.

"What?"

"I just figured out why you are acting like such a knucklehead."

"Why?"

"Because you don't know who LTO is, do you?" She laughed in disbelief as she secured her white-blonde hair behind each ear to prepare for his answer. "You don't even know what's going on here, do you?"

"Jah, but it's probably just another one of those Park Avenue boys with the Patagonia vests and the goofy pink whales all over their clothes," he said. "This will be like taking candy from a bunch of babies."

"I'm sorry to spoil your fantasy, Coco, but the founder of LTO Capital is *Piper Pearl!*" Alex screamed.

"*What?!*" Coco suddenly sat up in bed.

"*Piper Pearl* is the CEO of LTO Capital," she said.

"You mean your ex-boss at Allied Bank of England?" Coco asked. "The bastard who fired you for marrying me and then kept your $8 million bonus?"

"Yep," she said. "He started LTO with a bunch of his old Drexel buddies after he was fired from Allied Bank of England for inappropriate behavior with a female derivatives trader."

Coco first met Alex when she was working for Piper Pearl in the New York City–based investment banking division of Allied Bank of England. Their relationship began in a professional capacity when Alistair Gooding, the head of the ship finance in the bank's London office, threatened to pull the plug on Viking Tankers unless Coco found someone to refinance his loan.

With no other options, Coco had agreed to try his luck on Wall Street, and Alex had been the investment banker randomly assigned to manage the emergency bail-out junk bond offering. For Coco and Alex, it had been love at first video conference call.

Through a combination of charm, calling in favors, and dishing out heaping helpings of nautical nostalgia across dimly lit tables at Casa Lever and Polpo, Alex managed to close the deal. She rounded up a motley crew of intrepid investors whose dependence on ridiculously high yield compelled them to embark on the exciting, if ill-fated, journey aboard Coco's Viking Tankers debt offering.

The tanker market crashed just days after the five-hour closing dinner at Per Se in the Time Warner Center. Coco defaulted on the debt obligation after failing to make even the first of forty contractually obligated quarterly coupon payments, earning him membership into a rarified club of companies known as the NCAA — No Coupon at All.

Less than two months later, Coco and his new CFO, Robert Fairchild, took advantage of a loosely drafted bond indenture when they used the bondholders' *own money*, which was being held in escrow to fund future coupon payments, to buy back the bonds for fifty-nine cents on the dollar. Coco walked away with the money, the ships, the new CFO, and the girl — Alexandra Meriwether.

Coco and Alex's romance continued to flourish after the bond repurchase deal was done and dusted. During a weekend sortie to the Caribbean, she accidentally became pregnant. When she confessed to her boss, Piper Pearl, what had happened, and that she planned to marry the bad-boy Norwegian bachelor, Piper fired her and trousered her bonus.

The end of Alex's career as an investment banker marked the beginning of the happiest period of her life; she became mother to the twins and an ardent environmentalist working to protect the world her offspring would inhabit — starting with the extreme carbon-producing activities of her new husband.

"That's good news too," Coco said.

"How is that good news?"

"Because now we have an opportunity to get even," he said. "Possession is eleven-tenths of the law when it comes to ships in international waters."

"Coco, I still don't think you understand what's going on here," she said. "Your problem with LTO isn't going to get solved by an amend-and-extend negotiated over cold Chablis and black truffle penne at Claridge's like it does with the shipping bankers."

"I wouldn't break bread with that bastard even if he agreed to *forgive* my loan," Coco said. "We both know that shipping men have all the leverage once the money has been invested."

"People like Piper play by different rules," Alex warned.

"Piper doesn't know the bow from the stern," Coco said.

"No," she said, "but Rocky does."

"*Rocky?*" Coco asked. "What does that monster have to do with this?"

"Rocky DuBois was Piper's college roommate," Alex said. "They are good friends. Don't you remember anything?"

"Oh, no," Coco said as he started connecting dots and seeing an ugly picture coming into focus.

"And do you happen to know who Piper's bridge partner is?"

"Who?"

"A gentleman named Horace Buttersworth," she said.

"I *knew* it!" Coco screamed into the pillow. "I *knew* Horace rigged the tennis match!"

"*Now* do you see what's happening? This is a revenge trade, Coco!" she said. "Piper Pearl and Rocky DuBois are doing a Viking raid on *you!*"

"Are you saying this is like a hostile takeover?" Coco asked.

"No, Coco, this isn't *like* a hostile takeover," she said. "This *is* a hostile takeover."

Coco immediately closed his eyes, folded his hands together as if in prayer, and inhaled slowly and deeply.

"It is better to die with honor than live with shame," he said, repeating a line from the medieval Icelandic *Saga of Jomsvikings* that his father had taught him as a boy. "The battle begins now!"

Chapter 5

"I hate to kill your buzz, Viking warrior, but I've seen this movie and I know how it ends," his former investment banker wife said when she looked up from her second reading of the document. She was still dressed for date night, but she was all business.

"How does it end?"

"Not well, honey, not for you anyway," she said.

"The best movies have surprise endings," Coco said.

"So I'm assuming that RLB sold the loan to LTO at a discount?"

"Ten percent," Coco admitted.

"Wow! That's more than I would've guessed," she marveled. "LTO is going to foreclose on your loan as fast as they can and then sell your ships to Rocky DuBois on the cheap before the tanker market recovers. That's the game."

"Loan to own," Coco said.

"Exactly," she said. "At least they're upfront about their goals."

"But my loan is still current on interest and principal," Coco said. "How can they foreclose?"

"Because the most recent valuation certificate, which is included as an appendix to this horrible document, indicates that your ships are only worth $750 million in today' lousy market."

"Gerhard said that valuation was the reason RLB gave LTO the huge discount," Coco offered.

"Makes sense," she said. "And it means the Value Maintenance Covenant is blown to bits. That's how they are establishing the default."

"The VMC shall set the lender free," Coco said. "I know the tanker market is bad right now, but that valuation is still very light. My fleet was worth $1 billion one year ago, when I did the deal with RLB, and that was *before* we installed $150 million worth of scrubbers."

"Yes, but the initial valuation with RLB was done by Peder Hansen," Alex said, referring to the Norwegian shipbroker with whom Coco had practiced transactional monogamy for several decades.

"He's a generous man."

"And why are you acting surprised? It's not uncommon for ships to lose or gain twenty-five percent of their value in one year. Shipping is the most volatile hard asset business in the world — and that's *before* you add the multiplier effect of leverage."

"But who came up with the valuation for LTO?" Coco laughed. "I know it wasn't a sale and purchase broker in London or Oslo."

"It was produced by a website that uses an algorithm with dozens of different vessel specific inputs," she said.

"That's ridiculous," he said, laughing.

"It's objective," she replied. "A lot of asset lenders are using hard data instead of personal opinions when it comes to valuation."

"Jah, but then I'll just nominate Peder to provide a more robust valuation," Coco said. "He'll give them whatever number I need so everything looks okay after LTO averages the two valuations together."

"Nice try," she said. "But according to the loan agreement, the lender has the exclusive right to select the appraiser."

"So what will it cost me to make them go away? A one percent amendment fee? Exchanging heavy upfront fees for long-term debt restructuring has become its own industry."

"In your dreams," she said. "LTO is saying you can either pay off the $750 million loan at par, in which case Piper and Rocky pocket $75 million, or you can pay down the loan by $188 million within 30 days to reduce the senior bank leverage back to 75% and cure the VMC default."

"It's okay," Coco said. "I have been putting out fires like this ever since I bought my first ship. If I can't find a mutually agreeable solution, I'll just hoard all the freight income, stop paying expenses, deviate the vessels to borrower-friendly countries, and file for bankruptcy before they have a chance to arrest the ships."

"Oh yeah, Coco? And what will you do then?" she said with rising irritation.

"Then I'll flip Piper Pearl the keys and let him and Rocky put up the working capital and play the glamorous role of shipowner," Coco said.

"Oh, really?" she said, folding her arms across her chest. "That's what you think you're going to do?"

"Yup," he inhaled. "We'll see how much those guys enjoy being woken in the middle of the night with Somali pirate attacks and oil spilling onto Brazilian beaches and ships ramming Australian reefs and drunk captains and cocaine welded onto hulls and rogue waves and collisions with U.S. Navy ships and trade wars and hot wars and port strikes and drone attacks and —"

"You can't flip them the keys!" Alex growled through gritted white teeth. She had tried to remain calm as long as possible, but now she could feel herself starting to boil over.

"Why not?"

"Because you put *a personal guarantee* on the loan, Coco!" she screamed. "And you put the boys' trust fund on deposit at the same bank!"

"Oh, no," he said.

Alex had spotted the damning detail in the default notice he'd been hoping she wouldn't see. That explained why she was beating him over the head with the document. Quite rightfully too.

"*It's right there!*" she shrieked as she pressed her freshly painted red fingernail into the relevant clause in the document and shoved it toward Coco. "See!"

"I see it," he said.

"A personal-freaking-guarantee, Coco? Really? *Really? REALLY?*"

"Wow, did you actually read the fine print?" Coco said.

"*Someone* has to," she said. "Besides, what did you think I was doing in the bathroom for so long?"

"I thought you were getting yourself ready for date night, not reading my loan default notice!" he moaned.

"Coco, you have put all our family's assets at risk in the midst of a collapsing tanker market," Alex said. "I am not feeling especially relaxed or romantic!"

Chapter 6

"I know Piper is trying to take me down, but I have a very simple solution," Coco said. "You just need to trust me."

"Oh, really?" Alex challenged him. "And what's this simple solution of yours?"

"I'll just borrow the $175 million from the kids' trust fund, put the VMC covenant back into compliance, and do another bond offering in New York or Oslo to refinance LTO and pay back the kids," he said. "Problem solved."

"No, Coco, problem *not* solved!" she fired back immediately. "You are not touching that money just because some vulture hedge fund is shaking you down."

"But that cash is just sitting in negative interest rate bonds," Coco complained. "It would be insane not to put it to work defending my company from Piper and Rocky's hostile takeover."

"When we had the kids and got married, we made a deal that the money you made flipping those LNG carriers to the Chinese would be for the benefit of the children, and that now includes Maisy."

"Saving my company *is* for the benefit of the children," he said. "Once the tanker market turns, they will make a small fortune."

"Yeah, by starting with a large one," she said. "I don't think so. Besides, look who's back trading now. We had a deal."

"The kids are only nine years old," Coco said with a chuckle. "I think they'll be okay until I pay them back. When I was their age I dropped out of school and started working at a gas station to support my mom after my dad died."

"It's the principle of the thing," Alex said.

"Jah but $175 million *is* the principal!"

"Coco, taking money from the cookie jar is a slippery slope that business owners should always avoid," she said. "Especially shipowners. Once you start you never know when to stop."

"If it makes you feel better, honey, I can always lever-up *Kon Tiki* with some European bank and stick the $50 million in an offshore hidey-hole where no one will find it," he said.

"No you can't," she said.

"Why not?"

"Because that would be considered a fraudulent conveyance," she said. "According to the loan agreement, you are restricted from encumbering *any* of our assets without the written consent of the lender."

"Which is now Piper Pearl at LTO," he said.

"You got it."

"I could *kill* Fairchild!" Coco growled. "He should have paid closer attention to the documentation when we papered that little deal."

"Why do you blame Robert for everything?" Alex said.

"Because that's what I paid him for," Coco said. "To take blame."

"What you need, Coco, is to find a proper shipping bank to refinance the $750 million loan *without* a personal guarantee," Alex said.

"And who would *possibly* give me 100 percent financing on a fleet of old VLCCs in a falling market without any time charters or a personal guarantee?" he asked.

"There must be someone out there," she said. "How about one of the credit funds? Direct lenders are drowning in cash these days thanks to all the insurance companies and other investors who are desperate for yield."

"Alex, every shipping bank on the planet rejected my request last year, *including* the credit funds, and the market was pretty good back then. The only reason Gerhard did this deal was because I asked him for a personal favor."

"Yeah, and he asked *you* for a personal guarantee."

"He was my lender of last resort," Coco said. "Even with the personal guarantee."

"I bet Robert Fairchild could figure out how to get you 100 percent financing," Alex taunted him.

"I am *not* asking him for help after what he did to me. There is no human quality worse than disloyalty. It's like paying too much for a ship: No amount of hard work can ever truly make up for it."

"Come to think of it, Robert raised 100 percent finance for you *twice*," Alex said.

"I said *stop!*"

"He and I bailed you out with the $300 million junk bond when I was at Allied Bank of England, and then Robert got you another $150 million from Black Boulder Asset Management to buy the scrubbers."

"Enough about Robert Fairchild!" Coco insisted.

"Fine, but if you can't find someone to refinance the $750 million loan, you are going to have to sell your fleet — immediately," she said.

"*Sell my fleet!?*" Coco replied with a look of horror on his face.

"Yes."

"You want me to sell my fleet to one of my cannibalistic competitors at the bottom of the market?!" Coco shrieked at the mere suggestion of the sacrilege.

"As soon as possible," she said.

"Are you crazy? Ships are options with propellers. The dumbest thing you can do is sell them when the market is down. Smart shipowners buy on cannons and sell on trumpets. They buy when others cry! They plant seeds during the drought! They —"

"Spare me the shipping man platitudes," Alex said. "Smart investors know when it's time to cut their losses and sell. And that time for you is *right now!*"

As an investment banker, Alex had worked for plenty of clients who had held out for another five percent in a falling market only to live with the regret of never having gotten get their deal done. She had learned that when you had the right strategic reasons for selling, it was always wise to leave a few bucks on the table for the next guy; to use a squirt of greed to grease the closing.

"Why?"

"*Why?* Because if LTO ends up foreclosing and selling the fleet to Rocky, they will have no incentive to get top dollar for the ships because they can just come after your personal guarantee to make up the shortfall. Between a low sales price, default interest, and loads of inflated fees and legal expenses, you could lose the $175 million trust fund in the blink of an eye."

"Okay, but selling ships is a hell of a lot harder than buying them," Coco said, reciting a truth known to anyone who had ever really *needed* to sell a ship. "That's why we have so many multigenerational family shipping companies. They can't get out."

"You're going to try," Alex said.

"Alex, you seem to be forgetting that I have another $150 million of preferred equity *on top* of the $750 million of senior debt," Coco said. "Even if by some miracle I am able to sell the fleet for $750 million, LTO will get repaid in full, but Vinny Vitale at Black Boulder Asset Management will get completely wiped out."

"Life can be dirty when you live on the bottom of the food chain," Alex said.

"You Americans are brutal when it comes to destroying capital," Coco said.

"And you Europeans don't know how to take the pain and move on," she said. "I hate to sound insensitive, Coco, but Vinny is getting what he deserves for taking a second mortgage on ships that were over-leveraged even before he did the deal."

"It might be legal, but I think it's wrong to screw Vinny Vitale for supporting me and support Piper and Rocky for screwing me."

"The capital structure doesn't care what you think, Coco," Alex said. "And everyone knows preferred equity sits below senior secured debt in the cash distribution waterfall. Those are the rules of the game."

"Sometimes you have to change the rules to fit the facts," Coco said. "I only protect lenders who protect me."

"What are you proposing, vigilante financial restructuring?" Alex asked, yawning. "Is that what you're into these days?"

"I believe in justice," Coco said. "I believe in loyalty."

"Are you going to sell your ships and get rid of that personal guarantee or roll the dice and hope the tanker market picks up before LTO forecloses?"

Alex was exhausted from the conversation and the nonstop drama that came along with being married to Coco. He was like a volcano, building himself up and then blowing himself apart. Rinse and repeat. She wasn't alone in her fatigue. Coco's need to push everything and everyone to the limit had been wearing people down from the first time he climbed out of his crib, slid down the stairs, and made his first proclamation: "*Out!*"

He had exhausted his parents, teachers, lenders, charterers, investors, and more lovers than he could recall. But for those who stuck with him, hung on loosely during the whipsaw ride between boom and bust, euphoric and despondent, there was no human being on earth more loyal than Coco Jacobsen.

His pattern of generously giving loyalty and demanding it in return had been the key to his long-term success in a business famous for its comets — the self-interested dreamers and hustlers who briefly burned bright before disappearing into a vast universe populated by burned-out former ship-owners.

"Ever since the night Hilmar Reksten gave me a job when I was a kid, shipping has been my life," Coco said. "Shipping saved me. You knew that when you married me, so how can you ask me to sell my fleet and get out?"

"What about protecting me and the twins?" Alex said as she got off the bed and slowly walked toward the door. She picked up one of his blue button-down dress shirts and pulled it over her head. "What about us? Aren't *we* your life? Didn't *we* save you?"

"That's not fair," he said. "What you're doing isn't fair and it isn't nice."

"As your investment banker, I'm advising you to sell your ships before they are sold for you at a lousy price. I didn't expect this to turn into *Sophie's Choice*."

"A painful film," he said.

"Not as painful as this conversation," she replied. "You are going to sell the fleet or else there will be a consequence."

"A *consequence?*" Coco scoffed. "Are you threatening me?"

"Totally," she said.

As much as he valued and respected his wife's good judgment, the frightening truth was that Coco just didn't know how long he could survive without the adrenaline-pumping, dopamine-gushing, gut-wrenching thrill that came from buying, selling, and chartering big ships that operated in the spot market. There was nothing like the threat of death to make a person feel alive.

Coco thrived on the constant engagement with shipping friends and colleagues in all parts of the world. He was invigorated by merciless unpredictability of global commodity and financial markets. He was addicted to the rush that came from doing things like putting down just $5 million of working capital on a $500 million fleet that was hemorrhaging cash — based on blind contrarian faith that the market would turn. It might kill him in the end but living on the edge of billions and broke was what would keep him alive in the meantime.

Coco was no stranger to making big decisions, but as he stared into the pillow and avoided his wife's penetrating glare, he realized he had just been presented with the challenge of a lifetime. Not only was Alex asking him to do something he truly believed was commercially wrong, she was asking him to choose between the two things he loved most: his family and his ships.

Like most people, Coco wanted to be respected and loved, but those two things had suddenly become mutually exclusive. And if he played his cards wrong, he could lose them both. Most people would have hedged the risk, but Coco wasn't like most people. He was all-in, all the time.

"Your request is hereby *rejected*," Coco said, using the same brusque language he used when drawing red lines through the unacceptable terms of a time charter agreement. "What is your reply?"

Coco figured that by the time Alex and he had "lifted subjects" on their negotiation, he would have agreed to some combination of the following: keeping some ships, selling some ships and chartering-out some ships, taking in some contracts of affreightment, borrowing a bit of fresh money from the kids, and agreeing to a restriction on dividends and a cash sweep until the debt balance was paid down to a conservative level. The usual ingredients for compromise stew.

"Screw you!" Alex said.

"No counteroffer?" Coco asked.

"This isn't a sale and purchase transaction!" Alex said. "This is our life!" Then she turned around and began to move toward the walk-in closet of the master stateroom.

"Where are you going?"

"To sleep in Thor and Olav's room," she said.

Despite the fact that there were eight opulent bedroom suites aboard the yacht, the boys insisted on sleeping in bunk beds in the master bedroom closet, so they could be closer to Mom and Dad.

"Good idea," he said. "Let's both sleep on it and talk about this in the morning."

"I'm done talking," she said.

"What do you mean?" Coco asked, realizing that he had pushed too hard.

"I'm going to Miami in the morning," she said. "To see Maisy and attend an emergency meeting at St. Lucy's Academy."

"When are you coming back?"

"I don't know if I am," she said. "If not, I will send for the children and you will be hearing from my lawyer."

Chapter 7

Despite the fact that he woke up at 2:57 a.m. in the throes of a full-blown panic attack, with his heart racing and his sheets soaked with sweat, Coco had a great day on daddy duty. Like many Norwegians, he held a deep-rooted belief that parenting was an endeavor that should be shared among parents, hands-on and conducted outdoors in the most vigorous manner possible.

It was the first week in June, and the weather in the Bahamas was perfect for play. Cool in the morning and evening. Warm and breezy in the middle of the day. Deep blue sky and nonexistent humidity. After finishing home-schooling for the day at around 11 a.m., the three Jacobsen boys piled into the thirty-two-foot center-console Grady White that Coco had bought for fishing around the islands and making the occasional sortie to Miami.

Captain Ziggy kicked off the adventure with a top-of-lungs screaming, saltwater-soaking joyride through the waves around Paradise Island. Then they circled back to Captain's Beach for a picnic lunch in the shade beneath the blue canopy that Ziggy stretched between the T-top and the stainless-steel bow rail.

"When is Mommy coming home?" Olav asked sweetly as he looked up at his father. He had a peanut-butter-and-Nutella sandwich in one hand and a chocolate milk in the other, kindly assembled by Dominique, the French chef aboard *Kon Tiki*.

"Soon," Coco said, unconvincingly. He tried to remain positive for the benefit of the boys, but deep down he didn't know when, or if, his wife would come back. When she had made up her mind about something, it was almost impossible to convince her to change.

"But where did she go?" Thor asked.

"She went to visit Maisy in Miami," Coco said. "And she had to attend an important meeting at St. Lucy's Academy where she's on the board of directors."

"Just like Thor and I are on the board of directors and audit committees of all your offshore companies?" Olav said.

"Yes," Coco said with a smile.

"Is she cross with you, Daddy?" Thor asked.

"Maybe just a little," Coco said, pinching his thick fingers together.

"Then you better apologize," Thor said.

"I have and I will again," Coco said.

After lunch Ziggy slowly motored back to *Kon Tiki*, where Coco decided to show the boys what he did for his job. They spent almost two hours in the onboard command center where the tanker tycoon passed his days interacting with the dozens of shipbrokers, charterers, bankers, fuel suppliers, crewing agencies, offshore ship registries, insurance brokers, lawyers, ship managers, and shipyards who made their living keeping his fleet of thirty elderly VLCCs safe, employed, and, ideally, profitable.

The ten-by-ten chestnut-paneled, temperature-controlled, fireproof tomb had been carefully designed to accommodate the massive servers specified by its original owner, all of which the Norwegian immediately had ripped out in a Dutch shipyard. Coco had reclaimed enough square footage to install a custom-made bed so he could take an afternoon nap when he needed a break from the frenetic commercial activity. And if he and Alex didn't kiss and make up, his shipboard man-cave might become his new home.

As the boys ate the homemade orange popsicles Dominique had brought them, Coco took the opportunity to give them a primer on the global shipping industry. He started by pointing to the giant world map on the wall and describing the cargoes carried by the world's 80,000 oceangoing vessels, which were controlled by 11,000 different shipowners. When the popsicles were finished and both boys started yawning and rubbing their eyes, Coco walked them back to the master bedroom bunkhouse for an afternoon nap.

"Would you guys like me to read you a book while you fall asleep?" Coco asked as they passed through the bulkhead door and began to walk down two flights of dimly lit interior stairs.

"Yes!" they both said. "We love books!"

"What would you like me to read?" Coco asked as he collapsed with exhaustion onto Thor's bed. It wasn't easy being an old dad *sans* wife or au pair.

"Read this one, Daddy!" Olav said after he pulled a book off the shelf, handed it to Coco, and then sprung back up into his top bunk.

"*Mike Mulligan and His Steam Shovel,*" Coco read the title of the book as he examined the red cover. It showed a smiling face on an excavator's bucket. "Sounds very industrial. I like it already!"

Coco wasn't a strong reader in English, so he moved slowly through the children's classic. The story told the tale of Mike Mulligan, a man who spent his life operating his beloved old steam shovel, Mary

Ann. After many years of successful work together, Mike and Mary Ann faced a major threat when they were forced to compete with the more efficient modern shovels that were powered by gasoline, electricity, and diesel motors.

As he read the words, Coco's mind naturally drifted to the reality that new supertankers were being built with dual-fuel engines that could burn LNG, which produced one-third less carbon dioxide than heavy bunker fuel, while his ships were carbon-belching gas guzzlers.

Just like Coco, Mike Mulligan refused to give up on his old machine. He was forced to travel deep into the countryside where an old steam shovel like her could still find work. It hit close to home. Some of Coco's tankers were now so old that he was forced to trade them around North Africa and Southeast Asia, where oil terminals and charterers were more forgiving when it came to vessel age. The children's book was turning into his biography; he was terrified to find out how the story would end.

Coco enjoyed a moment of optimism when he read that Mike and Mary Ann were hired to dig the foundation for a new town hall. They accomplished the task in record time but worked so fast that they forgot to leave a ramp so that Mary Ann could get out of the basement of the new building. They had dug their own grave! Unable to escape, Mary Ann's engine was converted into a furnace to heat the building, and Mike Mulligan became the janitor of the town hall.

"That was intense." Coco sighed with exasperation as he closed the children's book and put it back on the shelf. "How did you guys like it?"

"It reminds me of you, Daddy," Thor said.

"*Me?* That's ridiculous," Coco said.

"No, really, you are like Mike Mulligan, and your old oil tankers are like Mary Ann."

"How so?" Coco played dumb.

"Because your business has been fun and exciting for a long time, but now you are getting toward the end and you have a big problem."

"Jah, but shipowners always have problems because ships always have problems," Coco said.

"No, Daddy, now you have a *serious* problem," Thor said. "An existential problem."

"An *existential* problem?" Coco repeated. "Where do you guys come up with this stuff?"

"Olav and I were talking during our tennis lesson this morning. We both agree that you need to buy some of those ships that install the offshore wind turbines."

"But I am a tanker man," he said with a laugh.

"Daddy, you are supposed to say tanker *person*," Olav said. "Without a gender."

"And why would I *possibly* buy ships that install offshore wind turbines?"

"Because the world is moving toward renewable energy like wind and solar," Thor said. "By the time Olav and I are old enough to drive cars all by ourselves, they won't run on gasoline anymore which means your tankers won't have anything to carry."

"And just look at what Mommy did to *Kon Tiki*," Olav added, and pointed out the window at the towering rotor sail and dozens of PV panels she had insisted on installing before they left London nine months earlier. "This vessel is almost carbon neutral."

"Did you just say *carbon neutral?*" Coco asked.

"As members of your board of directors, Olav and I would like to make a motion that you sell all of your tankers immediately."

"*Sell my tankers?*"

"Yes, or else you will end up Mike Mulligan," the boy said. "An old man living alone in a basement whose best friend is a furnace."

"But guys, the problem you describe is too far in the future to be concerned about now," Coco said, and thought of the conversation he had with Gerhard the previous day.

"Today makes tomorrow, Daddy," Olav said.

"And today is tomorrow's yesterday," Thor added.

"Did your mom put you up to this?" Coco asked suspiciously.

"It wasn't me," Alex said softly.

When Coco looked up, he was surprised to see his wife standing in the doorway. She was wearing blue jeans and a faded New York Yankees baseball cap and still had a backpack on from her trip to Miami.

"*Mommy!*" the boys cried out, bolting off their bunk beds and scrambling to hug and kiss her. No matter how bitterly he and Alex argued, Coco would never fail to appreciate how lucky he and the boys were to have her looking out for them.

"How long have you been standing there?" Coco asked.

"Long enough to see how smart my boys are." She smiled and opened her arms. "They gave you some good advice, Mr. Mulligan. I sure hope you take it."

"You're right," Coco said.

"Yes!" Thor shouted and pumped his fist like Federer. "Hooray for Daddy!"

"We are so proud of you!" Olav concurred.

"Proud of me for what?" Coco asked.

"For saying we're right," Olav said. "And for doing your part to make sure the earth doesn't die. You are going to help other people and helping other people is what superheroes do!"

"But I haven't done anything," Coco said.

"Not yet, Daddy, but you will," Thor said, and looked at his mom and twin brother. "We *all* know you will."

"Don't bet on it guys," Coco said.

Chapter 8

Later that evening, after the boys had finished their Impossible Burgers, taken their baths, and been tucked into their bunk beds, Alex uttered the fateful words.

"Coco, we need to talk," she said.

"I know," Coco said. "Let's go topside so the boys don't overhear us. Those kids have ears like bats."

As he silently trailed his wife up the interior stairway at the aft of the vessel, he couldn't help but wonder what was going to happen next. He and Alex had gotten into plenty of arguments over the years; it sometimes seemed to be how they communicated best. But their current game of chicken, her threatening to leave and his refusing to sell his fleet, was the highest-stakes disagreement to date. The only question was whether either of them would swerve before a collision caused a flaming wreck of marital destruction.

When they reached the exposed upper deck at the stern of the yacht, Alex sat down on one of the half dozen bright orange couches while Coco walked over to the outdoor wine cooler.

"I come offering peace," Coco said as he emerged with a frosty green bottle of Alex's favorite Montrachet in one hand and two large wine glasses in the other.

It was a clear and cool night, and Alex was dressed like she was still a student at Dartmouth. She was wearing faded khaki pants, gray rag socks, tan leather Birkenstocks, and a Patagonia jacket that resembled the coat of a freshly shorn sheep.

Despite her preference for shade and her diligent use of sunblock and straw hats, living on a boat in the tropics had bleached her shoulder-length hair white and turned her freckle-speckled face so brown that Coco could see only the flash of her teeth and the whites of her eyes in the dark night.

"You know I love that stuff," she said, "but do you really think a single-use glass bottle needs to travel 3,000 miles on a container ship?"

"Better than on an airplane," Coco said as he poured the greenish elixir. "How's Maisy?"

"She has good days and bad days just like the rest of us, but St. Lucy's Academy is in serious trouble," Alex said.

"Why?"

"Because the federal government is about to cut off funding for special needs schools like theirs. That's why they called the emergency board meeting. Unless they can think of something fast, they are going to run out of money in two months."

"How much are they short?" Coco asked.

"About $6 million a year," she said.

"That's $16,250 net per day," Coco remarked, habitually converting all figures into their daily time charter equivalent, net of brokerage commissions. Even the biggest shipowners boiled down the largest numbers to the lowest common denominator: the daily cash breakeven. It was the only figure that really mattered when determining whether you would make or lose money.

"Kind of amazing that just one of your VLCCs could change the lives of your niece Maisy and 74 other kids and their families," she said.

"Not in this market it couldn't," Coco said, deflecting her suggestion that he donate a supertanker to a special needs school in Florida. "Half my ships are operating below breakeven and the other half are sitting in Chinese drydock getting scrubbers installed. Which reminds me, was Camilla at the board meeting?"

"She sure was," Alex said.

"Did she mention the Scrubber Ships investment?" Coco asked, and held his breath.

"She sure did," Alex said.

"And?"

"Let's just say Camilla is trying hard to remain positive, but apparently Vinny Vitale has started watching the tanker market on his Bloomberg screen and he's freaking out."

"Investors who aren't comfortable sailing through rough weather shouldn't invest in shipping," Coco said. "It doesn't help a ship to have a frightened crew."

Alex first met Camilla Castro six months earlier when she joined the board of St. Lucy's Academy after her sister died and she became Maisy's legal guardian. Camilla, a thirtysomething Cuban American woman, spent every weekend at St. Lucy's supporting her disabled brother, Alvaro. The two women quickly became friends.

As they chatted on the sidelines of a Special Olympics soccer match against Fort Lauderdale, Camilla told Alex that she worked at an investor fund called Black Boulder Asset Management in New York City, where she had recently become the lead portfolio manager of their newly launched PURE ESG fund.

Camilla didn't say anything to Alex about the rumors on widely-read finance blogs that Black

Boulder was actually a beard for organized crime families who used the investment fund to launder dirty money. Nor did Camilla share the Wall Street scuttlebutt that Black Boulder–backed management teams often met with an "accident" if they failed to deliver the financial results they promised.

As a former investment banker, Alex couldn't help but to pitch Camilla on giving Coco $150 million to install scrubbers on his ships. Alex started the sales process by explaining that the International Maritime Organization (IMO), a unit of the United Nations, had recently begun enforcing a global regulation known as IMO 2020. It was a rule that placed a cap on the amount of sulfur dioxide particulate matter that ships were permitted to emit into the air.

This left shipowners with two choices: They could burn expensive fuel with low sulfur content, or they could continue to burn cheap fuel with high sulfur content and install a $5 million machine called a scrubber that removed the sulfur from the exhaust before it escaped into the atmosphere. The air-purifying scrubbers, Alex said, were an exciting ESG investment opportunity for Black Boulder to consider.

The next day, when Camilla was back in her high-altitude Park Avenue office, she shared the scrubber investment opportunity with Vinny Vitale, the hard-knuckle founder of Black Boulder Asset Management. Still on a high from having just liquidated his first ESG investment at a huge profit, Vinny was instantly intrigued.

Just as they had throughout the centuries, the risks, traditions, and enormous payoffs associated with trading ships at sea continued to capture the imagination of a wide range of people. There were former sea captains and mechanical engineers, scallywags and modern-day pirates, dreamers, drifters, grifters, and naive Wall Street hustlers who wanted desperately to believe that they had discovered an unknown industry of which they could take advantage. Vinny heard the siren song and gave Camilla the green light to proceed with the scrubber investment without having performed any analysis or due diligence whatsoever.

"Alex, I'm really sorry about the personal guarantee," Coco said.

"Me too."

"That was a stupid thing to do. I had no idea my RLB loan could end up in the hands of people like Piper Pearl and Rocky DuBois."

"For a person with so much experience, you can be very naive."

"I prefer to think of it as optimistic," he said.

"Of course you do," she said.

"It's a survival tactic for shipowners."

"I know, honey, but sometimes the light at the end of the tunnel really *is* a train," she said.

"But do you actually want me to sell my fleet at the bottom of the market?" Coco asked. "Is that really what you want?"

"No, but I don't think you have a choice," she said.

"Even if it would destroy my spirit? I don't think you want to spend your life living with a bitter old man who feels like a fool."

"I guess you could try to do some kind of a merger," she said. "Would you prefer that?"

"No, there's only room for one rooster in the henhouse," he said, highlighting the characteristic that was his greatest strength and also his greatest weakness — his need for absolute control.

"That's a pretty outdated way of thinking," Alex said. "In case you haven't noticed, success in the modern world is all about collabs."

"Collabs?"

"Collaboration," she said. "When people who have different talents come together to create something exceptional, something none of them could create on their own."

"I don't think that applies to shipping," Coco said.

"Of course you don't."

"The only thing that matters in shipping is price. And I really don't see why you are making this into such a big problem," Coco said. "I just need to buy some time until the market turns. I need a little runway."

"Unfortunately, you don't have enough money to buy a runway," she said. "So you need to develop a realistic exit strategy that's fair to *everyone*, including me and the boys."

"*Exit strategy?*" Coco repeated and swallowed hard.

He had heard the term "exit strategy" plenty of times before, but almost always when the person exiting was desperate. In his experience, there was no point in having a preplanned exit strategy in shipping; if you bought your ships for a low enough price, you could exit with a profit almost any time you felt like getting out. If you paid too much, you just had to decide when to take the pain.

"Real shipping men exit the industry feet first," he replied.

"That's exactly what I'm afraid of," she said.

"What's that supposed to mean?"

"Coco, your cardiologist said that two of the four gaskets in your heart are shot," she said.

"I know, honey, and that's exactly why I've been eating my vegetables."

"Pesto does *not* count as a vegetable," she said. "And for some strange reason you refuse to get the surgery Dr. Downs is recommending."

"Because I'm still in my prime," Coco insisted, diverting the conversation away from his childlike fear of doctors. "Just like my ships."

Coco had come to equate the age of his ships with his own remaining lifespan, which was why he was especially sensitive about what became of the vessels. He and his ships both needed to find a life-extending elixir, something that would allow them to trade for another ten years. He wasn't ready to scrap them…or be scrapped.

"Everyone dies at some point," she said.

"That's what Benjamin Franklin said about paying taxes," Coco said, smiling. "And you know I've never done that!"

"I think you're conflating correlation with causation," she said.

"I love it when you do the investment banker dirty talk," he said.

"I'm serious, Coco. If something were to happen to you, physically *or* mentally, I would have to spend the rest of my life cleaning up this A.D.D. Empire you've created. Now is the time to tidy things up, not put the last of our cash at risk."

"Jah, but come on, Alex, my business is very simple," he said. "I am just a truck driver."

"*Simple?*" she repeated with a laugh. "Coco, you have thirty old supertankers in the spot market, $750 million of defaulted debt, $150 million of worthless preferred equity, countless club deals and side hustles with your Norwegian buddies, at least

275 offshore special purpose companies, a mansion in London, a plane, a golf club in Surrey you've never been to, a yacht, two islands, one of which we can't even *find* at high tide, dozens of valuable oil paintings in museums and storage facilities all over the world and a personal guarantee in the hands of a guy who wants to crush you."

"Now I get it," Coco said. "I've spent my entire life collecting all that crap, and now you want me to spend what's left of my life trying to get rid of it all?"

"Yep," she said. "That's the way it works."

Chapter 9

"Okay, let's just suppose for a moment that I did manage to sell my fleet at a decent valuation," Coco said as he watched a pair of red and green running lights cruising along the coast. "I could pay off LTO and get rid of the personal guarantee, but then what? What would I do all day?"

Alex suddenly burst out laughing, which caused Coco to start laughing too; his wife's laugh was as contagious as a yawn.

"What's so funny?" Coco asked.

"Grace Fairchild called me this afternoon," Alex said, still giggling.

"You didn't answer, did you?"

"Of course I answered. She's my friend."

"What did she say?"

"Apparently Robert has been driving her absolutely nuts ever since you fired him."

"What's he doing?" Coco asked.

"According to Grace, he isn't doing *anything*," she said.

"What do you mean?"

"I mean apparently he wears sweatpants all day, grew a goatee, and spends most of the day on the couch watching Bloomberg, scrolling on his phone and mumbling about low bond yields."

"Good," he said. "Robert deserves to be sitting at home holding Herman after what he did to me."

"Coco, you must find it in your heart to forgive him for that."

"Treason is not a forgivable offense!"

"Grace begged me to convince you to hire him back and get him out of the house," Alex said. "She actually sounded quite desperate."

"I can't hire him back if I don't even have a business," Coco said.

"I never said you can't have a business, Coco," she said. "I just want you to get rid of the $750 million personal guarantee, and I don't want you to gamble our children's money on an over-leveraged fleet of old VLCCs in the spot market. Is that so unreasonable?"

"I can't be a shipowner if I don't own any ships," Coco said.

"You are really stuck in the past," she said. "Which is why I am going to offer you a special inducement for your good behavior."

"An inducement?"

"If you are a good boy, and do what I ask, I'm going to give you a reward."

"Coco likes rewards." The Norwegian giant smiled as he pushed aside a blue pillow and inched a little closer to his wife on the stylish orange couch.

"And I'm going to give you this gift every week," Alex whispered seductively into his ear.

"You are making me feel very uncomfortable, Mrs. Robinson," Coco said, doing his best imitation of Benjamin in *The Graduate*. "What are you going to give me?"

"Do you really want to know?"

"Yes."

"Are you sure you're ready?"

"I'm ready!"

"Okay," she purred. "I am going to give you a..."

"Tell me!"

"An allowance."

"A *what!*" Coco shouted as he jumped to his feet. "An *allowance! That's* what I get for selling my ships and sacrificing my life?"

"That's right."

"You mean like we give Thor and Olav if they flush the toilet, put their toys away, and vote my way on corporate board resolutions?"

"Using positive reinforcement to achieve behavior modification is effective for boys of any age," Alex said.

"That's ridiculous," Coco grumbled. He paused and then a few seconds later asked, "How much?"

"Two hundred and fifty thousand a week," she said.

"What! That's only a million a month!" he exploded. Coco slammed his left hand down on the couch, but the puffy pillows muted the desired effect.

"That's a lot of money, Coco."

"Not for me it's not," he protested. "All my shipowner friends get a lot more than that!"

"You don't know what your shipowner friends get," she said calmly.

"But it would take me years to save up enough to buy one supertanker!" Coco shouted.

"Which is exactly why you need to find an activity that requires smaller money," she said.

"But I've told you a million times," Coco said. "Shipping is the only thing I know how to do."

"I respectfully disagree with your self-actualization," she said.

"Huh?"

"I think the *real* reason you enjoy shipping is because you enjoy working with interesting people and because your superpower is that you are an amazing problem solver," she said.

"My superpower?" Coco said, memories flooding back.

"You're the best."

"The shipping industry does have the most interesting people in the world. And it is like one big never-ending problem," Coco admitted.

"So what's it going to be, Coco? Will you figure out how to get rid of the personal guarantee?"

Coco stretched out on the couch and closed his eyes. As he rubbed his temples, he thought about what he had learned from RLB, LTO, Peder Hanssen, his wife, and his children over the past forty-eight hours. The world really was changing, and he — and the entire shipping industry — were squarely in the crosshairs.

Although most people, the ones who didn't really know him or understand shipping, believed that Coco was some combination of crazy and lucky, that was not the key to his, or anyone's, long-term success in one of the world's most challenging businesses. The real key to longevity was the ability to process an enormous volume of information, spot opportunity, constantly reprice risk, and make quick decisions.

And that's exactly what Coco Jacobsen was doing as he gazed up at Sirius, the dog star, the brightest light in the vast southern sky. He was performing a series of complex calculations that produced an idea that surprised and excited him.

"I'll do it!" Coco declared, his left arm raised toward the starry sky.

"What?" she asked, perking up. "What did you say?"

"I'll do it," he said. "I will get rid of the personal guarantee or I will get rid of the ships. You have my word of honor."

"Really?" Alex asked, incredulous.

"Here's the thing, Alex," he said, paraphrasing the profound words Gerhard had said to him two days earlier. "When you're in a relationship that is important and valuable, sometimes you have to just go along with things even if you don't agree with them. I don't agree with your request, but I trust your judgment. I will do it to honor my love and respect for you."

"That is the most thoughtful thing you've ever said to me," she said.

"What can I say?" Coco smiled. "I'm a thoughtful Viking."

"You better move fast," Alex said, "because the tanker market is getting weaker and weaker, and Piper Pearl is planning to put your loan into foreclosure in twenty-five days."

"Of course I will move fast," he said, and leaned over to kiss her neck. "But not too fast. Just right."

"Perfect," she purred.

"And I promise to make you proud."

"How do you plan on doing that?" She smiled.

"I am talking pure, hot, and unadulterated carbon-reducing ESG," he whispered into her ear. He had a plan forming in his mind, but he didn't want to spoil the ultimate surprise by giving her any details yet.

"Keep going, baby," she said.

"I'm talking best practices when it comes to environmental, social, and, um…can you remind me what the "G" stands for?"

"Governance, baby," she cooed softly, and placed her wine glass on the table. "The G stands for 'corporate governance' — and good governance makes me wild."

"Then prepare to get wild," Coco said.

"How wild?"

"I'm talking about no conflicts of interest, no inter-company loans, and no related party transactions," Coco said as his wife sat down on his lap.

"Give me details," she growled. "I want *details!*"

"I will have policy manuals and handbooks," he whispered in her ear. "I will have limits of authority and auditors to audit our auditors' auditors."

"Oh God," she said.

"It's going to be so green that it will make you scream!"

"How green? Tell me!"

"Dark green!"

"Darker!"

"Hunter green!"

"Darker damn it! *Darker!*"

"BRITISH RACING GREEN!" he shouted at the top of his lungs.

"Yes!" she cried out so loudly that it startled an elderly security guard patrolling the marina. "A thousand times yes!"

Chapter 10

Coco Jacobsen was sitting incognito in the back corner of the Island House restaurant waiting for a twenty-four-year-old Greek woman named Athena Bouboulina to arrive from Boston. He hadn't felt so excited since the U.S. government put sanctions on Iranian oil tankers, causing charter rates to triple overnight.

It had been two days since his ESG epiphany on the upper deck of the yacht, and the afterglow was still burning bright. He had called the meeting with Athena as a first step toward executing his plan: to clean-up his old ships enough that he could raise money from investors seeking socially responsible investments.

If he could raise "green bonds" or find some other form of ESG capital to refinance his $750 million credit facility without requiring his personal guarantee, he would be home free; he could keep his ships and his family.

When Coco first moved his family aboard *Kon Tiki*, they spent a week in the Port Hercules marina in Monaco. One day, while Alex was getting the twins settled into their new floating home, Coco went ashore and had lunch at Yacht Club de Monaco with his friend and longtime business partner Captain Bouboulina, who brought along his granddaughter, Athena.

The passionate young woman had recently graduated from Boston Institute of Technology (BIT) with a dual degree in philosophy and mechanical engineering (with a concentration in ocean engineering) and had decided to dedicate her life to reducing the carbon emissions of the 80,000-plus vessels in the global seagoing shipping fleet.

When Athena courageously shared her hopes and dreams with Coco, he had been highly skeptical about her chances for success. Yet now here he was, less than one year later, in desperate need of her help. Power was shifting quickly in a world in which digital technology and ESG were tearing apart even the most traditional industries and putting them back together in ways no one could have ever imagined.

Coco had designed his incognito costume so that he would blend in with the restaurant's charter boat crowd. He had on dirty khaki shorts, a faded blue T-shirt, and dark sunglasses. His long black hair was stuffed into a tattered straw hat with an extra-wide brim.

He felt slightly sleazy meeting the young Greek woman in such a clandestine manner, knowing that onlookers might think they were witnessing a tryst, but there was no other option; there were half a dozen expatriate shipowners living on New Providence Island, and the last thing he needed was for someone to spot him with Athena and put two and two together. He'd be splashed on the front page of the *Ahoy Matey!* website within minutes.

As he waited for Athena to arrive, he took a moment to savor the stylish vibe of the Island House, which was located just outside the guarded gates of the Churchill Cay Club. He loved the energy of the place. The warm wind that wafted through the modern bar and restaurant. The clatter from the open kitchen. The dozens of pale yellow midcentury cylindrical chandeliers hanging from the soaring white coffered ceilings. The lush vegetation that surrounded the outdoor dining area. The small bar that was separated from the dining room by floor-to-ceiling wooden shelves on which hundreds of green wine bottles stood ready for service.

From behind his sunglasses, Coco sipped Sancerre and watched the action at the bar. It was packed tight with a multi-age and intercultural crowd. Billionaires next to boat bums. Locals alongside expats. It reminded him of the cantina scene from *Star Wars*, which he had watched for the first time with Thor and Olav a few days earlier.

Just as Coco spotted Athena passing through the gourmet shop at the front of the restaurant, one of his three phones lit up and started vibrating. When he looked down and saw the caller ID, he immediately felt acid rise into his mouth. Rocky DuBois. He normally wouldn't have answered the call, but he was so desperate for charters at the moment that he swallowed his pride and pressed the green button.

"What do you want, Rocky?" Coco said.

"Ah, it's always such a pleasure to hear your voice, Coco," Rocky said. "How is your soon-to-be-former life of luxury in the Bahamas treating you?"

"The weather is here, I wish you were beautiful," Coco sang the line from his new favorite song. Since starting his new life on the opposite end of the Gulf Stream, Coco had become obsessed with Jimmy Buffett's intoxicating island music.

"That's good, enjoy a laugh while you still can," Rocky said.

"Oh, and speaking of enjoyment, I am thoroughly enjoying the yacht that you generously bought me last time I took VLCC rates above $200,000 per day," Coco said with a cackle. "You have provided almost as much charity to the tanker market as your private equity buddy Horace."

After Coco had helped squeeze VLCC rates to astronomical levels in 2006, he cashed in some chips and bought the magnificent yacht *Dot Calm* for pennies on the dollar from the estate of a twenty-something Silicon Valley tech entrepreneur who had mysteriously perished while playing a video game.

Coco renamed the boat *Kon Tiki*, figuring that if the world went haywire, like if there was a pandemic or a social revolution or a nuclear war or a universal wealth tax or if all the glaciers melted, he could hunker down aboard a heavily armed and generously provisioned vessel and spend the rest of his life roaming the world like his Viking forebears had done.

"Take good care of that boat, Coco," Rocky said. "I don't want to find any deferred maintenance when Piper and I repossess it as part of your personal guarantee. And if you wouldn't mind keeping a few bottles of Johnny Walker Blue onboard, that would be terrific."

"What do you *want* Rocky?" Coco demanded. "Why are you calling me?"

"I'm just calling to let you know that I'm looking forward to taking over your fleet at the bottom of the market," Rocky said with a laugh, "and watching you cry like a big baby when the cycle turns. You will be remembered as the guy who bet too big and couldn't hang on quite long enough. Just like your idol, Hilmar."

"I'll *sink* my ships before I let you and Piper have them," Coco said.

"Ah, nice, so you are going to add *insurance fraud* to your long list of legal problems?" Rocky asked. "Whatever money you have left will be spent on lawyers."

"Screw you," Coco said.

"Actually, you're the one getting screwed this time," Rocky said. "I've finally got you by the short and curlies, and you can bet I'm not letting go."

Chapter 11

Athena Bouboulina peeled off her pink Elizabeth Taylor–style sunglasses and paused as her eyes adjusted to the dim light. Her presence instantly captured the attention of everyone in the bustling Bahamian brasserie.

The prosperous crowd was silently speculating about the source of her style. Pop singer? Movie star? Trustafarian? Few would have guessed from her shaved head, copious tattoos, aggressive body piercing, slashed blue jeans, and dime-store flip-flops that she was actually a brilliant mechanical engineer from BIT who was hell-bent on cleaning up the sooty shipping industry from which four generations of her family had shoveled in billions.

Coco rose from his seat, took off his sunglasses, and touched the brim of the straw hat. *Howdy, ma'am.* He was still rattled by Rocky's telephonic assault, but he managed to muster a friendly grin. Athena smiled brightly with contagious excitement as she made her way across black-and-white tiled floor of the busy dining room, maneuvering around an obstacle course of tightly packed tables.

"You look like a gangster sitting in the back corner with your big hat and sunglasses," she said, flashing a smile. "So exciting!"

"I've been binge watching *The Sopranos*," Coco admitted with boyish charm as he bent over and greeted her with a kiss on each cheek and then one more for good luck.

"But is someone out to get you?" she whispered.

"Several people," Coco said. "And another one will be very soon," he added, momentarily thinking about how Vinny Vitale would react to losing $150 million inside of ninety days.

"Thanks for coming down to the Bahamas on such short notice."

"My pleasure," she said. "*Papou* told me that you have some, um, travel restrictions."

"The shadiest people reside in the sunniest places," he said, and smiled and looked around the room. "How's your grandfather doing these days?"

"He's good, enjoying life in Monaco. But he is very worried about my uncle Spyrolaki," she said.

"Oh, no," Coco said with a laugh. "What sort of trouble has the black sheep of the Bouboulina family gotten himself into this time?"

"That's just it," she said. "Spyrolaki actually checked himself into the monastery at Mount Athos six months ago, and no one has heard from him since. We have no idea what's going on but it's very weird."

"Are you telling me that Spyrolaki gave up the Ferrari, the seaside villa in Kavouri, and the supermodel-turned-psychiatrist girlfriend to become a *monk?*" Coco laughed.

"Yes, and it's very troubling. But enough of our family drama. It's just so nice to be here with you now," Athena said as she arranged her sunglasses and iPhone on the heavily varnished wooden table. "I must admit I was a little surprised when my grandfather said you wanted to see me."

"Why is that?" Coco asked.

"Oh, I don't know, maybe because you literally laughed in my face when I told you that I've committed my life to decarbonizing the ocean shipping industry."

"I was trying to be helpful," Coco said.

"Helpful?"

"Honest," he said. "Sustainable energy always sounds good when oil is over $100 per barrel, but when prices collapse it's no longer economically competitive."

"Wake up, Coco, this isn't just about economics anymore," she said.

"Famous last words," he said.

"It's about the people in the streets, the consumers, who are *demanding* that corporations take better care of the environment."

"Good thing people in the street don't know anything about ships," Coco said. "Most people think food comes from grocery stores and petrol comes out of a pump."

"Yes, but they *do* know about the companies that charter the ships," she said. "The oil companies and commodity traders and grain houses and the manufacturers. ESG is here to stay, Coco, and even private shipowners like you and my grandfather can't escape from it for much longer."

"You're absolutely right," he said. "My bank sold my loan to a distress hedge fund because university students have been sleeping in their lobby to get them to stop financing the oil and gas industry."

"This is just the beginning," she said. "The tip of the iceberg, so to speak."

"But why are you so hung up on trying to save the world?" Coco asked. "As a member of the Bouboulina family, I suspect you don't need to work for quite a few generations."

"Have you ever read the book *Ethics* by Aristotle?"

"Aristotle Onassis wrote a book?"

"Different Aristotle," she said, chuckling.

"I must have missed that one," Coco said with a laugh. "But I did just finish an inspirational book called *Mike Mulligan and His Steam Shovel*. Do you know it?"

"We read *Ethics* during my freshman philosophy class at BIT," she said. "Aristotle believed that in order to be happy and lead a useful life, a person needs to develop a strong character. *Ethike arete.* So the book asks how man should live his life to achieve that."

"And this is how you are choosing to live yours," he said.

"Yes, and for the first time in my life I think I can actually make a difference," she said. "And the kicker is that reducing carbon emissions is actually the most fun, creative, and important task I've ever had the opportunity to work on."

"Really?"

"Did you know that by feeding cows lemongrass, they belch thirty percent less methane, which is more than *twenty times* more damaging to the atmosphere than carbon dioxide?"

"Maybe we should order some for lunch." Coco smiled and sat up in his chair. Athena's youthful enthusiasm was contagious.

"It's true," she said. "And this isn't charity work. There is now more money to be made in *reducing* carbon emissions than there is in *producing* it."

"I like the way you think," he said with a smile.

"My turn to ask the questions," Athena said. "Was it your wife or was it your kids?"

"Excuse me?"

"I'm just curious if it was your wife or your kids who convinced you to talk to me about reducing the environmental impact of your ships?" Athena asked again.

"Both!" Coco said with a laugh.

"Don't worry, you're not alone," Athena said, smiling. "Almost every shipowner I'm working with came to me because their family members encouraged them."

"You sound like a shrink," Coco said. "How's it going?"

"One of the things we've learned is that shipping is actually incredibly efficient considering how much work ships do," she said.

"Everyone knows that, but have you figured out how to make ships carbon neutral?" Coco asked.

"We're getting there," she said. "But our biggest problem is that we haven't been able to find any ships to use for the beta tests."

"I'm surprised," Coco said. "Sadly, there is rarely a shortage of ships in the world."

"We asked more than 100 shipowners, but not one of them would let us borrow a single vessel to install our equipment and make our modifications."

"*Borrow* a ship?" Coco repeated with a laugh. "They aren't sweaters. You could charter a ship, but the owner might not appreciate it if you do construction on their vessel."

"So I've learned."

"How about your family? Won't they let you use some ships? Between all the aunts and uncles and cousins, your tribe must have a couple hundred units."

"We do, but we are a traditional Greek family owner with mostly small bulk carriers and they aren't ideal for what I am doing," she said. "That's why I have decided to buy my own ships."

Coco tilted his head. He looked like a dog who had just heard a high-pitched sound. He was suddenly alert.

"Hold on, you're looking to *buy* ships?" Coco asked. "Do you have any money?"

"We just formed a new company called Beta Ships and raised $150 million in a round of Series A funding. We're in the market right now looking for appropriate vessels to retrofit with our environmental technology so that we can prove our concept for reducing fuel consumption and carbon emissions."

"Where did you find the capital?" Like any successful shipowner, Coco always tried to keep a close eye on new sources of funding.

"A man named Henry Husk and a bunch of his pals in Silicon Valley," she said.

"*Henry Husk?*" Coco asked, starstruck. "The technology billionaire?"

"Henry has many different business ventures," she said, "but what they all have in common is his belief in the power of science to make the world better."

"Wow," Coco said. "How did you find him? Did you use an investment bank?"

"He found me," she said.

"Henry Husk found *you?*" Coco laughed doubtfully.

"Yes." She smiled. "I took a class at BIT last year called 'Creative Destruction.' At the end of the semester, we had a contest where each student researched a heavily polluting industry and then presented their ideas for how to reduce its carbon footprint and make it more profitable by using technology and data. Henry Husk is an alum of the school, and he was actually one of the judges."

"And he liked shipping?"

"He *loved* it!" she exclaimed. "After he read my paper about the ocean shipping industry, he said he felt like he'd stumbled upon one of those lost tribes in the Amazon."

"Amazon." Coco laughed. "That's funny."

"Henry was so excited to get involved that he and some of his venture capital buddies gave us the money to go out and buy ships," she said. "And that's what we are trying to do now."

"I have an idea. Why don't you buy my ships?" Coco blurted out, the words escaping from his mouth before he even realized what he was saying.

Coco had called the meeting with Athena simply because he wanted to pick her brain about how he could raise some ESG money to refinance LTO, but he suddenly had a different idea. It was the kind of gut decision that was at the root of all his best moves.

If he could sell some of the equity in his ships to her newly funded company with its rock star investors, he might be able to hit the jackpot: extinguish his personal guarantee, go into business with the world's most exciting young entrepreneurs, make his ships carbon neutral, *and* keep some skin in the game. All at once, Coco Jacobsen felt the thrilling sensation of his missing mojo rushing back. It was game on!

"If a smart guy like you is a seller in a low market like this, I'm not so sure I should be a buyer," she said.

"Don't worry, it's not that," Coco said. "I'm getting some serious encouragement from my wife and the hedge fund from hell that just bought my senior loan."

"Remind me, what kind of tankers do you have?" she asked.

"VLCCs," Coco said, preparing himself for rejection.

"Cool!" Athena said.

"Cool?"

"Yes, those are exactly the type of ship we are looking for. How old are they?"

"The average age of the fleet is seventeen years young," Coco said, bracing for disappointment.

"Sweet!" Athena said.

"Sweet?" Coco repeated, confused. "Sweet" and "cool" were words he associated with ice cream, not elderly supertankers. "Are you saying you actually *want* big old oil tankers?"

"Let's just say that if this was Tinder, I'd be swiping right," Athena said.

"What does that mean?"

"It means I tried to buy some vintage VLCCs from the guys at Rowayton Shipping last week, but a Far East shipowner beat us to them."

"Hold on, if you specifically *want* old VLCCs, is that because you think you can make them carbon neutral?" Coco asked, incredulous.

"It's not that simple," Athena said, and then paused to take a painfully slow bite of conch ceviche before chasing it with a sip of Sancerre.

"Tell me," Coco said. He was now so excited about the potential transformation of his life and fleet that he was hanging on her every word.

"There are only two ways to make a VLCC carbon neutral," Athena said. "The first way is for the ship to burn a fuel that is carbon neutral, such as hydrogen, ammonia, nuclear, or methanol, or use batteries that are charged with carbon-neutral electricity like solar, wind, or hydro."

"Okay, can we do that?" Coco asked.

"Yes," she said.

"Great!"

"But probably not for at least another ten years," Athena said.

"Oh," Coco said. "But my ships and I don't have another ten years. What's the second way?"

"The second way is to burn fuel that produces CO_2, but then then capture and sequester that CO_2 before it escapes into the atmosphere."

"Okay, let's do that!"

"We're working on it," she said. "We are experimenting with different techniques such as cryogenically freezing the CO_2 and dropping it to the bottom of the ocean."

"That sounds like science fiction," Coco said. "Come on, don't you have any practical ideas?"

"There is no shortage of ideas when it comes to this stuff, but success is in the execution of the details."

"What are some other ideas?" Coco said.

"Well, we could pay a carbon tax on every ton of CO_2 that we emit into the atmosphere," she said. "That money could then be used to invest in the research and development of decarbonization technologies."

"I don't do tax," Coco said.

"Okay, well, we could purchase carbon offset credits like the airline industry does," she said, "to reduce our theoretical net carbon emissions."

"How does that work?"

"We would pay other people not to produce greenhouse gas," Athena said.

"Too much of a paper trail," Coco said. Ever since a bunch of his personal information got puked up as part of the Panama Papers, he was doing his best to go paperless.

"We could plant a forest or grow algae to offset our carbon production," Athena said. "You know, cultivate living things that naturally absorb carbon dioxide."

"I'm starting to lose interest," Coco said.

"But the thing I am most excited about is reducing fuel consumption by making simple hydrodynamic improvements to the vessels."

"Like what?"

"Basic plastic surgery," she said, and took a bite of bread. "Bulbous bow jobs, shaving down fat sterns, propeller enhancement, and installing ESDs."

"ESDs?" Coco asked. "You mean the music?"

"You are going to be a lot of work," Athena said with a sigh.

"That's what my wife always tells me," Coco said, smiling.

"ESD stands for 'energy saving device' — you know, like the Mewis Duct. We are looking at the EEDI."

"You lost me again."

"The Energy Efficiency Design Index," she said. "Environmental cost divided by benefit to society."

"I don't know about any of that stuff, but plastic surgery is proven technology," Coco said and looked around the room. "But don't you have any *bigger* ideas? *Bolder* ideas?"

"The end result is exciting, but the reality is that reducing carbon emissions requires lots of little changes and tons of hard work," Athena said. "It can be very tedious."

"I don't do tedious," Coco said. "I need something sexier and faster. Something that will get me excited."

"How much time do you have?" she asked.

"About twenty-three days," Coco said.

"*What?*" Athena exclaimed with a laugh. "The IMO is giving the entire world thirty years to fix this problem, and you are giving me twenty-three days?!"

"Yup," he said.

"That's insane."

"Real innovation is caused by real desperation — and my desperation is real, which means I'm a tremendous asset to you."

"I probably shouldn't even mention this to you because I know I'm going to regret it, but there is *one* thing that will immediately reduce carbon emissions in a very significant way. It will also cause charter rates to jump."

"Now you're talking!" he said, smiling as he rubbed his hands together.

"Before you get too excited, Coco, I should warn you that a lot of people, including the IMO, don't believe it's a long-term solution to decarbonization," Athena said.

"That's exactly what a contrarian like me wants to hear," he said. "What do you have in mind? Is it fast?"

"Actually, it's slow," she said.

"Slow?"

"I am talking about imposing a speed limit on ships," she said.

"Keep talking," Coco said, his unblinking eyes focused on Athena.

"The engines would have to be de-rated, of course, but slowing down ships by just four knots would immediately reduce CO_2 emissions by about thirty-five percent," Athena said.

"That's bold," Coco said.

"It's the biggest, cheapest, easiest fix we can make. Plus, if we were to slow down the fleet and then layer on wind assist technologies like rotor sails and kites..."

"And make improvements to the hydrodynamics," Coco added.

"And make sure the pistons are balanced, we will be able to significantly reduce emissions. Don't forget, there are more than 80,000 oceangoing vessels, totaling 1.2 trillion tons, so the potential for reducing climate damage is massive. This opportunity is a gift."

"So why isn't slowing down the answer?"

"Because some people think that since slow steaming reduces the capacity of the fleet, more new ships might be needed to make up for the lost capacity, which is actually *less* efficient than having fewer ships carrying more cargo by going faster."

"Let's give it a go," Coco said. "What do we have to lose?"

"It's impossible," she said.

"Why?"

"Because there are very few shipowners who can afford to push back against the major charterers and tell them that their ships won't go full speed," she said.

"Wait, but aren't the charterers the ones demanding that the shipowners be sensitive to ESG in the first place?"

"Sometimes."

"Then shouldn't they be ones *begging* to have a speed limit?" Coco said in a simmering rage.

"It's complicated," she said.

"It doesn't sound very complicated," Coco said.

"Well…"

"Jah, but I know one shipowner who would be happy to slow down his ships so his charterer would have to pay more," Coco added with a smile as he imagined breaking the news to his archenemy Rocky DuBois, who, despite their differences, was one of Coco's biggest customers.

"I know, Coco, but it can't be just you," she said, laughing. "The only way it would work is if you convince the *majority* of owners to slow down, and that's impossible."

"I've always enjoyed a challenge," he said.

Throughout his entire life, nothing energized Coco more than someone telling him he couldn't do something. It was why he was able to build a global shipping empire after spending just twelve months working as an apprentice shipbroker chartering Hilmar's ships. Maybe his wife was right after all. Maybe his superpower really was that he was a complex problem solver, not just a shipping man.

"But the good news is that if any sector can pull it off, it's VLCCs, because a relatively small number of owners control a relatively large percentage of the 800-vessel fleet."

"Perfect," he said.

"Trust me, it will still be like herding cats," she said.

"Then I shall be their shepherd," Coco said with a mischievous smile. "Meow."

Three Weeks Later

Chapter 12

The first day of Coco's new life began with great promise. He enjoyed a vigorous swim through the pale pink Bahamian dawn followed by a hot shower, a quintuple espresso, and a mountain of Dominique's heart-unfriendly bacon and eggs.

After suiting up for his sortie to the Marine Money Week conference in New York, where he would have a battle royal with Piper, Rocky, and Vinny, Coco reemerged topside. He had a Louis Vuitton backpack slung over his shoulder and a pair of loafers in his hand.

Coco set the bag down on the weathered teak deck and put on his green mirrored sunglasses to shield his eyes from the blinding sunshine. As he began to walk the fifty meters that separated him from his wife and twin boys on the stern, he took a moment to survey the spectacular surroundings of the Churchill Cay. Teal water. Pink villas. Green palm trees. Blue sky. Yellow sun. And a parking lot full of giant white yachts. His was the biggest.

He loved the place, but if his application for membership wasn't approved soon, he'd be forced to drop the lines and head back to sea in search of another paradise.

As he strode barefoot along the deck, Coco looked like a man in full — extreme in his strength, stature, confidence, virility, and influence — but when he caught sight of his beautiful wife and twin boys giggling in a plastic splash pool, he felt an uncontrollable urge to blubber like a baby.

Global travel had been a nonstop adventure during the forty-plus years it took him to build his empire, but now that he had amassed a fleet, a family, and a trust fund for his children, hitting the road was pure heartbreak. Even if a trip proved safe and productive, every day on the road was a day he would never get back — and he didn't have many of those to spare, especially considering his heart condition and the shitstorm he was going to unleash at the conference later that day.

But if his trip was successful, and achieved his goal, his long-term travel and personal stress would be greatly reduced in the future. It was just like the good advice Hilmar had given him on the frigid Norwegian night a million years earlier. *Always leave the party while you are still having fun, because that way you will have nice memories.*

"Good morning, Daddy!" Thor and Olav screamed, startling a team of gardeners pruning a mountain of roses 200 feet away.

The boys were playing in a blue plastic pool festooned with orange images of Nemo and Dory. It was positioned in the shade of the giant Marshall Islands flag flapping in the morning breeze. The boys had spotted the pool in a patch of detritus floating in the Sargasso Sea while playing I Spy during the transatlantic crossing.

At the urging of Coco's environmentally conscious wife, who had converted the ship's actual pool into an organic vegetable garden, the crew had dragged it aboard, washed it down, and filled it up. The boys had hardly gotten out of the water since. They used it even more than the elaborate recycled-cedar playset Alex had erected on the massive deck in the spot where the deceased internet billionaire's helicopter had once been lashed.

"Good morning, my beautiful boys!" the Norwegian giant boomed back. "And how are my independent non-executive directors on this fine June morning?"

"We are great!" said Olav, who often spoke on behalf of his brother.

"Why do you look so fancy, Daddy?" Thor inquired with concern. "Do you have a court date?"

"Where do you get these ideas?" Coco said.

"Then are you going to a birthday party?" Olav asked.

The boys hadn't seen their father wearing anything other than ripped shorts and T-shirts, often stained with grouper blood, in recent months. But today he was dressed in the uniform favored by Norwegian shipping men on travel: bare feet under Italian loafers, crisp white dress shirt from Sweden, faded jeans from America, and a blue British sports coat with a bright red Hong Kong hanky stuffed into the pocket for flare. Global. Sporty. Prosperous.

Coco took a moment to admire his sterling-silver cuff links sparkling in the bright morning sun. He had taken possession of 500 pairs of them, along with 175 custom neckties, several hundred engraved silver pens, and twenty-two large ships, after his hostile takeover of a courtly 200-year-old Norwegian company called Knut Shipping thirty years earlier. "Jah, I paid $300 million for the swag and got the ships for free," Coco famously said when he leaked the story to a reporter named Astrid at *Ahoy Matey!*

"I'm going to New York City," Coco said.

"Oh yeah, the land of the free money!" Olav exclaimed. "Are you going to collect more cash from Mommy's crazy bond investors?"

"Not this time," Coco said.

"Your father has sworn off Wall Street money," interjected Alex without looking up from behind the pink pages of the Financial Times. "He's in recovery."

Alex was reclining on a black lounge chair reading an article about the "conscious uncoupling" of China and the United States and the emergence of regional trade zones as the world deglobalized.

"Are you ever coming home?" Thor asked bluntly.

Coco immediately shot a concerned look at Alex, who peered at him over the top of her newspaper with one eyebrow elevated. Ever since he was born, Thor had demonstrated a preternatural ability to predict things before they happened, a gift that Coco knew would make him a good shipping man someday — though he also appeared naturally predisposed to a career in hostile interrogation.

"Of course I'm coming home," Coco said. "Why would you ask me that question, Thor?"

This was going to be Coco's first trip to Wall Street without his former CFO Robert Fairchild as his wingman, and it was sure to be messy. Coco had been feeling uneasy about the trip, but thanks to Thor's premonition, he was now even more concerned.

"I have a bad feeling, Daddy," Thor said. "A very bad feeling."

Chapter 13

When an uncontrolled splash battle suddenly broke out between Thor and Olav, Coco quickly retreated back to his wife's chair.

Alex was wearing pale-blue-and-white striped bikini bottoms, a tie-dyed Grateful Dead T-shirt, and the floppy yellow sun hat that Coco had bought for her in a tourist shop on Guadeloupe. Hanging from the chain around her tanned neck was a whimsical, sun-shaped golden charm made by Pablo Picasso. Coco had spontaneously purchased the item when a Sotheby's auction coincided with a romantic trip to Paris and an outrageously profitable vessel sale to the Libyans.

"I can't wait to come home," he said, leaned over and kissed her for a little longer than usual.

"Me too," Alex said tenderly, and wrapped her arms around his neck and pulled him closer to her. She was always a little sweeter before he left for an airplane trip. It was a subtle acknowledgement that, however slight, travel always involved a certain degree of risk, especially as Coco grew older.

As she stared up at her towering husband, Alex was suddenly struck by the ironic visage of the tanker king's silhouette against a backdrop of the ship's twenty-seven photovoltaic panels and the forty-foot-tall Danish-built cylindrical rotor sail. She quickly grabbed her phone off the tiny table next to her and held it up to capture the powerful image before it was lost.

"Smile and give me two thumbs up, honey," Alex said.

"Why?"

"Because you look very sexy right now," she said.

"I do?" Coco asked as he tentatively raised his thumbs and smiled.

"Yes, and also because I want to take your picture in front of the rotor sail and the PV panels," she said.

"But they are so ugly!" Coco whined.

"If we burned hydrogen like the yacht Bill Gates is building, we wouldn't need the wind assist," she said.

"Bill Gates is building a new yacht?" Coco gasped.

"That's the rumor."

"How long is it?"

"*How long is it?*" she repeated. "I think you're missing the point here, honey. The point is that the world needs to move fast to stop global warming before temperatures rise by another two degrees."

"How *long* is Bill's new boat?" he demanded through clenched teeth.

"I think it's about 112 meters," Alex said softly, and then immediately covered her ears.

"Argh!" Coco moaned. "These tech guys are killing me!"

Coco was irritated by how much the scale of money had changed during his career. In the old days, a global shipowner with $100 million in a Swiss bank account had some game. Now that was chump change compared to the herds of digital nerds prancing around with nine-digit VC funding, childish logos, and frivolous business models.

The swashbuckling shipowners of the 1950s and '60s — epic names like Onassis, Niarchos, Naess, and Reksten — were being eclipsed by eye-popping growth rates and outsized profit margins created by the tech entrepreneurs of the 2000s, people like Bezos, Musk, Zuckerberg, and Jobs. Coco knew that shipping's industrial glamor was at risk of fading into history, but he now had a plan to restore its pioneering splendor — and he was going to use some of Henry Husk's tech money to do it. You couldn't keep a good industry down.

"Don't worry, honey," Alex said, patting him on the knee. "Shipowners will always be a lot hotter than tech guys."

Click. Click. Click.

"These are keepers," she sang out joyfully as she inspected the soon to be iconic photos on the screen of her phone. "Eco Man would be proud of you."

Alex planned to email the ESG-friendly images to *Ahoy Matey!*, as well as to the *FT*, *Bloomberg*, and the *Wall Street Journal*, all of which were constantly on the prowl for B roll of the secretive shipowner.

"Are you okay, Coco?" Alex asked when she noticed that her husband was not acting like himself.

"I'll tell you tonight," he said. "If there even is a tonight."

"Come with me, honey," she said. "I want to talk to you."

Alex used Coco's hand to pull herself up from the lounge chair. They continued to hold hands as they walked across the teak deck to the starboard railing where the boys couldn't eavesdrop on their conversation.

"I know you don't want to sell your fleet, and I am sure that prowling around Marine Money Week trying to find a buyer isn't going to be easy," Alex said as she looked at Coco. "But I just hope you will remember what I told you the other night," she said.

"I will never forget what you told me," he said.

"Then repeat it for me."

"You told me that you like it when I — " he whispered in her ear.

"Not *that* part!" she shouted, and smacked his arm.

"Was there something else?" Coco asked innocently, fluttering his eyelashes. "Because I don't remember anything else."

"The part about you being a brilliant problem solver," Alex said.

"I liked the other part better," he said.

"Hey, you should double-check and make sure your flight is still going out on time," Alex asked.

"Why?"

Coco quickly checked his phone to see if he'd received a push notification about a cancellation or delay of his NetJets rental. Nothing.

"Because apparently there's a nasty low-pressure system brewing in the mid-Atlantic," she said. "The ocean is warmer this June than any time in history, and it's causing storms to form earlier than ever. Maybe even *hurricanes*."

"I'll be fine," Coco said. "There are no hurricanes in June."

"Oh, and by the way, Coco, this will be your last trip on a private plane."

"You want me to fly *commercial?*" Coco asked.

"Yep."

"Come on, honey, the tanker market is bad, but it's not *that* bad."

"This isn't about the tanker market," she said. "This is about each of us doing everything we can to reduce our own carbon footprint."

"I promise to do my part," he said, smiling. "And then some."

Chapter 14

"I'm very sorry, sir," the baby-faced NetJets pilot pleaded over his shoulder to Coco, "but there is absolutely *no smoking* permitted aboard this aircraft."

Coco leaned over in his seat and peered through the open cockpit door of the Embraer 300. He was horrified to see the young man hanging onto the controls like he was operating a jackhammer.

The tiny airplane was smashing through some seriously snotty weather en route from the Bahamas to New York. After the millions of miles he'd traveled by air, perpetually crisscrossing the planet to practice the equity-creating craft of aligning ships, charters, cash, and cargo, Coco Jacobsen had never experienced turbulence so violent.

"Jah, but Chris, I need this to calm my nerves," Coco called back. "You should probably smoke one too."

Alex had been right about the storm. When the little plane was cleared to take off from Nassau, the National Hurricane Center's spaghetti model showed the low-pressure system veering east and petering out over the sea.

But as the disorganized storm moved north, the unusually warm Atlantic Ocean shoved it west and gave it a second wind. Now the mess of low pressure was pushing the airplane around the dirty air like a dog with a tennis ball.

"I'm just following the rules, sir. And please address me as Captain Christopher. That's company policy," he added through gritted teeth as the airplane rolled onto its side while simultaneously nose-diving.

"Progress is made by people who break the rules, not by people who follow them," Coco shouted back above the rushing roar of heavy weather and hardworking jet engines.

"Thank you, sir. I'll keep that in mind."

"Just look at your own president," Coco called out. "He isn't afraid to color outside the lines to get things done."

"I think it's best if we don't discuss politics," Captain Christopher replied.

These liberal millennials were driving Coco absolutely batshit. He knew he was going to have to get used to them, because they would inherit the world, but he couldn't help but wonder: When did the world get overtaken by all these carbon-fearing, rule-following, digitally obsessing, radically transparent, environmentally over-reacting, kale-worshipping, texting-instead-of-talking, social-media-scrolling, fake-meat-eating, hater-hating, food-tracing, journal-keeping, hash-tagging, meme-loving, best-practices-following, Venmo-paying, phone-addicted, afraid-to-own-a-car, still-living-with-their parents *weenies?*

In Coco's book, the only good thing these passive-aggressive youngsters had brought to the party was the social acceptance of yoga pants that looked like they'd been applied with a spray can. Now *that* was real progress.

"Fine, I snuffed it out," Coco said, after he had smoked the cigarette down to the filter and dropped it into the dregs of a beer can.

"Thanks for your understanding, Mr. Long-Johnsen," Captain Christopher said. "We appreciate it very much."

"Please, Chris," Coco said. "Call me Harry."

As much as Coco was unaccustomed to, and irritated by, being told what to do, particularly by some punk kid he was paying by the mile like an Uber driver, he couldn't help but giggle every time he heard the alias Harry Long-Johnsen. The name sounded just Scandinavian enough to obscure its delightfully adolescent humor. Until the day he died, Coco Jacobsen would remain a kid at heart.

Although the Norwegian shipping magnate was mostly amused by Rocky's trumped-up charges of felony bunker theft, he was annoyed that the threat of arrest diminished the quantity and quality of his visits to New York, his favorite city in the world. When he did travel to America, he never stayed overnight, couldn't fly commercial, and always traveled under a phony name to reduce the possibility of being arrested.

During a brief break from the white-knuckle turbulence, Coco's enormous brown hands removed the white napkin from the inside pocket of his blue blazer. It was a crude diagram of the deal he had cooked up with Athena.

After more than forty-five years in shipping, during which he had metamorphosed from petrol-pumping eighth-grade dropout to the world's largest owner of elderly supertankers, his legendary run as an independent tanker owner was about to be dramatically transformed. As long as he didn't die in a stupid plane crash first.

During their long lunch at Island House, Athena and Coco had spent hours in the back corner scheming and dreaming and sipping Sancerre and scribbling a deal structure, shipping style, on the back of white paper napkin. As with every transaction that needed to remain confidential, they'd even given the deal a code name, Operation Greta, in honor of the daring teenage Swedish environmentalist.

By the time the early birds had begun to filter in for dinner, Coco and Athena had devised a solution that would solve both of their problems and create vast new opportunity; it was a plan that could only be executed at the annual Marine Money Week conference in New York because that was the only time and place during the entire year that all the key dealmakers with decision-making authority from all over the world would be together. But the window to execute Operation Greta was extremely small, and they couldn't afford for anything to go wrong. There was zero margin for error.

According to the hieroglyphics on the napkin, Coco would enter into a memorandum of agreement (MOA) to sell Scrubber Ships' entire thirty-ship fleet to Athena's company, Beta Ships, for $750 million net. The concept of "net" was especially important in shipping transactions because the sums were large and it was customary to have millions of dollars in commissions paid to a variety of brokers and intermediaries, some of which were even affiliates of the buyers and sellers themselves.

Coco believed the selling price was low, especially considering the $150 million of new scrubbers, but he was planning to substantiate it with the internet-generated appraisal that LTO Capital sent him to prove his loan was in default. When he sold the fleet and paid off LTO in full, two things would happen:

His personal guarantee would be released, and Vinny Vitale's $150 million would disappear.

Coco felt sick about damaging Vinny so quickly and completely, especially since the guy hadn't done anything wrong, but Coco was choosing to put family first.

The biggest obstacle was that Henry Husk's investor group had only seeded Athena's with $150 million of equity. That meant Coco would have to help her arrange $600 million of debt financing in order to close the deal.

Coco knew all too well that his assets weren't appealing to commercial banks. That's why he was planning to take advantage of the Chinese vessel leasing market, the only source of capital of which there was more supply than demand at that moment.

There would be more than a dozen Chinese ship leasing companies looking for deals at Marine Money Week, but Coco had his sight set on one in particular — CSLC, China Ship Leasing Corporation, which was run by the volatile Chen stepsisters. It took a long time to complete due diligence and conclude a first transaction with a Chinese vessel leasing company, but since Coco had already been approved by CSLC on a previous transaction that didn't close, he knew that they could move quickly...but only if they wanted to.

Back to the plan. Once Athena had taken delivery of the vessels from Coco, she would modify the ships with the carbon-neutralizing accoutrements she had invented at BIT and use her Boston buddy's artificial intelligence and natural-language-processing software systems to optimize the chartering.

When it was all said and done, the outcome would be brilliant for Coco; *Kon Tiki* and the kids' $175 million trust fund would be forever safe from creditors, neither Rocky nor any of his other competitors would get their hands on Coco's ships at the bottom of the market, and Coco would look like an ESG god to his wife, children, and the world at large.

As an equity kicker, Henry Husk and his friends had agreed to give Coco a silent, springing interest in Beta Ships; once they got their $150 million of initial equity back with a ten percent annualized return, Coco would be entitled to claw back twenty-five percent of the common shares.

But there was a problem: He had to execute the complicated, multistep transaction without the help of Robert Fairchild. Coco was about to find out if what Alex said on the yacht was correct, that a talented CFO was worth their weight in gold.

The cabin was suddenly plunged into darkness as the aircraft collapsed into 5,000 feet of sickly black clouds. The violence of the jolt toppled the beer off Coco's small table, shattered a cabinet full of plates and glasses, and yanked the latch of the flight deck door off the wall, causing it to smash open and closed incessantly.

Coco hastily shoved the diagram of Operation Greta back into his blazer pocket, gripped the armrests, and sucked in a breath so deep that he felt like his lungs might explode. For a man who needed to be in control, sitting in the back of an out-of-control rent-a-jet with two kids at the wheel wasn't much fun.

"Hey, Chris," the Norwegian shouted. "Is the bad weather almost over?"

"Actually, we have just been advised that it's about to get quite a bit worse," he called over his shoulder.

"How can it get worse when we are nearly tits-up already?"

"Because Tropical Storm Harold has strengthened into Hurricane Harold, and we are approaching the eyewall."

"We're flying through a *hurricane?*" Coco shrieked.

The big Norwegian immediately cupped his hands around his bugged-out eyes and smushed his giant face against the small oval window. He was hoping to see the twinkling orange lights of industrial New Jersey, suggesting he might survive this jinxed journey. But what he saw instead was the horrifying image of the dim white light bulb on the tip of the stubby little wing flexing forty-five degrees in an eerie green washing machine of tropical wind and water. It looked like it could snap like a brittle twig.

"Can we please take a smoother route when we go back to the Bahamas tonight?" Coco pleaded. "I don't mind if it costs more."

"You're funny, Harry," Captain Christopher chuckled nervously through clenched teeth.

"I wasn't joking."

"We aren't going back to the Bahamas tonight."

"Oh, yes, we are," Coco shouted. "I reserved this pitiful little airplane for the round trip today."

"Oh, no, we aren't," Captain Christopher replied.

"I promised my kids I would be home tonight," Coco said. "And I literally *can't* spend the night in America because of a, um, legal technicality."

Coco suddenly had visions of the NYPD arresting him on Rocky DuBois's warrant and hauling him down the center aisle of the Marine Money Week conference in handcuffs. He feared the image might replace the one of him grinning behind his sunglasses that *Ahoy Matey!* used as their file photo whenever they wrote something about him, which was almost every day.

"I'm sorry, sir, but this aircraft isn't leaving the ground until tomorrow afternoon at the earliest," he said.

"Why not?"

"Because it will require a complete analysis as a result of the lightning strike."

"Lighting strike!" Coco shouted.

"We didn't want to scare you," he said.

"Is that why the lights went out?"

"If you are looking for something to blame, Harry, you can blame it on climate change. It was 108 degrees in Miami today, and the sea hasn't been this warm since they started keeping records."

After less than thirty seconds of stability, Coco's testicles dropped into his ankles as the plane suddenly shot up, climbing even steeper than it had after the slingshot takeoff in Nassau a few hours earlier. He felt like he was riding a roller coaster.

"Does this thing have one of those black boxes?" Coco shouted to the pilots through the intermittently open door.

"Of course we do," Captain Christopher said. "That is compulsory under FAA regulations."

"Good," Coco said and removed the transaction structure of Operation Greta from his sport coat pocket, unbuckled his chest harness, and staggered like a drunk toward the cockpit. "I want you guys to stick this in there."

He figured that if he perished on the airplane, maybe Robert Fairchild could salvage the deal and save Alex the misery of unwinding his affairs under the sword of Piper Pearl and Rocky DuBois. Calling Robert back into his service was the last thing in the world that he wanted to do, but he figured he could live with it so long as he was dead. He would put the deal structure in the black box and write Robert an email that he would hopefully send before the plane smashed into the ground.

"You must remain in your seat," Captain Christopher shouted.

"What difference does it make where I am when this thing hits the ground?" Coco replied as he kept walking. "I just need you guys to put this in the black box."

"We can't do that," the pilots replied in unison, as if repeating a refrain in church.

"Why do you guys always say 'no' to me?" Coco asked.

Before Captain Christopher could explain that the black box was actually concealed in the tail of the aircraft, his co-pilot said, "Good news, Mr. Long-Johnsen. We have just been informed that we'll be on the ground soon."

"I don't appreciate your choice of words," Coco snarled as he clicked the seatbelt closed and pulled it tight.

"One more thing," she added.

"No more beverage service?"

"We're going to have to ask you to assume the emergency landing position."

"What!" Coco screamed. "You mean the *crash* position?"

"Please bend forward as far as you can," Captain Christopher said.

"So I can kiss my ass goodbye?"

Based on the gift that Hilmar had given him that frigid Norwegian night fifty years earlier, Coco always figured it was only fair that he would die young. His life had been a feast, he wasn't entitled to have the gravy too.

But like many naive fatalists, a seriously frustrating situation arose when he approached the age of sixty. That was when Coco fell in love with Alex, became a father, funded the $175 million trust fund — and realized that his most enjoyable and meaningful twenty years might actually still be *ahead* of him.

"We need you to place one hand on top of the other and do not interlock your fingers," she said, reading the instructions off of a laminated placard.

"*Holy shit!*" Coco shouted, his blue eyes bugging out.

As Coco squeezed the temples of his humongous head between his knees, he was startled by the comforting thud of the landing gear being dropped beneath his feet, followed by the mechanical buzz of extending wing flaps. He was thrust forward when the aircraft suddenly decelerated, stabilized, and fell oddly silent.

The Norwegian involuntarily unclenched his sphincter as he peered over Captain Christopher's shoulder and saw two rows of white landing lights glittering like a Christmas tree. Maybe he was going to make it after all. Out of the frying pan at Teterboro and into the fire at Marine Money Week.

Coco prepared to hear the soothing squeak of rubber on runway, followed by the relieving scream of reversing Rolls-Royce jet turbines, but he experienced something else entirely. With just fifteen feet separating him from terra firma, a wind shear swatted the fifty-two-foot aluminum cylinder onto the asphalt runway like a mouse caught in a snap trap.

The violence of the impact cracked the airframe, blew out the tires, and caused Captain Christopher's head to smash against the jagged knobs and dials on the instrument panel. As the lightweight airplane went careening sideways off the runway at 160 miles per hour, Coco hugged the sketch of Operation Greta against his chest like it was a teddy bear.

Through the open cockpit door he could see that the runway lights had vanished. They were now speeding through the foul weather toward a grove of mature pine trees eerily reminiscent of the Bergen forest where his mother took him cross-country skiing under the moonlight as a boy. As he prepared for impact, Coco Jacobsen realized he hadn't taken Hilmar's advice after all. He had stayed at the party too long.

Chapter 15

"I am going to *kill* Coco Jacobsen!" Vinny Vitale growled through gritted teeth from his sprawling corner office on the forty-fifth floor of 268 Park Avenue.

It was the middle of the day, but Hurricane Harold had darkened the sky so completely that it seemed like dusk. As the wind gusts violently slammed against the floor-to-ceiling windows of his unlit lair, Vinny stared at the Scrubber Ships financial model. His jaw hung open with disbelief.

With his trusty Babolat tennis racquet white-knuckled-gripped in his right hand, he leaned into the haunting blue light of the two monitors and slowly slogged his way through the Excel spreadsheets. Page by page, row by row, column by column, cell by cell.

He clicked the mouse like he was firing a handgun, *bang-bang-bang*, as he highlighted the outrageously overstated assumptions in yellow. He felt like he was shining a flashlight on the gruesome details of a crime scene. And there was worse to come. Camilla hadn't updated the Scrubber Ships model in almost a month, and according to his Bloomberg screen the tanker market had been getting worse by the day. It was going to be a bloodbath.

Vinny rubbed his throbbing temples and looked out across the eerie and abandoned forty-fifth floor kingdom that he controlled. The lights were off, the air conditioning was turned down, and the foyer's towering flower arrangement, an obscene display of Rome-moments-before-the-fall decadence, had been hauled off to a landfill. Even the omnipresent aroma of freshly brewed coffee and stale food delivery were conspicuously absent.

An asset management company without people was as haunting and useless as a carnival without kids, Vinny thought. On any other afternoon, Black Boulder would've been buzzing like a Bangkok bordello. His army of wealth-seeking Wharton grads would be pounding out PowerPoints that promoted potential transactions and provided performance reviews of existing investments.

Surrounded by the glittering lights of magical Manhattan, the air was normally thick with private equity dirty talk — jargon spoken against the backdrop of econometric erotica flashing and blinking and scrolling on a dozen giant televisions tuned to Bloomberg and CNBC.

There would be idle uttering about asymmetric risk and accretion; leveraged recaps, hurdle rates, credit arbitrage, and creating alpha through value-add; synergy realization and leverage capacity. The high-functioning men and women would speak in mysterious acronyms like WACC and IRR, ROI and NAV, ROCE and QOA, and the mother of them all: MOM, an homage not to the women who lovingly carried them and painfully pushed them into the world, but to something even more sacred and brutal — *the multiplication of money*, the merciless metric by which all fund managers were ultimately judged.

But today the office was empty.

The majority of midtown offices had been evacuated around noon when the NYPD closed down the transportation system and ordered people to go home and shelter in place to avoid potential injuries caused by the bizarre June hurricane currently bruising the Big Apple.

Vinny tried to piece together the confluence of random events that culminated in the financial tragedy of Scrubber Ships. He vividly remembered when Camilla Castro, one of his most ambitious and enigmatic MDs, surfaced the "opportunity" during the Monday morning meeting a few months earlier. She had been incredibly excited to have fortuitously met the wife of a Norwegian shipping tycoon who needed money to install exhaust-cleaning scrubbers on his fleet of supertankers. To Vinny it seemed like serendipity. It was a perfect fit for his newly launched PURE ESG fund.

As the storm raged outside, Vinny processed the speed and severity of the capital incineration. And he began to think about how he was going to take down Coco Jacobsen. After all, making an ill-timed, unsecured investment in a fleet of over-leveraged old VLCCs may have been an uncomfortable pimple on the ass of one of the mega private equity funds, but for a firm the size of Black Boulder, it spelled trouble. With a mere $500 million of assets under management, the failure of a $150 million investment in Coco Jacobsen might be terminal. Everything Vinny had worked so hard to build was now at risk of evaporating.

Vinny had thought he was alone on the dark forty-fifth floor, but when he saw the light in Camilla Castro's office go on, a sadistic smile stretched across his face. He couldn't wait to hear what she had to say for herself. He needed someone to pay, but first he needed some answers.

Chapter 16

Camilla Castro may have looked like a million bucks in the tattoo-tight blue dress and the charcoal *kajal* that set off her vivid green eyes, but she knew she was in deep shit. The moment she updated the Scrubber Ships financial model and refreshed the workbook, her screen lit up with high double- and even triple-digit red numbers.

At least she was alone, she thought. As she cast her eyes around the deserted and dimly lit office, she vaguely considered the idea of renting a car and bolting back down to Key Biscayne and never coming back. She would take a pay cut, but she could easily get a job at one of the big international banks in Miami, serving wealthy Spanish-speaking clients from Latin America while enjoying the good weather and seeing Alvaro all the time.

Her dream of making a killing in New York City so she could support her little brother was quickly turning into a nightmare from which she wanted to wake up. You were never too young to have an exit strategy, she thought.

Camilla had been walking east across forty-fourth street to shelter in place at her Tudor City apartment when she received the email from her go-to London shipbroker, Fergus. She immediately turned around and headed back to the office. Fergus had sent her the current vessel appraisals and cash flow numbers she needed to freshen up the Scrubber Ships Excel file. Once she had updated the financial model, she planned on emailing it to Vinny so he could blow off steam while he was out of the office.

Camilla suddenly lost her breath when she noticed a single glass office light up across the deserted prairie of dark cubicles. It was the southwest corner. The one with the great all-day sunlight, the unobstructed view of the Statue of Liberty, and the only fully functioning tennis backboard in a midtown Manhattan skyscraper. It was Vinny's Corner, which meant she was screwed.

She was in shock as she watched the five-foot-three-inch money manager rise in front of his floor-to-ceiling bookshelves packed tight with golden tennis trophies and gaudy Lucite deal toys. As Camilla watched Vinny exit his office and start heading in her direction with a tennis racquet resting on his beefy shoulder, she felt a geyser of cortisol gush from her adrenal glands. It was telling her it was time for fight or flight — but it was too late for flight. Fighting for her life was her only remaining option, and Vinny Vitale was a formidable opponent.

Camilla appeared to keep her eyes on her computer screens, but like a driver pretending not to watch the police car in the rearview mirror, her eyes were fixed on her boss. His body was so jacked up on supplemental human growth hormone, protein powder, testosterone top-ups, and extreme fitness that he waddled. As he moved closer, he awakened one slumbering motion-sensor light after another — flashes counting down to the moment of her reckoning over the shipping investment gone wrong.

Vinny rounded the final corner and entered the hallway that ran around the perimeter of the forty-fifth floor. It was an eight-foot-wide moat of cool beige carpet that separated the managing directors like

Camilla from the legion of nine-to-five staffers who served them.

As he moved down the backstretch, Camilla struck a professional pose; she twisted her shiny black hair into a loose bun on top of her head, secured it with a yellow number-two pencil, and narrowed her eyes as she focused on the screens. She tried to look composed, but her heart was racing.

Camilla Castro had conflicting emotions when it came to Vinny Vitale. Although he was known on Wall Street for inflicting violence on people who failed to perform as they had promised, he had always been supportive and encouraging of her. She didn't want to be naive, but she didn't want to be judgmental either. Lord knows she wasn't perfect.

But no matter how unsure she felt about him, there was no question about why he was coming to see her. He had been demanding to know how Black Boulder's investment in Coco Jacobsen's company was performing. It wasn't going to be pretty.

Chapter 17

Despite the four decades he had spent running money, Vinny Vitale would never look, sound, or smell the part of a midtown money manager. His short stature, muscular body, thrice-broken and never professionally repaired nose, Queens patois, and street-fighting approach were as unusual in the rarefied world of institutional asset management as the way he had entered it — through a hole in a chain-link fence.

As one of their many illicit ventures, Vinny and his twin brother, Otis, had hacked a hole in the fence that separated Big Jimmy's Tire Emporium from the grounds of the US Open tennis campus in his native land of Flushing Meadows. The V Bros' petty hustle involved smuggling penny-pinching preppies into the annual tennis tournament for a fee, but the enterprise proved life changing.

When business was slow one sweltering late August afternoon, as the humidity thickened the air and the temperature climbed above 100 degrees, Vinny and Otis violated the Dealer's Code; they climbed through the hole and took a taste of their own product.

The first match they saw took place on one of the remote practice courts. Vinny watched in awe as a spirited John McEnroe smashed multiple racquets and released a wide range of profanities at the balding French referee before losing to a seventeen-year-old wunderkind from Ireland named Davenport Kirkpatrick.

Otis's interest in tennis was limited to watching ladies' singles matches and scavenging for loose change beneath the metal bleachers, but that afternoon Vinny learned that he possessed a superpower — the ability to compile data and compute probabilities. Without premeditation or planning, he instinctively divided the tennis court into zones on the back of a discarded US Open program. Then he meticulously scored each shot like his grandfather did at Mets games, noting in which zones each ball bounced before a point was won.

After the professional tennis carnival moved out of town and high school started up again, Vinny couldn't get tennis off his mind. As part of a math project, he sat at the kitchen table and crunched the data he had mined at the US Open.

Vinny used the statistics to prove that when a tennis ball was returned *from* a certain place on the court *to* a certain place on the opposite side of the court, it had a higher or lower probability of winning the point. The experiment sounded basic, but the fact that it was measurable and repeatable meant it was genius.

Vinny wasn't content counting other peoples' points. He needed to be in on the action. So through a combination of deadlifting barbells, hitting millions of yellow balls against a cinder block wall at the local Catholic church, nurturing his naturally obstinate personality, and leveraging his proprietary algorithms, Vinny Vitale became a tennis star.

At age fourteen he entered the New England championships qualifier through the back draw and ended up beating the Ukrainian number-one seed in the stunning triple tiebreaker that was televised on Channel 11. At sixteen years old, Vinny advanced to the quarterfinals of a national tournament in Delray Beach, Florida, losing a close match to a then unranked German ginger named Boris Becker.

At seventeen the circle was completed when Vinny qualified to play in the US Open. He was knocked out in the second round by a fifteen-year-old Russian, but the American's ascent from the mean streets to top-flight tennis proved to be good fodder in local and international newspapers.

A knee injury, combined with his hot temper, prevented Vinny from playing professional tennis on the ATP circuit. But his hometown celebrity helped him land a well-paying job teaching tennis to rich kids at an exclusive Hamptons country club. Vinny had been planning to enroll at a local community college after Labor Day that summer until the father of two kids in his tennis class, who was a partner at Bear Stearns, asked to speak with him privately.

The remarkably good-natured and kind investment banker had been intrigued by an article he'd read in the country club's summer newsletter, which someone had left in the changing room. The article described Vinny's method of using statistically generated techniques to win matches against players who were, by all other measures, better than him. Vinny knew how to win ugly, punch above his weight.

"You're a smart kid, Vinny," the banker said as he approached him in the tennis shack between lessons. "But it isn't smart to play games that only one person can win."

"There's always a winner and a loser, Mr. Baldwin," Vinny said as he took a break from stringing racquets and accepted an iced tea.

"Not on Wall Street," Mr. Baldwin said, smiling. "On Wall Street the pie just keeps getting bigger because the value of the stock market increases over time."

"Must be nice when more than one person can win," Vinny said with a laugh as he resumed stitching neon green string through grommets of a racquet.

"In game theory, it's what we call a *win-win*," Mr. Baldwin said. "And I want you to be a winner, Vinny. I want you to come work on my convertible bond desk after Labor Day."

Figuring he could always go back to school if Wall Street didn't work out, Vinny instantly accepted the invitation. Mr. Baldwin proved to be a loyal friend and devoted mentor, until he choked to death on a hunk of prime rib at 21 Club at the age of fifty. That's when Vinny decided to start his own money management business. He collected his first assets from a group of "family offices" controlled by business owners he knew from the old neighborhood.

He named his firm Black Boulder on the brazen belief that it would one day grow even bigger and stronger than Blackstone and BlackRock. But thanks to his impulsive investment in Coco Jacobsen's Scrubber Ships, he was about to get crushed into gravel.

Chapter 18

"It's so great to see you, Vinny," Camilla said as her boss moved within earshot, the aroma of his Dolce & Gabbana cologne preceding his arrival.

"Don't be so sure," he replied. He placed one hand on each side of the door and leaned in to have a look around. "To be honest, I'm kind of surprised to find you here, Cammy. Everyone else is gone."

"I could say the same thing about you," Camilla replied. "What's the boss doing here during a hurricane?"

"I think you know exactly why I'm here."

"I do?"

Vinny subtly scanned the young woman's personal space with the curiosity of a parent passing a teenager's off-limits bedroom. The ten-by-ten warren was standard issue for a midtown private equity managing director making $375,000 per year plus a guaranteed bonus of at least that amount — double what many doctors made and more than ten times the compensation of a teacher of the same age, education, and experience.

There was the usual cream-colored linen wallpaper on two sides and glass walls on the other two. One glass wall faced the hallway, which allowed for a combination of good lighting and Vinny's binocular surveillance of what was on her screen. The other wall had a magnificent view of the prickly green points of Saint Patrick's cathedral, the *New Yorker* sign illuminated in glowing red light bulbs, and across Times Square toward the Hudson River and the plains of New Jersey — all of which were presently obscured behind the thick green snot of Hurricane Harold.

As he examined Camilla's office, Vinny was unnerved by the dearth of personal effects. He couldn't recall ever seeing an occupied office so sterile. It was weird. Even the legions of auditors and summer interns brought more decor.

There were no photos of wrinkly grandparents or mushy-faced newborns swaddled in pink-and-blue striped hospital blankets. There were no sunburned noses and smiling faces on Hamptons beaches, no shots of boyfriends or brothers or bridesmaids or husbands or horses or parents or puppies. There were no Yankee foul balls, no trinkets from Asian business trips, and no matchbooks from the Delano Hotel or Nobu.

The only objects on her credenza were a massive stainless-steel Yeti, an iPhone charger, a rolled-up blue yoga mat, and a pair of AirPods. As a man perpetually afraid of losing his best talent to a bigger firm that paid better, Vinny couldn't help but notice that Camilla's office was decorated for a quick escape. She could fit all of her non-digital possessions into a shoebox.

"I'm here because I have to finish my letter to our investors," Vinny said. "And the only thing I need to calculate the performance of the fund is the current valuation of the Scrubber Ships investment."

"What a coincidence," Camilla said. "I was literally just updating the numbers in the Scrubber Ships financial model."

"Great," he said.

"Um, yeah," she stammered. "Hey Vinny, would you like to come into my office and sit down?"

"Only if I am invited," he said.

"You are," she said, smiling warmly. "Cordially."

"So how's it looking?" he said as he entered and sat down next to her desk.

"I'm not going to lie, Vinny," she said solemnly. "The losses are steep."

"How steep are we talking?"

"Today's low charter rates have caused the value of the vessels to drop dramatically, since ship values are a function of the perceived amount of free cash flow they will generate."

"I get it. So what number should I put into my Q2 report to investors?" Vinny asked. "I need to calculate the return in order to figure out our carried interest."

"Based on the vessel values I just received, the value of our investment in Scrubber Ships is approximately..." Camilla paused as she looked at the screen and performed a few phony calculations on an improvised Excel calculator.

"*How much?*" Vinny asked with impatience as he squinted his eyes in concentration as if preparing to receive a 125-mile-an-hour serve from an ornery Eastern European teenager.

"Zero," she finally said.

"*What?!*"

"Zero."

"Wait, are you saying that our return on investment is zero?" Vinny asked.

"No, Vinny, what I'm saying is that our *principal* is currently worth zero," she said.

"Is this some kind of joke?" he demanded.

"I wish it was," she said.

Vinny knew the Scrubber Ships situation was bad, but he had no idea it was *this* bad. After a prolonged period of silence during which Vinny Vitale's nostrils flared and a symmetrical set of thick veins, remarkably reminiscent of lightning bolts, pulsed on his temples, he began to methodically adjust each of the strings on his Babolat. Once all of the strings were in order, he raised the tennis racquet high above his head with both hands and smashed it against the floor.

"But there's no need to be alarmed," she said.

"No?"

"All I'm saying is that if the ships were sold today, our preferred equity piece would not be worth anything because the value of the fleet is the same as the outstanding balance of the loan secured by the vessels. The ships are worth about $750 million, and the balance of the senior loan is $750 million, and that doesn't include our $150 million of preferred equity."

If what Camilla was saying was true, then Vinny Vitale was toast. The $7.5 million annual management fee that Black Boulder generated was a nice skim, but it wasn't nearly enough to sustain him. After paying Wall Street salaries and Park Avenue rent, his take-home pay wasn't enough by half to cover the $150,000 after tax dollars that Vinny, his wife, and their five beautiful daughters devoured each month.

Vinny needed the carried interest. He was desperately depending on it. That was the real reason he had made the outsized bet on Scrubber Ships. If the deal with Coco Jacobsen went wrong, Vinny would be looking for a job as a $15-an-hour barista at Starbucks while his former peers were dispensing investment advice to the masses, writing their memoirs, and donating libraries and hospitals to be named in their honor.

"We must be getting scammed," Vinny said.

"Don't worry, Vinny. Coco would have to be crazy to sell the ships in today's lousy market," Camilla said calmly. "He would lose all of his equity."

"Maybe he *is* crazy?" Vinny said. "Did you ever think of that? He seemed a little crazy the one time I met him."

"The only time you guys got together you ended up swimming in a fountain in Cannes as the sun was rising," Camilla replied. "That was like something out of *The Wolf of Wall Street*."

"I know," he sighed, shaking his head back and forth. "That's what sucks about this."

"What?"

"I really liked that guy," Vinny said. "I think we could have been friends."

"You are both loyal, self-made, and hardworking men," she said. "Hopefully that means you can find a way to work things out."

"But how can we be down 100 percent? I've been in the money business four decades and I've never lost 100 percent of my money on anything!"

"Shipping is powerful medicine," Camilla said. "If the dose isn't appropriate, it can be lethal."

"It's going to be lethal alright," Vinny said.

"Look, Vinny, I just want you to know that if someone needs to take the fall on this investment, it will be me," Camilla said. "I'll take the bullet."

"I respect that, Camilla, and I just want you to know that we don't use bullets anymore," Vinny said.

"Okay," she said stoically. She just hoped it would be quick.

Camilla knew she'd made a mistake. Had Alex and Coco not been her friends, and had they not shared a common need to make sure St. Lucy's Academy continued to operate for the benefit of Maisy and Alvaro, she might not have recommended the Scrubber Ships deal to the investment committee in the first place. She didn't admit it to herself at the time, but she had a conflict of interest; Coco and Alex were a related party, a hallmark no-no of the "G" in PURE ESG.

She had conveniently overlooked two fundamental flaws in the investment thesis. The first was that there was no way of predicting the future price of oil, which meant it was impossible to know the future price difference between low-sulfur fuel and high-sulfur fuel. That meant it was impossible to accurately forecast the economic value of the scrubbers.

The second problem was that the leverage on the fleet was much too high considering the fact that the ships were not on long-term charter and there wasn't any form of personal guarantee on Black Boulder's preferred equity slice if the market turned down. Those two factors, taken together, created a cash flow stream and capital structure that was too fragile to withstand the heavy blows of shipping's consistent volatility. The returns would appear to be lower on paper, but she couldn't help but wonder if shipping was a sport best played without any leverage at all.

"But Vinny, we haven't actually lost any money," Camilla said. "It's an unrealized loss. The only way we would lose the money is if Coco decides to sell the ships now. And like I said, if he sells the ships now, he will lose all his equity," she said. "Why on earth would he do that?"

"Why on earth would anyone be in this zombie industry in the first place?"

"We'd need to hire a behavioral psychiatrist to answer that question," she said. "It's complicated."

"No, it's simple. Get me Robert Fairchild on the phone right now," Vinny shouted. "He's the one who convinced us to do this fraudulent transaction, and he's the one who is going to get me my money back."

"I can't," she said.

"Why not?"

"Because Coco told me that Robert retired from Scrubber Ships shortly after we made our investment," she said quietly.

"*Retired?*" Vinny said, stunned. "Hold on, are you saying that *my* $150 million was *his* exit strategy?"

"I hadn't thought about it that way," she said.

"Oh, and you think it was a *coincidence?*"

"Yes," she said and then paused. "I don't know. Maybe not."

"Do you happen to have Robert Fairchild's home address?" Vinny asked, his eyes penetrating hers as he demanded a truthful answer.

"Yes," she said.

"Can you write it down for me?"

"I guess so," she said.

After Camilla had reluctantly transcribed the information from her phone onto a scrap of paper, she handed it to Vinny. The moment he took possession of it, she recognized that she had just made a terrible mistake and put Robert's life at risk.

"Thanks," he said. "This deal was supposed to be *my* exit strategy, not his exit strategy! I thought I was going to retire on a Gulfstream, but if this investment goes wrong I will be retiring in an *Airstream!*"

"Never give up, Vinny," Camilla said calmly. "You are stronger than you think you are." It was one of the many important lessons Alvaro had taught her without knowing it. "The more challenging the situation, the closer we come to truth."

"I ain't giving up, and I ain't backing down either," Vinny said, and used his mangled tennis racquet to push the telephone across the desk toward Camilla. "If you can't get me Fairchild, then get me the big guy. Get me Coco Jacobsen!"

"I can't call him either," Camilla said. "Not right now."

"Why the hell not?"

"Because he's on an airplane heading to New York," Camilla said.

"I hope he doesn't die in a plane crash before I get a chance to kill him," Vinny said. "Why's he coming to New York anyway?"

"Because he's giving the closing keynote address at Marine Money Week this afternoon. Apparently he has a major announcement to make."

"What the hell is Marine Money Week?" Vinny snarled.

"It's the biggest shipping finance conference in the world," she said. "And it happens to be taking place at the Montclair Hotel today."

"During a *hurricane?*" Vinny asked.

"Shipping people are social creatures. They prefer to do business in person," she said. "It's a three-day event, and today is the last day, which means everyone arrived in New York before anyone even knew there would be a hurricane. Since all the flights out are canceled and the NYPD has issued a shelter-in-place order, the organizers figured it would be best to just go ahead with the final day of the event as planned."

"That's the best news I've heard all day," Vinny said, staring blankly out the window into the rain-filled sky.

"It is?"

"Oh yeah," he smiled, returning his eyes to hers.

"I'm glad you're happy."

"Get yourself ready to go, Camilla," he said. "I'm going to ask one of my associates to meet us at the Montclair Hotel in one hour."

"The associates and analysts all went home for the day," she said.

"It's not that kind of associate," he smirked.

"Then what kind of associate is it?"

"The kind that can show Mr. Jacobsen just how hard we play the money game here in New York," Vinny said, and waddled out the door.

Chapter 19

"Bless us, O Lord, and these thy gifts which we are about to receive," Robert Fairchild said after folding his fingers together, closing his eyes, and solemnly lowering his head — just enough to expose the beginnings of a bald spot of which even he was not yet aware.

He may have looked like a middle-aged man at peace, but the inner Robert Fairchild was suffering from some major-league agita. As honored as he was to be kicking off his father-in-law's eightieth birthday lunch, he was frustrated to be missing out on the Marine Money Week conference taking place at the Montclair Hotel just a few blocks away.

It would be the first time he hadn't attended the annual socio-corporate affair since first stumbling upon the shipping industry ten years earlier. While running Eureka! Capital, a midtown hedge fund, he had accidentally typed the letters BDI into Google instead of the stock quote box on his Bloomberg screen.

He had been looking to check the share price of a crappy little life sciences company called Biodynamics Incorporated, ticker BDI, but what he found instead was an altogether different BDI, the Baltic Dry Index, which ended up being a door into a parallel universe: the bizarre and wonderful world of international ocean shipping. His life hadn't been the same since.

Just as Robert was about to wrap up his father-in-law's birthday blessing, he lost his train of thought when a torrent of text messages and phone calls came cascading onto the iPhone he'd stashed in his corduroys against his wife's strict instructions about possessing the device at dinner.

"Are you having a heart attack, Dad?" inquired his perpetually hungry thirteen-year-old son, Oliver, as he ripped open a dinner roll and pushed a pat of butter into it with the tip of his index finger. "You look really weird."

"That's *gross!*" his wife, Grace, recoiled. "Use a knife!"

"Sorry," the boy said, and licked his finger. "All clean!"

"I'm fine," Robert said as the vibrating stopped. "Don't worry."

"If you're fine then get on with it," Grace urged.

"Yes, we have a hungry boy over there," his father-in-law, Oscar, said, smiling proudly at Oliver.

"Okay, sorry," Robert said. "Bless us, O Lord, and these thy gifts which —"

Just as Robert attempted to resume the pre-meal blessing, the device hidden in his pocket emitted another tantalizing tickle. Someone was desperately trying to reach him, which was unusual. He hadn't received a lot of incoming communication since Coco dumped him.

He was torn by the stimulation of the device. On the one hand, his father-in-law's eightieth birthday meal was no time to take a phone call. On the other hand, as a former shipping man, he knew that inappropriate moments were exactly when the best and worst things happened.

Physically unable to resist the vibrating any longer, the forty-nine-year-old man rose from his family table, folded his blue cloth napkin into a tidy square, and uttered words that were not officially part of any blessing.

"Amen, gang," he said solemnly.

Grace's eyes popped open. "*Excuse* me? Did you just say *'Amen, gang'?*"

Robert avoided her glare. He didn't need to see his wife to know that her face displayed a haunting mélange of dumbfounded and homicidal as she watched her potentially soon-to-be-former husband move away from the table. Her delicate eyebrows were up, her beautiful brown eyes were open wide, and her normally inviting, glossy-pink lips were agape with shock.

"Where do you think you're going?" she demanded.

"Little boy's room," Robert said. "Is that okay?"

It had been many years since Robert had been able to sit through an entire meal, enjoy a movie, participate in a meeting or conference call, watch a television show, or even take a leak without having his phone involved. The compulsion had only gotten worse since he'd lost his job. When he couldn't get away with the filthy act of self-indulgence in public, he developed the coping skill that so many people used: excusing himself to use the bathroom to check it in private.

"Not in the middle of the Lord's Prayer it's not," she said.

"Nature calls," he said. "Besides, your name is Grace, why don't you finish it?"

"Hold it," she said.

"I wish I could," Robert said with a sigh. "That's the whole problem, right Oscar?"

On the way out of the room, Robert scooped his Pinot Noir off the dining table so he could bring it with him — to enhance the imminent pleasure of checking his iPhone. After all, the only thing more satisfying than cruising his screen was doing it while simultaneously doing *something else* that required his attention, like watching a movie or talking on the phone — maybe even *two* other things.

"I mean *STOP!*" Grace snapped.

Robert had made it halfway across the living room when his wife jumped to her feet and went into attack mode. She scurried across the room and intercepted him before he had a chance to escape. She put one arm on each side of the wooden door jamb to block his exit. He was caught in a roadblock.

"Spread 'em," Grace demanded, and motioned toward the built-in mahogany bookshelf on both sides of the casement door.

"Excuse me?"

"Put one hand on *Diary of a Wimpy Kid* and the other hand on Bruce Springsteen's biography," she said calmly but sternly. "Then spread your feet and close your mouth."

"I believe stop-and-frisk is illegal in New York," Robert said.

After he had assumed the position, Grace pried the wine glass from her husband's hand, finished the considerable remains of his favorite Oregon Pinot Noir in one large gulp, and slammed the empty glass on the built-in bookshelves. It was showtime.

"What is she doing?" Oscar whispered to his grandson, leaning across the table.

"Pat down," Oliver replied casually.

"Drugs?"

"Nah, she wants to see if Dad has his phone hidden on his body."

"Does he?" Oscar asked.

"What do you think, Grandpa?" Oliver laughed.

While Grace was occupied searching her husband's body, Oliver stole a sly glance at the device he had surreptitiously stowed under the dining room table with a flap of silver duct tape. An avid, some might say compulsive, online gamer, Oliver felt compelled to check in with his virtual comrades several times each minute — an interval remarkably similar to that of his father looking at his iPhone. When it came to technology addiction, the cat was in the cradle chez Fairchild.

With his daughter and grandson distracted, Oscar fished a giant iPhone from his pants pocket. The old man's dopamine was gushing as he blasted through half a dozen apps: scanning the Apple-curated news, perusing the radar map showing the vector of Hurricane Harold, searching the local movie listings, tracking an incoming Amazon order, and swiping at Tinder — to see if any fresh ladies had been added to the seventy-plus age category in the last twenty minutes. *Bingo!*

Back at the main event, Grace went to work searching her husband's body. She commenced the pat down procedure at the cuffs of his blue gingham shirt and green cashmere sweater. She worked one arm at a time. Her hands moved slowly over his left wrist, applying massage-quality deep tissue pressure as she moved up his forearm.

Her blood pressure spiked when she reached his left armpit, momentarily mistaking a matted tuft of hair for an electronic device. False positive. She repeated the procedure on his right arm. Nothing. Satisfied that there was no contraband concealed above his waist, Grace fell to her knees to have a look down under. She started the process again, just above his suede bucks, and worked her way up his sockless ankles and calves en route to his groin.

"You'd make a terrific TSA officer, honey," he said as her probing advanced slowly up his right leg.

"Be quiet."

"You could at least buy me a drink first," Robert said.

Grace did not respond to his flagrant use of flirtation as a form of distraction, nor did she alter the course of her examination. To the contrary, the moment Robert shifted the angle of his hips slightly while pretending to sneeze in a fashion that was uncharacteristically dramatic, she knew she must be close. The bobber was twitching.

And then she felt it.

The thin rectangular device was wedged deep in the front left pocket of his trousers, so close to his plumbing that she might not have probed the region in the presence of her old father and young son. But tonight she was taking no prisoners; she would have resorted to amateur proctology had she thought it might produce a phone.

"Gotcha!" she shouted as her hands aggressively seized the device, along with a grab bag of skin, half a testicle, some pubic hair, boxer shorts, and a clump of corduroy.

"Ouch!" He shrieked in pain and jumped back.

When Grace spun around and triumphantly hoisted her digital kill above her head, she saw her eighty-year-old father and thirteen-year-old son reflexively, if clumsily, attempt to stash their own unauthorized devices beneath the table. At that moment, Grace had an epiphany: It was over. She wasn't going to spend the rest of her limited days on earth policing this bullshit. She was done.

"I know I won't be able to win the war against these weapons of mass distraction," she said as she marched toward the window. "But I'll be damned if I can't cause some casualties along the way."

When she reached the bank of windows, Grace examined Robert's iPhone with genuine curiosity and focus — as if she were trying to locate ringworm larvae in a piece of dog crap before bringing the Ziplock bag to the vet. How could something so small wreak so much havoc? she wondered.

"What are you doing?" Robert asked calmly.

"This is the instrument of the devil," she replied.

"Don't you think that's a wee bit extreme?"

"Is it? Look at the logo, Robert," she said, and held up his phone. "It is an apple with a bite taken out of it. How much more obvious could it be?"

"Interesting observation, Mom," Oliver acknowledged with a kindly nod.

"Robert, you promised you wouldn't bring this thing to the dinner table."

"Yes, but —"

"Not to church, like you ever *go* to church; not while in the middle of a parent-teacher conference; not while driving; and not in the bedroom."

"I adhere to those rules," he solemnly swore.

"Oh, really," she said, hand on hip, eyebrow elevated. In case he didn't remember the event, she added, "Let's not forget the *Aristotle Incident*."

Robert regretfully recalled the time Grace busted him using his phone during Aristotle Onassis/ Jackie O. role-play shortly after he'd bought a 1977-built freighter from Spyrolaki and renamed it *Lady Grace* in honor of his wife.

"Are you *ever* going to forgive me for that?"

"I can forgive," she said as she placed his iPhone on the radiator, "but unfortunately I cannot seem to forget. It's become a recurring nightmare."

Grace lifted the black iron latch, crouched slightly, and pushed the window up with both hands. As the glass slowly slid open, a gust of Hurricane Harold's wind and rain instantly infiltrated the apartment. It riffled papers, ruffled curtains, and caused Oliver and Oscar to look up startled from their devices. She stuck her arm out the window and held Robert's device twenty floors above Park Avenue.

"What do you think you're doing?" Robert asked.

"We're having a family exorcism," she said, "which is the closest thing we have to church these days."

"This isn't funny," he pleaded as he moved toward her. "I need that thing. It's my lifeline to the world."

"Do you see me laughing?" she said.

"Can I at least see who was trying to reach me?"

"No."

"Maybe it was Coco," Robert said.

"Yeah, right," she said. "He hasn't returned a single one of your calls or texts since he fired you. Alex isn't even calling me back."

"He didn't fire me," Robert said as he moved toward her with his arm outstretched. "I retired. Now give me back my phone. Please."

"You *better not* have retired," Grace said.

"It was kind of a misunderstanding," he said.

"Well, don't misunderstand this, Robert. If you take one more step, I'll drop it."

"Yes, officer."

"And look what you've done to that kid," she said, motioning toward Oliver, who *again* tried unsuccessfully to stash his iPhone under the table.

"What did I do?" Robert asked.

"It was bad enough when you used your phone when you came home from work, but now that you don't even *go* to work it's worse than ever. This kid is going to grow up thinking daddies are all addicted to their phones, and that's not good."

"I am *not* addicted to my phone," Robert said with self-righteous indignation.

But as vigorously as he would protest the accusation, Robert knew that he really was addicted to his iPhone. In the diagnostic parlance of psychologists who specialized in treating the growing epidemic of screen and social media addiction, he was known as a "constant checker," and his symptoms had indeed flared up since he'd stopped working for Coco; the less he had going on, the more compulsively he scrolled, desperately hoping it might magically produce something stimulating or profitable.

On a typical day he would handle, touch, scroll on, stroke, check, swipe, stare at, cradle, and sometimes just lovingly fondle the device in his pocket close to 500 times — ten times more than the average teenager.

"This thing has stolen more from you than it's given you," she said.

Then Grace did something she wished she'd done a long time ago; she opened her hand and set the evil device free.

"Fly away, little phone!" she cried as she leaned out the window and watched the iPhone tumble through the stormy weather. It bounced high off the building's iconic green canvas awning before disappearing into a puddle on the northeast corner of Eightieth and Park. The beast was finally dead.

Chapter 20

The terrifying landing at Teterboro Airport, during which Captain Christopher crapped in his khakis after his head smashed against the instrument panel, had probably subtracted a few more years from Coco's actuarial clock — but he was lucky to be alive.

The deep swale that separated the runway from the adjacent pine forest was full of water, compliments of Hurricane Harold. The swampy watercourse miraculously brought the projectile airplane to a soggy stop just fifty feet shy of a deadly impact. As Captain Christopher was being hauled away in an ambulance, muttering something about "best practices," Coco jumped into an Uber to make the twelve-mile journey to Manhattan.

Once he had checked into the Montclair Hotel, the first thing Coco did was make a dozen unsuccessful attempts to reach Robert Fairchild by text, email, and telephone. After he gave up, he took a scalding hot shower in the Presidential Suite before getting ready to go downstairs to Marine Money Week.

With his face just a few inches away from the gilt-framed mirror in the steamy bathroom, he inspected his attempt at manscaping. He slowly rotated his head from side to side, closely examining the bloody nicks blooming across his leathery face while attempting to run his fingers through hair that was just a few twists away from dreadlocks.

The cruel LED lighting provided a haunting illumination of his face. From afar, the Norwegian appeared as mentally and physically fit as ever. But zoom in close and it was a different story altogether. The punishing life of a crude oil tanker owner — characterized by excessive quantities of stress and the gratuitous use of alcohol needed to blunt it, working around the clock to triage an endless array of operational and financial problems, incessant international travel, and not nearly enough sleep, exercise, or healthy food — was starting to take a toll.

He wanted to leave the shipping party while he was still having fun. Go crawling back to *Kon Tiki* and never leave again; hibernate in the islands, get healthy, spend time with his family, pay attention to the weather, and train for next year's Churchill Cay tennis tournament — so he could kick Horace Buttersworth's bony ass.

The Norwegian tanker tycoon hardly recognized his own reflection in the hotel mirror. Living in the tropics had toasted his naturally brown skin to the same texture as the puckered hide of the Louis Vuitton duffle bag unzipped on the giant bed and nearly the same shade as the black Viking battle helmet tattooed on his right bicep. The three hours each day he and Ziggy spent poling a skiff over the sand flats in search of elusive bonefish had given him a menacingly muscular physique.

But despite his castaway appearance, Coco's piercing blue eyes were sharper and more alive than they had been in years. In just three hours he was scheduled to deliver the closing keynote address at the thirty-third annual Marine Money Week conference. In his five minutes of remarks he would forever change his life, identity, and legacy — and maybe even change the centuries-old way that ships were owned and operated.

As Coco was inspecting his face, a crashing sound exploded in the living room of his hotel suite. He was startled by the explosion — and it took a lot to rattle the self-made oil tanker magnate. It wasn't in his nature to be paranoid, but the truth was that some very bad people were not happy with him. In one fluid motion, he spun around, squared his shoulders, widened his feet, and raised his fists. It was a stance he had learned as a little boy in Bergen, where he'd been bullied. That was before Coco grew tall and strong and wealthy.

With huge, tight fists in front of his face, Coco slid his bare feet silently across the white woolen carpet as he moved down the long hallway. When he paused to listen for the intruder, he noticed for the first time that the expressionist artwork lining the walls depicted scenes of maritime activities in the era when sailing ships still filled New York Harbor and docked at Manhattan's many piers. No matter what happened in the future, Coco would always be proud to have been a shipping man. It was the closest connection to the history of human progress that still existed in the modern commercial world — and it was hidden in plain sight.

Coco knew he might need a weapon. As he approached the large living room of the suite, he reached around the corner and wrapped his left hand around the cylindrical silver lamp on the end table next to the yellow sofa. He yanked the clear plastic electrical cord from the wall, ripped off the shade, and gripped the lamp in his giant hand. Then he raised it over his head like a club and slowly peered around the corner.

Normally the $25,000-a-night suite would have afforded spectacular views across the southern part of the 840-acre Central Park. The canopy of electric-green budding treetops, the red neon Essex House sign glowing atop the hotel, the Woolman skating rink, the horse-drawn carriages hauling tourists and new lovers across the park, the twin peaks of the Time Warner building, the oxidized-green mansard roof of the Plaza Hotel, and the traffic oozing down Fifth Avenue and across Central Park South, fourteen floors below. But today he couldn't see anything but the ghostly mass of gray water vapor that had been stalking him all the way up the Eastern Seaboard.

When Coco moved slowly into the large living room of the suite, he was startled to see that one of the four massive windows was wide open. The eighty-mile-an-hour gusts of Hurricane Harold were violently slamming the window against the wall. The large sheet of safety glass was cracked into a spider web of fractures, and there was a deep dent in the pale yellow-and-blue striped wallpaper where the latch had been striking the wall. The puddle on the floor had turned the white carpet brown.

Still clutching the shiny lamp over his head, Coco moved across the living room and slowly approached the window. He leaned outside and looked up to inspect the eve of the roof above. Nothing. Then he surveyed the shallow terraces of the neighboring room. Nobody. He pulled closed the broken window and latched it, hoping the cracked glass would hold together and continue to keep out the weather.

BANG! BANG! BANG!

Coco was startled by the aggressive pounding on his door. He walked barefoot back down the long hallway. When he peered through the peephole, he saw the distorted outline of a familiar face that he'd last seen during a bitter disagreement. It was Pratap Bhat, the undisputed heavyweight champion of the global vessel scrapping market.

Known in the shipping industry as a cash buyer, Pratap bought more than 300 ships for recycling annually. In recent years he had used his substantial retained earnings and unique position in the market to amass a working fleet by buying ships intended for scrap and continuing to operate them.

Sometimes he could squeeze one cargo out of them en route to a subcontinental demolition yard; other times he could trade them for years if the market paid enough to justify the cost of ongoing maintenance. Ships were like cars or boats or any other piece of machinery: They were as good as their original construction and subsequent maintenance. And there were plenty of examples of charterers who preferred twenty-year-old Japanese-built ships over newer ships that had been poorly maintained, consumed too much fuel, or had been built by inferior shipyards.

"What the hell do *you* want, Pratap?" Coco called through the door.

"Ah, thank you for the very kind greeting, my friend," Pratap said with a warm smile. "I have missed you too. It has been a long time."

"Not long enough," Coco said.

"Don't be so silly my friend. Open the door."

"How did you know I was here?" Coco said as he reluctantly unhitched the chain that locked the door.

"I have my sources," Pratap said. "But don't worry, this will be our little secret. And not our only secret, either," he added as he entered the suite.

"You've always been good at keeping secrets," Coco said. "Especially from me."

"My God, man," Pratap marveled at Coco, examining the Norwegian's castaway appearance from his almost-deadlocked hair to his savagely tanned feet. "You look like you just stepped off the set of *Pirates of the Caribbean*. This is so very cool!"

He may have been of average height and build, but Pratap Bhat had a large and stylish presence. He was wearing a perfectly tailored royal blue suit with a bright red hanky stuffed into the breast pocket. His white shirt was opened just enough to expose the gold chain hanging around his neck and his moustache had been grown long and waxed Dalí-style since the last time Coco had seen him, when Coco stormed out of high tea at the Burj Al Arab hotel in Dubai. Pratap's thick, wavy black hair had turned salt-and-pepper over the past year, and his teeth were a bit brighter and whiter than his eyes.

Pratap Bhat was a legend in the vessel demolition market. Like a dreamy-eyed speculator migrating west during the American gold rush and or the internet boom, Pratap was just eighteen years old when he piled onto a crowded bus in his hometown of Hyderabad and headed for Alang, the ship demolition capital of the world.

His plan was to work for the summer on the beaches where massive oceangoing ships that had reached the end of their useful economic lives were rammed ashore at high tide and then deconstructed by hand. The steel that was harvested from the dead ships was fed into mini mills and used to satisfy a substantial portion of the country's domestic steel requirements in an enviably efficient manner.

Pratap sauntered onto the beach with a red bandana wrapped bandit-style around his mouth and nose and a blue-flamed blowtorch in his left hand. He immediately went to work brutally dismembering a 487-foot Greek-owned freighter named *Endless Prosperity* — one chunk at a time.

Pratap's plan was to work in the vessel demolition facility for a few months and return home with a year's worth of money to share with his family, but then he fell in love — with the mysterious world of cargo ship demolition.

He worked his way up through the ranks. He spent thousands of hot days ripping apart vessels and just as many cool nights sitting beside an open fire learning about the economics of vessel recycling from the elder scrappers.

By the age of twenty-three he had saved, begged, and borrowed enough cash to buy his own ship — a dead freighter named *Blue Mountain Express* that had been lying on a Jamaican quayside for more than three years after the DEA discovered it had been hauling large quantities of ganja to New Orleans in addition to the bauxite listed on the official bill of lading.

Pratap paid a paltry $50 per ton for the Sinsemilla ship, which was market price at the local scrapyards in Brownsville and the Dominican Republic. But the name of Pratap's game was arbitrage. He managed to finagle the certifications needed to tow the vessel back to the Indian Subcontinent, where scrap ships commanded a higher price. But instead of scrapping the ship immediately, he kept the vessel at anchor for more than three months, living aboard and waiting patiently for a spike in virgin steel prices that would, in turn, lift scrap steel prices.

When the per-ton price spiked after China unleashed a trillion dollars of stimulus aimed at steel-intensive infrastructure development projects, Pratap fetched a lofty sum for the freighter, generating a $500,000 windfall. That gave Pratap the seed money he needed to carefully build a billion-dollar empire over the next three decades.

"What do you want, Pratap?" Coco asked.

"Can't I visit an old friend?"

"Do you actually think we are friends after what you did to me on *Viking Alexandra?*"

"But why are you cross with me?" Pratap said with a laugh. "I paid you the full market price for that ship."

"Because I sold you that VLCC for scrap, and you ended up operating it for another six months after you took delivery in Jeb Ali. You even stole a cargo from me at Ras Tanura!"

"Come on, Coco, you are the one who *invented* the scrap-n-trade when you dressed up in a cash buyer costume and bought a fleet of old VLCCs from the Great Dane in Copenhagen and then proceeded to operate them for five more years," Pratap said.

"Jah, but that was different."

"That was genius," Pratap said. "I will never be your equal when it comes to combining theater and shipping, but I will always try."

"That wily old Dane was pretty surprised when his old ships kept coming back from the dead lowballing cargoes," Coco said with a laugh.

"You outfoxed the fox on that one," Pratap said. "But seriously, I want you to know that I really was planning to recycle *Viking Alexandra*, until the Americans put all the Chinese and Iranian tankers on the naughty list, which caused charter rates to skyrocket to $225,000 per day just as we were bringing the vessel from Jeb Ali to the demo yard."

"You got lucky," Coco said.

"I can resist many things, but making $10 million on two voyages isn't one of them," he said with a smile.

"That was my ten million," Coco said.

"Coco, we all know that selling ships shortly before they increase in value is very painful, but you should be happy that you don't own that ship in today's market," Pratap said. "You'd be losing your shirt."

"I have thirty other shirts," Coco said. "What do you want from me, Pratap? Why are you here?"

"I'm here to help you, my friend," he said, smiling.

"Help me?"

"I gather you are having some financial issues," he said. "I thought you might need to raise some cash."

"Who told you I need cash?"

"I heard those savages at LTO bought your loan," Pratap said.

"Who told you that?"

"I read it yesterday in the new issue of *Ahoy Matey!*," Pratap said. "That was poor manners for Piper Pearl to send his grandson down to the Bahamas to hand you the foreclosure notice during tennis. I am also a tennis player, by the way."

"There are no secrets in this town," Coco said, perpetually stunned by the transparency in the U.S. capital markets. It was a far cry from the cloak-and-dagger world of private European banking, where people could still keep a secret.

"Everyone knows that the VLCC market is very weak and your ships are very old. When you consider the challenges of getting competitive financing on an old fleet of tankers these days, I thought you might be interested in selling me some of your ships now to raise a bit of liquidity."

"I'm not selling my ships by the ton," Coco said, and he slammed the door, momentarily imagining a hunk of his own flesh on a scale in a butcher shop.

"Suit yourself, mate, but I am warning you. You should scrap them now, while the prices are still firm," Pratap called out through the closed door. "ESG is going to make vessel recycling more expensive very soon."

Chapter 21

Coco removed a fresh blue button-down shirt from his duffle bag, pulled it over his head, and started to head downstairs to the conference. It was T-minus three hours until his life-changing keynote address, and there was no turning back now.

Coco was electrified with nervous excitement. Like a homerun hit in extra innings or a soccer goal scored with zero time left on the official's clock, the sum total of his entire life was being compressed into one do-or-die moment.

As he exited the elevator at the lobby of the Montclair Hotel, Coco removed the tarnished silver H.A.R. money clip, a cherished gift from his mentor and idol Hilmar, and peeled off a $100 bill.

"Have a nice day," he said as he pressed it into the hand of the elderly operator.

"Oh my God!" she said slowly, stunned by his gesture. "Is this for me? Really?"

There comes a time when giving money to people who need it is a lot more fun than amassing more of it, Hilmar had told him. Although performing random acts of generosity initially felt wholly unnatural to Coco, going against the deep-rooted instincts of every bad-market-fearing, penny-pinching shipowner, Coco grew to love it.

"Do something nice for yourself, dear," he replied, humbled by the look of joy on her face. "You deserve it."

After he exited the elevator, Coco turned left and began walking toward the hotel entrance on Fifth Avenue. His heart jumped when he saw an NYPD officer, accompanied by a massive German shepherd, guarding the hotel exit. Whoever had told Pratap that Coco was at Marine Money Week might have also told Rocky, who would have been thrilled to call the police to enforce the outstanding warrant for the "Cappuccino Bunker Caper." Fortunately, the officer was distracted from scrolling on his phone and didn't see him.

Coco made a quick right and ducked out of the main hallway before the distracted cop spotted him. He entered a rotunda covered with trompe l'oeil murals and slowly ascended the spiral staircase that led to the grand ballroom where Marine Money Week was being held.

As he climbed the stairs and looked down, he saw a dozen different clusters of shipowners and shipping bankers and lawyers huddled together doing business in small groups. When he reached the top of the stairs and looked down, he noticed a pride of bearded young Norwegian dealmakers looking up at him like they were worshipping a god. Coco smiled and waved.

When it came to hard assets, the shipping industry had more transactional velocity than any other single market in the world. There were a variety of reasons for this, but it boiled down to the fact that ships, cargo, and offshore U.S. dollars were all fungible commodities. When taken together, shipping was the most "perfect" market in the world.

Anyone could transact anything with anyone, anywhere, anytime. A Greek could sell a ship to a Norwegian, finance it in Paris, and charter it to a Korean, who might sub-charter it back to a Greek, possibly even to *the same* Greek who had sold the ship in the first place — so long as there was a spread to be skimmed.

In a therapeutic effort to calm his sizzling nerves, Coco rejected the recommendation of his Parisian pulmonologist and decided to smoke a Marlboro. Before arriving at the conference registration desk located just outside the double doors that led into the grand ballroom, he turned left and walked down a deserted flight of stairs. When he got to the bottom of the stairs he stopped and peered around the corner at the hotel's Sixty-First Street entrance. He was relieved to see that there was no police presence.

Coco pushed through the hotel's revolving door and emerged beneath the Montclair's iconic illuminated marquee. The scene was post-apocalyptic, and he was surprised that there was suddenly very little wind. The normally buzzing and obscenely prosperous block of Sixty-First Street between Madison Avenue and Fifth Avenue was a ghost town. The rain had temporarily let up, the air had a putrid smell, and the sky had turned an eerie shade of green; Coco was standing in the eye of Hurricane Harold. A dozen trees were down, and countless snapped limbs and fallen branches littered the sidewalks and were strewn across the street.

To his right, Madison Avenue was deserted. Most of the lights in the street-level shops and the offices above them were dark. To his left, he saw a blue-and-white NYPD cruiser slowly patrolling Fifth Avenue barking orders through a PA speaker, reminding civilians of the 10 p.m. curfew and admonishing them to remain indoors while the strong winds made deadly projectiles out of everyday objects.

But no matter how shitty the weather, how short the trip, or how awful the agenda, Coco always felt energized being on the streets of New York City. Over the course of his peripatetic life, the Norwegian had been everywhere, owned everything, seen all there was to see, and done just about everything there was to do — from island-hopping in the Caribbean and Mediterranean to spring skiing in the Alps to surfing the best breaks from the Maldives to Maui. He had stayed in the best hotels, owned the best art, real estate, and cars, and consumed copious quantities of the best food and wine. But spending time in New York City in June had become his single favorite moment of the year — for both pleasure and business.

When it came to actually operating vessels, New York was no longer a major shipping hub. The oil companies, grain houses, commodity traders, and shipowners had left New York long ago; they had migrated to leafier and more tax-efficient places like Switzerland, Greenwich, Houston, London, Vancouver, Singapore, Hong Kong, Athens, Oslo, and Bermuda. But when it came to finding new money to finance ships, there was no city in the world that held a candle to New York. It was the world's capital of capital — since more than half of the assets on the planet ultimately resided in American-controlled bank accounts.

Although it might literally kill him in the end, the hot money Coco had been able to source in New York had completely changed the trajectory of his life and business. While the traditional purveyors of European and Asian ship finance were focused on forgoing a high return for the sake of preserving principal and servicing multigenerational relationships, the U.S. capital markets were something altogether different;

they were a wild and exciting accessory that could give even the most conservative capital structure a bit of pizazz.

The U.S. had deep vernal pools of capital that sometimes sought risk rather than desperately trying to minimize it. The U.S. didn't provide the most dollars to the global shipping industry, which comprised more than 80,000 ships worth $1 trillion with an annual demand for capital of $200 billion, but in some ways it provided the most important dollars: the marginal dollars that kept the business interesting.

Coco had to give Robert Fairchild credit for helping convince him that shipowners who didn't take the time to cultivate relationships with U.S. investors would find themselves at a significant disadvantage over time. He wouldn't admit it in front of Fairchild, but his former CFO had been right about that, and a lot of other things too.

But it wasn't just the money that attracted Coco to New York; it was also the spirit of the place. No matter what chaos and crisis had defined his year, spending time with Alex in New York in June always invigorated him. He loved anonymously wandering the streets and getting lost in Tribeca, SoHo, and the nooks and crannies of Greenwich Village. He enjoyed stumbling upon galleries and clothing boutiques and having long, rosé-enhanced rooftop lunches in the warm midday sunshine. New York City always exhausted him long before he exhausted it.

"*Coco!*" a voice cried out.

Coco was surprised to hear someone call his name. He had just scanned every inch of Sixty-First Street from Fifth Avenue to Madison Avenue, and there hadn't been a single sign of life besides the patrolling police car. When he turned to see who it was, he was relieved that, as if by magic, his old friend Freddy Fingers had appeared beneath the illuminated marquee of the Montclair.

"Freddy!" Coco exclaimed as they embraced before stepping back and admiring each other. The two men had enjoyed a long-term bromance, a form of mutual respect among males who had managed to survive in the shipping jungle over an extended period of time. "What are you doing here?"

Coco hadn't seen Freddy, the British-born, flamboyant CEO of NASDAQ-listed shipping company Justice Shipping Limited (JSL), since an annual shipping-bank-hosted Christmas party at a hotel in Knightsbridge a couple of years earlier. Coco might not have recognized him if he'd passed Freddy on a crowded street. He looked healthier now than when they first met years earlier in a Houston cabaret while courting charters from a crusty Houston oil man named Rocky DuBois.

Freddy's thinning hair, historically worn scruffy long, had been chopped off, offering more detail of the shape of his skull. Like many men, he looked less bald without any hair than he did with some. His fitness regimen had sharpened his facial features and given him several inches of height as he stood straight. He was wearing a dark blue custom suit and tiny, round, gold-rimmed glasses in the style of Steve Jobs. Despite the horrific shipping markets, Freddy Fingers looked better than ever.

"I have been waiting for you," Freddy said.

"In a hurricane?" Coco said.

"Whatever it takes to get a moment with the world's most famous shipping celebrity," he replied.

"How did you know I was going to be in New York?"

"I have my sources," Freddy said.

"You and everybody else," Coco said with a laugh. "How are things at JSL?"

Freddy had named his company Justice Shipping and painted a scale on the smokestack of each ship to reflect the fact that he always owned exactly the same number of large tankers and large bulk carriers. It was the perfect balance of non-correlated tonnage, the perfect hedge, or so he thought until both markets went into the crapper when China and the United States divorced after twenty years of mutual benefit.

"It's been a challenging decade," Freddy confessed. "From 2000 to 2010 the shipping business was great, but from 2010 to 2020 it's been pretty awful. My share price has gotten crushed, and my investors aren't happy."

"That's exactly why *I* would never do an IPO," Coco boasted just as the gusts resumed, providing soothing relief to his sun-torched skin. "Having short-term investors in long-term assets isn't a perfect marriage."

"Don't bullshit a bullshitter," Freddy said, laughing. "Everyone knows the real reason you weren't able to IPO your LNG ships is because you couldn't pass a background check thanks to Rocky DuBois."

"Jah, but that turned out to be a blessing," Coco said. "By the way, is Rocky here?"

"He's having lunch with Herbjorn at the Chatham Bar inside the hotel as we speak," Freddy said. "Broker talk is that Rocky has twenty cargoes to lift out of the Arabian Gulf before summer. He could fix them all now at today's super-low rates, but apparently he's holding out to take us shipowners down by another $5,000 a day."

"But we're already below breakeven," Coco said.

"This is what gets the old guy off," Freddy said. "It's really sick."

"I think Rocky is going to have a long, hot summer," Coco muttered under his breath.

"I hope so, but it's not looking good for the shipowners. The list of available tonnage building up around the load ports is getting longer by the day."

"Don't believe everything you read," Coco said.

"Coco, I need to ask you a favor," Freddy said abruptly.

"I'm not in a very good position to help anyone right now," Coco said.

"Indeed, I heard LTO bought your loan," Freddy said. "That Piper Pearl is a nasty old wanker. He owned some of my bonds at one point. I bought back his paper at par just to get him at my hair."

"You don't know the half of it," Coco said, declining to divulge that Piper was actually fronting for Rocky, who was planning to steal his ships and then rob his family. "So what's up Freddy? What do you need?"

"As you know, Coco, owning big bulkers and big tankers has historically been an effective way to diversify."

"The scales of justice," Coco said. "When one market is cash-flow negative, the other one is usually strong enough to make up the shortfall."

"That was always the theory, but it doesn't seem to be holding true anymore," Freddy said. "Now that China dominates the shipping market, when they sneeze the entire industry catches cold."

"Look on the bright side, Freddy, distressed markets like we have today are exactly when guys like us should be buying ships as we did in the 1980s. New ship orders will slow down, and when demand picks up we will take control of the market again. It's the shipping cycle."

"Earth to Coco," Freddy said with a laugh. "The eighties were *forty years ago*. Back when we did deals with Marc Rich and wore Hermès neckties and flew on the Concorde and had big bellies from all the three-martini lunches with oil companies," Freddy said. "The world has changed, man. Hard assets are the new herpes."

Coco recalled when Alex had told him that he needed to stop living in the past, telling the same old shipping stories decade after decade without modernizing his goals, strategy, and tactics. Even a quintessential shipping man like Freddy Fingers was starting to lose interest, which was an encouraging confirmation of the announcement he was going to make later that day.

"Everything is cyclical," Coco said.

"Not everything," Freddy said, shaking his head back and forth. "Some changes are systemic."

"Hard assets will come back into fashion someday," Coco said.

"The fun thing about hard assets is *asset play*, buying low and selling high. The problem is the key ingredients for asset play are gone. There's not enough cheap bank debt, equity risk appetite, or global trade growth. We are zero for three at the moment, and I don't see any of those things changing. That means we are playing a free cash flow game now."

"Free cash flow is nice, but that's what creates the problems," Coco moaned. "When there is free cash flow people start ordering more new ships that kill the market and force the old ones to get scrapped."

"When I got into this business, we used to say that operating a ship was the pain in the ass thing we did after we bought it and before we sold it," Freddy said. "But now, with the asset play gone, the business of operating ships is just hard work."

"It's more fun when we are making money."

"We aren't exactly fashionable in a world in which the largest taxi company owns no taxis, the biggest hotel company owns no hotels, and investors can make double-digit returns by buying Amazon and Apple and going on vacation. That's why I need your help."

"What can I do for you?" Coco asked.

"I need cash flow, mate," Freddy said. "And I need it now."

"Don't we all," Coco laughed.

"No, this is different. If I can't show my investors some contracted future cash flow, I am going to have to cut my dividend," Freddy said.

"So cut your dividend. That's no big deal," Coco said. "That's what owning a cyclical business is all about. When there's no cake, you don't eat cake."

"That's okay for a private company like yours," Freddy explained. "But I promised my investors *yield* when I converted my company into a master limited partnership."

"Why did you do that?"

"I did it to get a better valuation," Freddy confessed. "It's not like the old days, Coco. It's not good enough to just make money anymore. Everyone wants to know about your capital allocation policy."

"What does that mean?" Coco asked.

"Capital allocation is what you promise to do with the spare money," Freddy said.

"You should tell your investors they should be grateful if there *is* any spare money," Coco said.

"That's not how it works," Freddy said. "Nowadays they want to know if you will pay down debt or buy more ships or pay a dividend or buy back your own shares."

"I am a simple shipowner, but I don't see why giving away the capital you need to survive and grow should make a company *more* valuable," Coco said with a laugh. "Steroids can be good but not on a long-term basis."

"It looks like the steroids are working for you," Freddy said, squeezing Coco's bicep.

"I've been trying to get a bit healthier now that I have a wife and the twins to look after," Coco said.

"Is that why you are smoking a cigarette with me? Don't you know every cigarette takes seven minutes off your life?"

"Yes, but the seven minutes I give up are the worst ones because they come at the very end, when I am suffering," Coco said. "I would happily exchange those lousy seven minutes for seven very enjoyable minutes smoking this cigarette with you right now." Coco smiled.

"Everything's a trade with you," Freddy said. "Here's the thing, Coco, if I eliminate my dividend, the MLP investors will be forced to sell more stock than the market can absorb and the price will drop by twenty-five percent."

"That's when the Freddy Fingers premium will become the Freddy Fingers discount. And that's when the real shipping men like me will come into the market and take a nibble," Coco said, smiling, "when it is cheaper to buy your paper than it is to buy more steel. I might even take a bite so big that it makes you question the depth of our friendship."

"You don't get it, Coco, this isn't a game. If my share price crashes, I will have a serious problem," Freddy said. *"Personally."*

"Why?" Coco asked.

"Because I margined my own stock," he confessed.

"You didn't." Coco laughed.

"I did."

"And what did you buy with the money?" Coco asked.

"Options," Freddy said after a period of silence.

"On what?"

"My own shares," he confessed.

"You *didn't!*" Coco laughed and slapped his thigh.

"I did."

"That's so awesome!" Coco chucked. "You leveraged your shipping shares to buy more leveraged shipping shares in a highly leveraged shipping company?"

"Yes," Freddy admitted.

"Well, no one can accuse you of not drinking your own Kool-Aid," Coco said.

"Come on, Coco. I need your help," Freddy pleaded.

"I'm just as screwed as you are," Coco said. "We shipowners all rise and fall on the same tide."

"I really need a hit of long-term cash flow, man," Freddy suddenly sounded like a junkie. "I need it so bad. Won't you please charter-in some of my ships on fixed rates for three to five years? I promise to make it up to you when the market is better."

"I can't help you, Freddy," Coco said sternly. "Not this time."

"But I have plenty of cash," Freddy begged.

"If you have so much cash, then use it to pay the stupid dividend," Coco said.

"The investors won't let me," Freddy complained. "I have $150 million of unrestricted cash on my balance sheet, which is more than I have ever had, but the investors want to see my ships generating free cash flow, not just paying out cash as dividends."

"Then just use the $150 million to buy back your shares," Coco said. "That's what I did with my bonds. It worked out great."

"Come on, Coco, you owe me. Don't you remember when I chartered all those Aframax tankers from you for seven years, just so you could access the cheap money in the Japanese leasing market?"

"Yes."

"I lost my ass on those ships," Freddy said.

"Don't worry," Coco said, laughing as he inspected his friend's rump. "Your ass has never looked better."

"How about when I paid you $125 million for that Korean VLCC when it was worth less than $100 million, just so it would increase the broker valuation of your entire fleet and get your covenants back in compliance without you having to cough up any cash?"

"I appreciated that," Coco said.

"Today is no different. I have cash, and you need cash. There must be some way we can work together."

"I don't think so," Coco said.

"Have it your way," Freddy said as he pulled a tiny silver pistol from the inside pocket of his suit jacket.

"What the hell are you doing?" Coco cried.

Freddy pointed the miniature handgun up in the air and rotated it back and forth as he closely examined both sides of its antique finish and mother-of-pearl handle. Then he pointed it three inches away from Coco's mouth.

"This won't hurt a bit," Freddy said, and squeezed the trigger.

Chapter 22

"That little toy looks so real," Coco said as he moved his unlit Marlboro into the orange flame flickering from the barrel of the Sharper Image cigarette lighter. Once Coco's cigarette was lit, Freddy turned the incendiary device onto his own cigarette.

Coco and Freddy both felt a surge of optimism as the tidal wave of fresh nicotine made its way through their bloodstreams. As they smoked in silence, a pair of bright white LED headlights turned left off Madison Avenue onto Sixty-First Street. They watched as the triple-black, pimped-out Mercedes Sprinter with darkened windows and Virgin Islands license plates reading *STALKER* inched toward them.

As if maneuvering through a minefield, the armored vehicle slowly made its way around the downed trees and snapped limbs that had fallen in the Hurricane. When the vehicle finally stopped in front of the marquee of the Montclair Hotel, Freddy and Coco exchanged puzzled glances and shrugged their shoulders as they each sucked on their cigarette like big babies on a warm bottle of milk.

They were the type of dudes who might roll up to Marine Money Week in an assault vehicle like the one idling in front of them, which meant they were naturally curious about which member of their own species was about to emerge from the backseat.

The men watched in silence as the driver, whose physique and demeanor suggested a recent retirement from the Israeli military, stepped down from the car.

Offering them a wink and a smile, the chauffeur lightly tapped his left breast twice, just to let them know he was armed.

As they speculated as to which of their shipowner friends might be about to disembark, they watched a black stiletto heel attached to a lithe leg emerge from the mysterious vehicle before being planted on the sidewalk.

"*Buenas tardes*," Camilla Castro said with a heavy Cuban accent as she air-kissed Coco once on each cheek — and then a third time for friendship. What was left of Freddy's cigarette hung from the lower lip of his open mouth.

"Tell you what," Freddy whispered out of the side of his mouth. "If you agree to charter some of my ships and give me enough guaranteed cash flow so that I can pay my dividend, I agree not to tell Alex about this friend of yours in Manhattan."

"Thanks," Coco whispered back. "But who do you think introduced me to her in the first place?"

"Seriously?"

"Yup."

"You have a very generous wife," Freddy said, and Coco nodded in agreement.

"She charged me a finder's fee," Coco said.

"Still."

"Freddy, I'd like to introduce you to Camilla Castro, from Black Boulder Asset Management," Coco said as Camilla and Freddy extended their hands toward each other. "Camilla, this is my friend Freddy Fingers. He is the CEO of Justice Shipping Limited."

"*Encantado*," Camilla said.

"*Igualamente señorita*," Freddy replied, and turned to Coco. "And where did the two of you meet?"

"At St. Lucy's Academy," Camilla said. "My little brother, Alvaro, goes to school there with Coco and Alex's niece, Maisy."

"That's a lovely thing to have in common," Freddy said.

"But now Coco and I have a different kind of relationship," she smiled.

"Pray tell," Freddy smiled.

"It's purely financial," she said.

"It's purely ESG," Coco said and winked. "Camilla is the portfolio manager for Black Boulder's PURE ESG fund. She's the one who gave me the money I needed to buy the scrubbers for my ships."

"It wasn't a gift," Camilla reminded Coco. "It was a loan."

"You told me it was equity," Coco said with a laugh. "And *equity* is another word for *gift* in the language of shipowners."

"It is *preferred* equity," she clarified. "There is a difference."

"Big difference," Freddy said. "Been there, done that, paid the coupon, got the T-shirt."

Freddy's sweet schoolboy crush on Camilla was killed the moment Vinny Vitale's Gucci-loafer-clad foot poked out of the car and stretched toward the sidewalk. Camilla, Freddy, and Coco watched in silence as the size-eight, gold-festooned shoe hit the ground followed by 180-pounds of menacing muscle shrink-wrapped in faded designer blue jeans and a black cashmere turtleneck with matching blazer. Vinny had a Babolat tennis racket in one hand, a giant phone in the other, and a five-inch dollop of puffy white hair sitting atop his powerful sixty-three-inch body.

Although Vinny's diminutive size sometimes caused him to be momentarily mistaken for a child, his youthful height was dramatically offset by his fast-growing facial hair, muscle-bound body, neck as wide as his head, fingers flashing with golden bling, and nose that looked like it had been ripped off, stepped on, and then reaffixed by someone who was late for a train.

But every one of Vinny's unusual physical characteristics immediately yielded to the bright sparkle in his blue eyes — the result not of any profound emotional sensitivity, but of the overactive tear ducts that he had tried unsuccessfully to have corrected several times at the Hospital for Special Surgery on the Upper East Side.

"Gentlemen," Vinny said with a wide smile that exposed the almond-size gap between his two front teeth. His head bobbed up and down as he spoke. "You guys enjoy hanging around outside in a hurricane?"

"We are happy being anywhere we are permitted to smoke," Freddy said, and put his arm around Coco. "Cool van."

"Wanna buy it?" Vinny said.

"I'm not sure how I'd get it back to London," Freddy said.

"You can put it on the deck of one of Coco's unemployed oil tankers," Vinny said.

"There's an idea," Freddy said. "What are all those antennae on the roof?"

"This pig was owned by a hedge fund I financed that specialized in using satellite surveillance to predict corporate earnings. They monitored things like how fast corn fields were growing and how full fuel terminals were, how many cars were in Walmart parking lots. They even counted barges on rivers and ships loading cargo."

"It's hard to keep secrets these days," Freddy said.

"The snooping part worked great, but one of the math geniuses made a coding error in the hedging strategy, and the whole thing blew up in about thirty seconds. Which is why I had to repo the pig — and take a few other, um, actions against the management team that let me down."

That was the moment when Freddy Fingers realized who Vinny actually was. He swallowed hard. It was Vinny Vitale, Wall Street's biggest villain.

"It's great to see you again, Vinny," Coco said, smiling. "That was some night out we had in Cannes. We should do it again some time."

Vinny took a step toward Coco and silently glared up at the Norwegian, his eyes darting back and forth across Coco's face.

"I'm not sure how many more nights you have left," he said.

Camilla stepped into the space between Coco and her brooding boss and said, "Vinny and I are greatly looking forward to what you have to say."

"I only speak the truth," Coco said.

"Truth?" Vinny laughed.

"I'm sure you'll be terrific, Coco," Camilla said sweetly as she took hold of Vinny's arm and started to direct him toward the entrance of the hotel. "*Buenos suerte*, Coco."

After Freddy and Coco watched Camilla and Vinny disappear through the revolving door of the Montclair Hotel, Freddy took one last drag of his cigarette and tossed it into the fast-moving current of dirty water rushing toward an overflowing sewer on Sixty-First Street. He squinted behind his round spectacles as the blue smoke coming from his nostrils and mouth was quickly swept away on the humid wind.

"Vinny's last name isn't *Vitale*, is it?"

"Yes! Have you heard of him?"

"Indeed," Freddy said.

"Great."

"Not really. I hate to ruin your day, Coco, but do you have any idea who that guy is?"

"The only thing I know is that he gave me $150 million to buy scrubbers for my entire fleet, and between you and me, it's looking like he won't see a penny of it ever again," Coco said.

"I came here today to ask for your help in solving my problem, but you have much bigger problems than I do," Freddy said, sighing as he shook a fresh cigarette out of the box. "I'm worried about paying my dividend, and you should be worried about your life."

"That's ridiculous," Coco said. "You're the one who told me that when it comes to investing in shipping, it's caveat emptor — buyer beware."

"It's also *borrower beware*," Freddy said. "Shipowners need to know who they are taking money from in order to understand what might happen if things go wrong."

"I think investors are basically all the same," Coco said dismissively. "Money is a commodity just like ships and cargo."

"Vinny Vitale is a different beast," Freddy said. "Do you have any idea where that gentleman gets the capital that he manages?"

"Probably the same conservative pension funds and insurance companies and endowments that everyone else in this town gets their money from," Coco said. "Right?"

"Wrong," Freddy said. "It's never been proven in court, not yet anyway, but the word on Wall Street is that Black Boulder's capital is dirty."

"How can capital be dirty?"

"His limited partners include a dangerous group of politically connected labor unions, Catholic dioceses, private credit unions, and certain 'family offices' associated with septic hauling and waste management."

"Sounds good," Coco said.

"No, Coco, *not* good. Don't you know what that means?"

"Not really," Coco said. The subtleties of American organized crime were lost in translation to the Norwegian.

"That means he might be investing money for the *mafia*," Freddy said.

"Like *The Sopranos!*" Coco announced. "Alex and I love that show. She says I remind her of Tony Soprano. Powerful yet sensitive."

"Then you must know what Tony Soprano does when someone doesn't pay back the money they owe him?"

"Jah, but the Wall Street guys don't do that," Coco said with a laugh. "Maybe he will hit me with his Blackberry?"

"I recently heard a rumor about a Silicon Valley CEO who lost the money Vinny had invested in him," Freddy said, leaning in close so no one could overhear the conversation.

"What happened?"

"Apparently the guy was stripped naked and strapped down in an abandoned New Bedford warehouse where a hundred hungry lobsters picked at his genitals for *two days*."

"Ouch," Coco said, instinctively touching his own.

"And there was an investment banker here in New York who sold Vinny a tech IPO that went bad after less than twelve months of trading. Want to know what happened to him?"

"Probably not."

"He was run over by a commercial fishing boat while waterskiing off Montauk," Freddy said.

"What's your point?"

"What's my point? My point, Coco, is that you have climbed into bed with a very dangerous man," Freddy said.

"Can you please use a different expression next time," Coco said.

"You can default on all of your other obligations, even your banks if you need to, but whatever you do, Coco, make sure you don't default on Vinny."

"Thanks, Freddy," Coco said. "I'll keep that in mind."

Chapter 23

Coco appeared to be moving in slow motion as he lumbered up the carpeted stairs two at a time. When he reached the top, he turned left and took a few steps toward the grand ballroom where the Marine Money Week conference was in full swing.

As he peered through the open doors at the rear of the room, Coco was surprised to see that despite Hurricane Harold, which was causing the elaborate crystal chandeliers to literally swing from side to side and occasionally flicker, there was a standing-room-only crowd in attendance on the final afternoon of the three-day conference.

Even at the significant distance, Coco could see the elevated stage was packed tight with a panel of the biggest European shipping bankers. They were veteran lenders from Paris, Rotterdam, London, Hamburg, and Oslo whose employers had been financing ships for centuries. But now they were tasked with financing the industry's transition to carbon neutrality, a disruption many believed was the biggest since ships switched from sails to steam engines.

Through the open double doors 150 feet away, Coco could hear Pierre DuFault from Versailles Bank bemoaning the shipping industry's relatively low returns in light of the risks and regulations, but Coco knew firsthand that skilled lenders made money more consistently than shipowners did.

When it came to ship finance, there was more to the story than just economics. The reality was that most serious shipping bankers and banks, especially the European ones, had the same level of engagement, personal responsibility, and dedication to the industry as the shipowners. Their business wasn't purely about maximizing the economic benefits of a particular transaction at a specific moment in time, but about respecting the value of past and future relationships.

That was one of the reasons why so-called tourists — the investors, lenders, and owners who visited the shipping market for a fast buck and a quick exit — didn't always experience the same degree of reciprocal sacrifice that existed among the lenders and borrowers who were in it for the long haul.

Just as Coco was casually cruising past the cloakroom on his way to the grand ballroom, he felt a claw-tight clamp on his bicep. He looked down to see the muscular Vinny Vitale resplendent in black cashmere. The diminutive fund manager effortlessly yanked the six-and-half-foot-tall shipping tycoon into the cloakroom and shoved him into a rack of coats, pressing his body against the wall with his tennis racquet.

Coco stared down at Vinny. As the Norwegian was considering how he would reply to the assault, he took a moment to savor the smell of the woolen coats that had come in from the rain. The earthy aroma reminded Coco of his childhood home — and his first job, on a sheep farm, when he was just eight years old.

His mind was instantly awash in memories of when his mom and dad were still alive and they all lived in the tiny house by the fjord. He remembered the hot summer nights when they would all sleep on his parents' bed watching a little black-and-white television because it was the only room that had a breeze from the sea.

Coco missed being a little kid, which might have been one of the reasons he refused to stop acting like one. In fact, until the moment he'd married Alex and become father to Thor and Olav, he would've traded all the worldly possessions he'd amassed to go back in time. Back to those endless summer days when his parents were still alive. When there was no school and no expectations, no responsibilities. Before he learned just how filthy and brutal and complicated and unsatisfying the world could be sometimes.

"Jah, but I also play tennis with a Babolat," Coco finally said. "This is a good omen. Maybe we can play tennis together some day."

"Let me give you some advice, Viking man," Vinny seethed as he pressed the racquet beneath the Norwegian's chin.

"That would be terrific," Coco said with a laugh. "Good advice is so hard to find these days."

"Don't do anything or say anything in your speech that will damage the value of my investment in Scrubber Ships," he hissed. "Got it?"

"Let's call it Viking Tankers," Coco said. "Would that be okay?"

Even under his present duress, he still couldn't believe how ridiculous the name Scrubber Ships was — or that he'd allowed Fairchild to greenwash his company just to get his hands on the ESG money. Anything for a deal, that's what Fairchild always said.

"I don't know how much you know about me," Vinny continued, "but trust me when I tell you that my investors and I do not have a sense of humor when it comes to losing money. You can do a Google search if you don't believe me."

"I don't do Google," Coco said.

Coco's natural instinct was to beat the living crap out of Vinny Vitale and bury him half-dead in a shallow grave of wet woolen outerwear — which is exactly what he would have done pre-Alex, before she had subtly modified his various maladaptive behaviors.

She encouraged him to delay his own gratification to the maximum extent possible. To take five deep breaths before responding. To flex his muscles and then relax them. To get a good night's sleep before replying to an irritating email or phone call. To match every negative thought with a positive one. To count his blessings on the string of worry beads Captain Bouboulina had given him. And to practice empathy when he came across unhappy people like Vinny Vitale.

Had someone taught Coco these valuable skills earlier in his life, he might have avoided certain events, such as confronting Rocky DuBois during his family's Thanksgiving dinner after Rocky made a bogus claim of *force majeure* on an out-of-the-money charter. But he wasn't going to look back with regret, because Thor and Olav had taught him that today makes tomorrow, and today is tomorrow's yesterday.

He didn't know exactly what all the stuff meant, but he took it to mean that having a successful life was like driving a car: You had to keep your eyes on the road, constantly adjust the speed and direction for changing conditions, and not spend too much time looking in the rearview mirror or else you would smash into something coming at you.

"It seems like something is bothering you, Vinny," Coco said after he had completed his five deep breaths. "Let's talk it out, so we can feel better together. Stress is the cause of anger, and inflammation is the cause of pain."

"There's nothing to talk about," Vinny said.

"How about your feelings?" Coco said. "How do you feel right now?"

"I feel like *killing you* is how I feel right now!"

"Maybe we should talk when you are in a better headspace," Coco said as he removed Vinny from his arm and began to walk out of the cloakroom. "I don't want you to do or say anything you will regret."

"The only thing I regret is giving you my $150 million," Vinny said.

As Coco began to exit the room, savoring the triumph of his own mature behavior, he suffered a sudden and inexplicable relapse. He was just a few steps from successfully extricating himself from the altercation with grace and poise when he involuntarily turned around and marched toward Vinny. He grabbed the little beefcake under the armpits and hoisted him halfway up the wall.

"*Boys!*" shouted Elaine Marstons, the chief Marine Money Week conference organizer, after she popped her head into the cloakroom and saw that Coco had Vinny pinned against the wall. Vinny and Coco looked at her with guilty fear in their eyes. They'd been busted.

"It's just a friendly chat, Elaine," Coco said sweetly. "Everything is under control."

"But he's *hurting* me," Vinny said. "And he's so much *bigger* than me."

"Coco, put that man down *this instant!*"

"I'm sorry, Elaine," Coco said sheepishly, lowering Vinny's body until his blinged-out loafers returned to the carpeted floor.

"We expect better behavior from our keynote speaker," she said. "Now you are going to apologize to him, Coco, and you are going to mean it."

"Not fair. He started it," Coco complained, and looked at Vinny, who flashed a gap-toothed smile.

"And I am going to finish it," Elaine said.

"Fine," Coco dramatically exhaled with defeat. "I'm sorry, Vinny."

"That wasn't so hard, was it?" Elaine said, and smoothed her hair in case it had been tousled in the tussle.

"Not at all," Vinny said.

"If you gentlemen have some business to discuss, may I suggest you avail yourselves of the deal room? It has a pleasant, trattoria-like atmosphere and is conveniently located just across the hall. There is continuous coffee service and an appealing selection of freshly baked —"

"Eh, it's kind of a private matter," Vinny said.

"Ah, yes, well if confidentiality is what you require, we have a small private dining room you can use," Elaine said.

"That would be wonderful." Vinny smiled kindly at Elaine. "We would like to use your private dining room. There are a few more things I'd like to say to Mr. Jacobsen in a more private setting," Vinny said. He didn't want any witnesses.

"That would be lovely," Coco said, and looked at his watch, "but unfortunately I have to give my speech soon."

"Oh, no, you don't," Elaine said.

"I don't?"

"No, you have plenty of time until your Keynote," Elaine said. "Matt is always running late."

"Wonderful," Vinny said.

"Please, follow me, gentlemen," she said.

Just before the unlikely threesome entered the Deal Room, Vinny aggressively pinched Coco by the elbow to prevent him from bolting. He flashed a phony smile to the hundred-plus ship finance deal junkies who watched in awe as the shipping industry's biggest, tallest, and swarthiest whale was being forcibly escorted toward the back of the room by a blinged-out, miniature muscle man wearing designer jeans and a black cashmere turtleneck sweater.

"Holy smokes," Mick Stronghold leaned forward and whispered to a table of lease-seeking clients. "I think that dude is Vinny Vitale."

"Who is Vinny Vitale?" his friend Pedro asked.

"He's a bad hombre," Mick said. "I've read about him on all the Wall Street blogs."

"Bad as in good?" Pedro asked.

"Bad as in *psychotic*," Mick whispered. "They call him the Butcher from Bridgehampton."

The deal room remained hauntingly silent as awareness of the infamous Vinny Vitale's toxic presence spread like a noxious odor. The enthusiastic deal junkies pressed the pause button on hotly contested debates: Did the shipping industry have too much capital or not enough? Would the economic cold war between the U.S. and China result in the regionalization of trade and a reduction in long-haul shipping? Will zero interest rates cause ship prices to inflate? Would digitization actually put shipbrokers out of business? Is LNG green? What will it take to get institutional investors excited about shipping again? Is residual value insurance a real thing? Is it better to be public or private? Will new ships ordered today be obsolete in ten years due to changing emissions regulations? George did *WHAT?!* To *WHO?!*

Camilla Castro burst through the double doors of the silent deal room. She was breathing heavy as she scanned the surroundings. When she spotted Coco and Vinny about to slip into the private dining room, she moved toward them as quickly as her high heels would allow.

She reached them seconds before they disappeared through a strange sliding doorway. Camilla ducked into the private room and pulled the heavy wooden pocket doors closed behind them with a loud and ominous thud.

"I'd like to be a fly on the wall in there," Pedro said.

"Oh no, you wouldn't," Mick said.

Chapter 24

Without saying a word, Coco, Camilla, and Vinny sat down on opposite sides of the round table as if they were settling in for a game of poker, which, of course, they were.

The white tablecloth was littered with logo-festooned items left behind by the previous occupants of the hot-sheets deal chamber. There were silver mint tins sponsored by an accounting firm. A tiny blue flashlight compliments of a ship registry. Several pens provided by an international law firm and a notepad covered with chicken-scratch IRR calculations of whatever shipping investment had been pitched in the room previously.

"I am really sorry about what happened in the cloakroom," Coco broke the ice as he held up his hands in surrender.

"What happens in the cloakroom, stays in the cloakroom," Vinny replied.

"*Que Va?*" Camilla laughed and dramatically threw her arms into the air. "I go to the ladies' room for five minutes and you *chicos* can't control yourselves?"

"Vinny started it," Coco said, pointing.

"Come on, boys, let's stay calm and get down to business," Camilla said as she placed a plastic bottle of water in front of each of them. She knew the most significant contribution she could make to the present situation was to provide an abundance of good humor and charm that might prevent Vinny from killing Coco.

"Fine," Coco said.

"Coco, why don't you start by giving us a quick update on our investment in Scrubber Ships? We all know the market has been weak, but how are things going with the business?"

"I've never seen it so bad," Coco said gravely, thickening his accent and slowly shaking his huge head back and forth as he slipped into the role of down-and-out Norwegian shipowner.

"*Not* a good start," Vinny said as he hoisted his tennis racquet into the air to communicate to Coco that it could be used as a weapon.

"The tanker market has been terrible ever since you made your investment in the scrubbers," Coco said. "Timing is everything in this business, and yours was very bad."

"No shit, Leif Erikson," Vinny said. "What we want to know is *why*."

"Bad shipping markets always start the same way," Coco said. "Too many ships and not enough cargoes."

"Too many ships?!" Vinny snapped. "But you specifically told us the order book for new VLCCs is smaller than it's ever been."

"The order book for new ships *is* small," Coco said.

"So what's the problem?"

"The problem is that the existing fleet is *huge* and very young."

Vinny turned to Camilla. "You didn't ask about the *current* fleet size when doing your due diligence?"

Vinny knew all along that he should have taken a more active role in the tedious task of performing due diligence on the Scrubber Ships investment, but he had been so swept up by the excitement of ESG investing and so intoxicated by the romance of the maritime industry that he threw caution to the wind.

"How's the demand side?"

"It's gone negative for the first time in decades," Coco said.

"Why?"

"Like every tragedy, there were a combination of things that came together to create disaster," Coco said.

"Like what?"

"Trump's trade war with China, the European recession, and India's efforts to reduce air pollution. The increased use of renewable energy like wind and solar isn't helping fossil fuel demand either," Coco added. "There was also a coup d'état in Venezuela, and a Saudi oil refinery was bombed by ISIS drones in the Arabian Gulf."

"Holy crap! Are you telling me all that stuff happened since we made our investment?" Vinny asked.

"That was just the last couple weeks," Coco said.

"It sounds like a blockbuster movie."

"This is a humbling business," Coco said. "When weak demand caused oil prices to hit a twenty-year low, OPEC cut oil output, which means fewer barrels of oil will be needing a ride on ships."

"I'm going to be the one doing the hitting," Vinny said, tapping his racquet again.

"Don't be silly, Vinny," Camilla said calmly, patting him on the arm. "Let's talk about a happy subject," she continued with a smile. "How are the shiny new scrubbers working out? Our impact investors are very excited to be part of such an exciting ESG initiative that will dramatically improve the air quality for people who live near seaports."

Vinny was frustrated that his investment in Scrubber Ships wasn't performing well, but Camilla was right, at least the scrubbers themselves were ESG. That would make the investors a bit more forgiving about the subpar financial results.

"To be honest, we haven't switched them on yet," Coco said.

"*What?!*" Vinny screamed, his blood pressure rising. "Why not?"

"Oil prices are low, which means that ships with scrubbers aren't commanding much of a premium these days," Coco said.

"Okay, but if there is any premium at all, why haven't you turned them on?" Camilla asked.

"There has also been quite a lot of resistance to the open loop scrubbers."

"Hold on," Vinny said. "Are you saying the $150 million of scrubbers that we put into our PURE ESG fund aren't even *green?*"

"It depends who you ask," Coco said. "But some people feel that a machine specifically designed to flush concentrated sulfur effluent into the sea isn't green at all."

"Oh, shit!" Vinny said and turned to Camilla. "And we even named the company Scrubber Ships!"

"It's better than Nauti Shipping," Camilla reminded her boss, "which is what you originally wanted to name it."

"I'd be more than happy to change the name back to Viking Tankers," Coco offered again.

"Coco, it sounds like it's been a perfect storm," Camilla said calmly.

"Yeah, the perfect *shitstorm*," Vinny added.

"But I'm sure it's nothing we can't manage, right Coco?"

"Yes and no," Coco said. "If it was just the tanker market we might be able to sail through the snotty weather. The problem is that I am also having a bit of a financial crisis at my company as well."

"What kind of financial crisis?" Vinny asked.

"Do you remember Reeperbahn Landesbank?" Coco asked.

"Of course," Camilla said. "RLB. That's the German bank that has the $750 million first preferred ship mortgage loan on the Scrubber Ships fleet."

"*Had*," Coco said.

"What do you mean, *had?*"

"RLB informed me a few weeks ago that they sold our loan to a distressed debt investor here in New York."

"But I thought you and the German dude in Hamburg were best friends," Vinny said. "You told us you two had some kind of *special relationship.*"

"Gerhard wasn't involved with the loan sale. The bank's ESG task force made the decision to sell my loan after LTO made an unsolicited offer to buy it," Coco said solemnly.

"Holy shit!" Vinny shrieked. "Are you saying they sold your loan because it *wasn't* ESG?"

"Exactly," Coco said. "Believe it or not, it was the most polluting loan in the bank's *entire loan portfolio*. And it's a big bank."

"Arghhh!" Vinny jumped to his feet and repeatedly smashed his tennis racquet against the floor. "The Scrubber Ships investment is supposed to be the crown jewel of our PURE ESG Fund!"

"I never said it was ESG," Coco said innocently. "I don't even think there is an official standard for what ESG actually means."

"That jackass Fairchild was the one who said it was ESG," Vinny said. "Then he retired the moment you guys stole my money. Don't worry, we are going to pay him a visit tonight if you don't give me my dough back."

"Fairchild may not work for me anymore, but if you insult him you are insulting me," Coco said. "And I don't think you want to insult me."

"But Coco, why is it a problem that RLB sold your loan?" Camilla asked calmly, trying to minimize what she knew was a potential issue. "The terms are the terms. They can't just go into the loan agreement and change them."

"The problem is that the new guys just served me with a default notice," Coco said.

"A *default notice?*" Vinny shrieked.

"They are saying that if I don't pay down the loan by $188 million, or pay off the loan at par, they are going to foreclose on the vessels," Coco said.

"How could you let this happen?" Vinny moaned. "How is this even possible?"

"VLCC values have collapsed, and we blew out our VMC covenant. Look at this," Coco said as he removed $750 million valuation proffered by his new lender and pushed it across the table. "No one was expecting the ships to lose $250 million of value in two months."

"So then pay the $188 million of equity to fix the VMC default!" Vinny said. "Why are we even talking about this? They are your ships. This is your responsibility. Act like a grown-up and deal with it!"

"They are *our* ships, Vinny," Coco said. "Remember you are the equity too."

"Give me a break, everyone knows that preferred equity is just debt in drag," Vinny said.

"I would pay it, Vinny, but I can't," Coco said.

"But you *specifically* told me that you would reserve $175 million of cash liquidity to use to support the deal if it became necessary," Vinny said.

"I know, but now my wife won't let me use that cash," Coco confessed.

"Just a reminder, Vinny," Camilla interjected. "We agreed with Robert Fairchild to accept 200 basis points of additional preferred yield in exchange for not having Coco's personal guarantee. That means Coco isn't legally committed to support our investment with outside money. It would be more of a moral commitment."

"Did you say your *wife won't let you?*" Vinny laughed.

"Ever since our twins were born and my heart disease started getting worse, my wife has refused to let me take the $175 million out of the piggy bank. She only allows me to spend $1 million per month, and that wouldn't help us much in this situation. We are burning more than $1 million every *week* in this terrible market."

"Hold on. Wait. Let me get this straight," Vinny said. "The global tanker king is on an *allowance?*"

"I get a lot more than my kids," Coco said defensively.

"My wife tried to put me on an allowance last year when my assets under management started dropping," Vinny said, laughing.

"Maybe you should have listened to her," Coco said.

"All I know is, I gave you $150 million less than three months ago to install the scrubbers. That should make the ships *more* valuable, not less valuable," Vinny said.

"It doesn't work like that in shipping," Coco said. "The amount of money you put into an asset has nothing to do with what it's worth."

"How is *capex complicated?*" Vinny shrieked.

"Because the new lender has decided to value the ships on a charter-free and scrubber-free basis, assuming they will be sold through an orderly liquidation," Coco said.

"I smell a rat, Cammy," Vinny said. Losing money irritated Vinny, but getting hustled drove him into an uncontrollable fit of violent rage. "And you know what happens to rats, right?"

Chapter 25

"Come on, guys, let's stay constructive here," Camilla said. She felt like a coach trying to give an inspiring halftime pep talk to a team that was getting slaughtered. "You are both smart guys, surely we can figure a way out of this that will make everyone happy. Coco, would it be helpful if Vinny and I spoke with the new owner of the loan and tried to work with them?" Camilla asked.

"I'm afraid not," Coco said, looking down solemnly.

"Who the hell bought the loan?" Vinny shouted so loudly that the deal junkies next door overheard him.

"As I said, it's an investment company here in New York," Coco said as he riffled through his manila folder trying to dig out the default letter that Alex had clubbed him over the head with aboard *Kon Tiki* during the date night from hell.

"What's the name?"

"They are called LTO Capital," Coco said. "Apparently the LTO stands for 'Loan-to-Own.' Have you ever heard of them?"

When Coco said the name, Vinny emitted a haunting and high-pitched whimper. It sounded like he'd been sucker-punched in the gut. Of course Vinny had heard of them; they were a dangerous gang of former junk bond traders infamous for doing whatever it took to seize control of hard assets, even if that meant spending many years and millions of dollars on litigation. Vinny could kiss his retirement goodbye if he decided to fight them; he would die in a deposition chair in some dumpy courthouse.

"Okay, let's cut the crap," Vinny said. "What are you saying, Coco?"

"I think I just said it," Coco said.

"Do you actually have the balls to ask me to put in *another* $188 million after you lit my first $150 million on fire just a few months ago?"

"I'm not making any promises here," Coco said, "but the fresh $188 million would allow you to get common equity at the bottom of the market cycle. That's how serious shipowners make money."

"I thought *you* were a serious shipowner?"

"It's really up to you if you want to defend your investment," Coco said. "It doesn't matter to me anymore."

"What do you mean it doesn't matter?" Camilla asked. "This is your company. You have spent decades building it. How can it not matter?"

"Because I'm going to lose all of my equity no matter what happens," Coco said.

"Well I don't have another $188 million to throw at this problem," Vinny stated.

"That's what I figured. And that's why I wanted to be the one to tell you that I've decided to sell my fleet and retire."

"*Sell your fleet and retire?*" Vinny screamed. He snapped his thick neck to glare at Camilla. Everyone was retiring except him!

"It's time for me to leave the shipping party," Coco said. "I'm going to spend what time I have left with my wife and watch my boys grow up."

"What the hell!"

"I have no other choice," Coco said. "I just gave you the right of last offer, and you declined. What else can I do?"

"Let's stay calm here, boys," Camilla said. "Coco, how much time do we have to find a solution?"

"What do you mean?" Coco asked.

"She means when are you planning to initiate a process for selling the ships on the market? Are you going to hire an investment banker to explore strategic alternatives? Are you going to put a book together and broadly market the business to financial and strategic buyers? Are you going to consider a leveraged recap whereby the —"

"It's already done," Coco said simply. "It's over."

"What's done?" Vinny barked. "What's over?"

"The sale. The buyer is here at Marine Money Week. I am planning to lift subjects and sign the rest of the paperwork this afternoon immediately following my keynote address."

"But I wasn't even notified," Vinny said.

"I'm notifying you *right now*," Coco said. "All I need to complete the transaction is your signature consenting to the sale. My lawyer, Gerry Coyote, is here at Marine Money Week, and he has the necessary paperwork in his hotel room upstairs."

"*Today?*"

"Right now, man!" Coco said, picking up his phone. "Let's just get it over with, before I make the announcement in my speech."

"Are you being serious, Coco?" Camilla asked, suddenly afraid for her own life. "You actually made a deal to sell the fleet without even telling us? I thought we were partners? I thought you were a loyal person? That's just not right," she said.

"Sale and purchase deals happen fast when they are done between serious shipowners," Coco said, turning his eyes to the ground in shame.

"Did you bring a resolution to the board?" Camilla asked.

"Yes, both of the independent directors have voted in favor of the transaction. I have their signatures right here," Coco said, removing a piece of paper festooned with the boys' choppy signatures.

"Who the hell are the independent directors?" Vinny demanded.

"Their names are Thor and Olav," Camilla said.

"Who the hell are they?" Vinny asked.

"They are both Norwegian-American gentlemen," Coco said. "They sit on the board of many other companies."

"How much did you get for the ships?" Vinny asked.

Coco felt lousy going against the moral code by which he had always done business, of only screwing people who had screwed him first, but he had no choice. Vinny was nibbling at the bait. All Coco needed to do was follow the procedure that Ziggy had taught him: set the hook with a forceful tug, reel him in with unwavering confidence, and then toss him into the cooler, where his glittering scales would turn dull gray as he suffocated.

"That's the good news," Coco said brightly.

"Finally," Vinny exhaled, enjoying a brief break from the emotional turbulence. "Some good news."

"Considering the current market conditions, I managed to get a very good price. The net proceeds of the sale will be more than enough to pay LTO the $750 million and also cover the various brokerage commissions, advisory fees, and legal expenses, and clean up some outstanding shareholder loans. So we don't need to worry about coming out of pocket at the closing."

"Out of pocket?" Vinny asked, confused. "What do you mean?"

"No, we won't have to come out of pocket," Coco said. "That's what's so great."

"How much do I get?" Vinny demanded.

Vinny knew he was looking at a loss, but if the proceeds from the sale of Scrubber Ships were enough to ensure that he still got a chunky carried interest thanks to the highly profitable leveraged recap of CheapSleeps, his first ESG investment, he might be tempted to throw in the towel, move on, and execute his own exit strategy.

He might not be able to live in a stucco mansion on Ocean Avenue in Palm Beach, but unless the Scrubber Ships investment was a *total* disaster, he would still have enough dough to buy a place on the Intercoastal Waterway in Delray with a swimming pool and a dock deep enough for the Donzi.

"As the *preferred* shareholder, you get 100 percent of the proceeds after the senior loan has been satisfied," Coco said.

"I know how a cash distribution waterfall works," Vinny said. "What I want to know is how much money will I *get* from the sale."

"Once LTO has been paid, the remaining proceeds will be applied first to your $15 million of unpaid PIK interest and next to the repayment of your $150 million of principal," Coco said.

"*How much friggin' money, Coco?*" Vinny asked again slowly.

Coco opened his manila file again and riffled through a few documents until he found the sources and uses table. The figure he was looking for was circled in red crayon.

"Aha, here it is," he said. "Once the sale is completed, Black Boulder Asset Management will receive a wire transfer of immediately available funds in the amount of..." Coco paused.

"Yeah?"

"Three thousand six hundred eighty-seven dollars and twenty-three cents," Coco said.

After a painful period of silence, Vinny said, "I think you're missing some zeros."

"Oh, there are plenty of zeros, Vinny," Coco said enthusiastically. "But unfortunately they are located on the wrong side of the decimal point."

"Are you saying that I am going to get back thirty-six hundred bucks on a $150 million investment?!" Vinny shouted.

"And some loose change," Coco said.

"My *loafers* cost more than that!" Vinny screamed as water began to stream from his hyperactive tear ducts.

"Don't cry, Vinny," Coco said as he offered him a used paper napkin that had been left on the table. "If it makes you feel better, I lost all of my equity too."

"Equity!" Vinny growled as he mopped up his tears with the sleeve of his cashmere turtleneck. "You never *had* any equity! *I* was the friggin' equity!"

"Preferred equity," Coco clarified. "There's a difference."

"Not when a deal goes wrong there isn't," Vinny said.

"True that," Coco said.

"Hey Cammy, how much keyman life insurance do we have on this Viking slob, just in case he meets with an accident?"

"The same amount of keyman insurance we keep on the CEOs of all our portfolio companies," she replied with regret in her voice.

"Two times the amount of our invested capital," Vinny said.

"That's correct," she said. "I just paid the premium on Coco's life a few weeks ago, so I know there is no question that the policy is valid."

"Nicely done," Vinny said, turning to examine Coco as if he might not ever see him again. "Hey, Coco?"

"Yes?"

"It looks like you're the two-bagger I needed to complete my own exit strategy, to Palm Beach," Vinny said.

"What's that supposed to mean?" Coco asked.

"It means you're finished, Mr. Jacobsen," Vinny said. "Have a nice time in hell."

"I'll look forward to seeing you there," Coco replied.

Chapter 26

Coco Jacobsen was rattled to the core when he retreated from his disastrous come-to-Jesus talk with Vinny Vitale. He had successfully reeled the beast into the boat, only to learn that it was going to kill him. Of all the investors in New York, he had ended up with the one backed by the Godfather.

For the first time since Alistair Gooding at Allied Bank of England threatened to pull the plug on him ten years earlier, Coco felt like he was in the kind of trouble that he might not be able to wiggle his way out of. He was out of control, and this time it involved more than just money. It was his life. It was his family. It was everything.

The other unanticipated disappointment had been not having Robert Fairchild with him. Going through financial distress was always anxiety-inducing, but going through it without a wingman was lonely as hell. The real fun of doing deals was working together and bonding with people who were on your team. People who shared your goals and incentives. Your values and vision and sense of humor. But now he was utterly alone.

As Coco was exiting through the deal room door, he glanced over his shoulder and spotted the Chen sisters from China Ship Leasing Corporation arguing at a table in the far corner. They were partially obscured by the shiny black lid of a Steinway grand piano. When he looked at the women, a smile stretched across his giant face.

Most people would have seen two sophisticated, impeccably dressed, and ultra-professional women in their mid-thirties having a spirited discussion, but Coco saw a ticket to his new life; he saw a $600 million pile of cash, the emancipation from his personal guarantee, and the potential salvage of his sinking marriage.

He had to convince the Chen sisters to lend Athena $600 million so she could complete the acquisition of his fleet. It was step two in his supposedly simple plan, and step one had been a disaster. He badly needed a second-half rally.

Coco strode confidently across the deal room, leaving dozens of admirers and inquirers swirling in his wake as he made his way toward the constantly quarrelling Chen sisters. Step-Irish-twins born eight months apart to a powerful shipping patriarch father, Rebecca and Roberta were now co-CEOs of one of China's largest vessel leasing companies.

When it came to building a healthy portfolio, they made an excellent team. Ironically, their most profound professional synergy was the fact that they were opposite in almost all respects. They had trouble sitting together at meals, needed to be physically separated during meetings, and always selected seats on opposite sides of first-class airplane cabins when they had no choice but to travel together.

An article in *Ahoy Matey!* detailed the afternoon that Rebecca was restrained on an Alitalia flight from Milan to New York when she and her sister came to blows over the length of the repayment profile of a loan to an Italian container line. Rebecca wanted it *lunga*, Roberta wanted it *corta*.

Many believed that Chinese leasing companies like theirs had single-handedly saved the shipping industry from ruin. Companies such as the Chen's had collectively invested more than $50 billion in shipping at a time when the industry was desperate for capital after European banks like RLB left the market, having suffered large losses on aggressive loans consummated during China's demand boom of 2003–2009.

It was during that six-year twilight zone of trade, after China joined the WTO, that an overnight doubling of demand for seaborne commodity transportation caused ship values to quintuple — and commercial banks to fight for the opportunity to lend money to shipowners.

The raging party was followed by a horrible hangover. As the aggressive loans came due five to seven years later, the amount of the balloon repayments grossly exceeded the value of the collateral. The "prosperity" of the 2000s shipping markets ended up destabilizing the industry and destroying value for the next decade.

There were different theories about why Chinese financiers like the Chens had come to the rescue of shipping just as bankers were exiting. Some surmised that deploying huge sums into ships was an efficient way for China to get their country's surplus of dollars into circulation. Others speculated that their presence in ship finance was just a step toward China's longer-term goal of having a meaningful role in all aspects of the shipping industry.

And the country was well on its way; China was already producing the most competitively priced ships in the world and was the single largest user of ships as well. The Chinese employed container vessels to export all kinds of finished goods, from electronics to clothing to furniture to toys. They used bulk carriers and tankers to import virtually every major commodity the country needed to develop infrastructure and industry, including oil, gas, chemicals, iron ore, coal, and grain.

In less than a decade, shipping had become synonymous with China. But whatever the motivation, the fact was that China had a lot of dollars to put to work, and the shipping industry was always hungry for dollars, so they made good bedfellows.

"Hello ladies!" Coco boomed to the Chen sisters as he popped up from behind the piano.

"Coco!" cried the petite Rebecca as she jumped up from her chair and hugged him, her hands barely touching as she wrapped her slender arms around his giant body.

Rebecca's hair was chopped short. She wore miniskirts and high heels and liked partying with friends and clients until sunrise. When it came to ship finance, she favored deals that involved large, old ships capitalized with a combination of high single-digit fixed return debt and a right to profit sharing when the charter markets got frothy. She called it "debt with benefits."

"Who's ready to play Let's Make a Deal!?" Coco announced, a reference to an old American game show he had watched on television with Alex. "I know I am!"

"Oh, hi, Coco," Roberta sighed without mustering the energy to rise from her chair.

Roberta's shiny black braided hair stretched in a straight line halfway down her back. She always wore tailored business suits and flat shoes and rose at sunrise for prayers and daily preparations. Her ship finance fetish was new, environmentally superior ships secured by decade-long "hell and high water" contracts with the industrial behemoths that dominated the market for oil, gas, and iron ore. Nothing got her more excited than a loan-to-value ratio below fifty percent coupled with a long-term charter with a BBB counterparty.

Taken together, the two sisters represented opposite ends of the broad spectrum of different strategies among Chinese leasing companies. The challenge was that each Chen sister had a veto right over the other, and finding transactions that appealed to both of them at the same time was almost impossible.

"Your patience with me is about to be rewarded," Coco said to Rebecca while ignoring Roberta's diss.

"Bring it on, brother!" Rebecca said.

Rebecca had been keen to do a transaction with Coco for many years, and they had even gotten a deal approved a year earlier, but it never closed because Coco wasn't able to finalize the long-term charter to the oil company that Roberta required.

"Don't do us any favors," Roberta said with agonizing boredom as she stared blankly at her phone.

"Speak for yourself, Grandma," Rebecca said.

"What did you just say to me?"

"When it comes to ship finance, you act like such an *old lady*," Rebecca said, batting her long eyelashes at Coco. "If you are so afraid of risk, you should finance airplanes or real estate."

"I'm not afraid of risk, Rebecca, but I want to remind you that we aren't a cash-for-clunkers program."

"Just ignore her, Coco," Rebecca said, smiling. "What do you need?"

"I'm looking for a $600 million term loan secured by a first preferred mortgage on my entire fleet," Coco said. "Just a plain vanilla first mortgage facility. Nothing fancy."

"How much is that old fleet of your even worth in this lousy market?" Roberta asked. "Valuations on elderly tankers have taken a huge hit lately. The old ships suffer most in markets like this one."

"I received an appraisal for $1 billion not too long ago," Coco said, referring to the stale valuation that Peder Hanssen prepared for the wealth management people at RLB about a year earlier.

"I remember that one, Coco, but as you know from last time, our standard operating procedure is to get *fresh* valuations from a panel of five independent shipbrokers. We throw out the highest valuation and the lowest valuation and then we average the remaining three valuations and back-test them against historic data to determine the standard deviation."

"I forgot about that," Coco said.

"And I hope you have some time charters this time around," Roberta said.

"Roberta, darling, time charters are against my religion," Coco said.

"That's a pity, Coco darling, because spot market ships are against mine," Roberta said, yawning. "What is the age of the vessels at this point?"

"They are perfectly seasoned cougars in the prime of their lives," Coco said.

"How old?"

"Seventeen years, on average," Coco said.

Roberta scratched out some quick calculations on the law-firm-logoed notepad in front of her. "That means they are seventy-five years old in people years based on their current age relative to their total useful life," Roberta said.

"You mean like *dog* years?"

"Exactly," she said. "I don't know what you're into, Coco, but seventy-five years old isn't a cougar in my book."

"Play nice," Rebecca said to her sister.

"Honestly, Coco, I think your time would be better spent speaking with Pratap Bhat than us," Roberta said. "If this market stays down much longer, your ships will be getting ready to take a long nap on a Bangladeshi beach. But look on the bright side, maybe they will be reincarnated as something nice, like rebar."

"Enough, Roberta!" Rebecca snapped. "You will treat my client with some respect."

"Respect? You mean the way you spoke with the CEO of Mollusk Oil when he was sitting at this table a few minutes ago?"

"That beast gave *us* a term sheet, telling us that we were going to charge him LIBOR plus lint to finance his fleet of new Aframax tankers," Rebecca said. "I don't think that was very respectful of us or our capital."

"Yeah, well, it takes a lot of bloated loan margins and nonexistent profit sharing to make up for the kind of principal losses you are going to rack up with your old ships in the spot market," Roberta snapped back.

"Operating older ships in the spot market is the only way to make money in this business," Rebecca retaliated.

"Yeah, until you don't."

"Hey, sister, all our deals would lose principal if you bothered to account for currency risk and inflation," Rebecca said. "You lose all self-control the moment you see a BBB credit rating. It's embarrassing. The only reason we aren't broke is because we borrow below the benchmark LIBOR rate that we charge our customers."

"Oh, yeah, well, your balance sheet has been used more times than —"

Smack.

Coco was stunned when he watched Rebecca slap her slightly older half-sister across the face. Roberta answered the assault by tossing her long braid over her shoulder, wrapping her arm around Rebecca's head and pulling her sister's cranium into a headlock.

"*Ladies!*" Coco shouted as he pulled the half-sisters apart. "Let's show some self-control."

"What do you know about self-control, Coco?" Roberta said. "You've never seen a source of capital that you didn't fall in love with."

After Roberta released her grip on Rebecca's head, the two women shouted at each other in Mandarin for five minutes, mesmerizing the deal room occupants. Everyone knew Chinese vessel leasing had become highly competitive in recent years, but the Chen sisters were taking it to a new level.

"Are you okay?" Coco asked Rebecca after Roberta stormed out of the deal room.

"Oh, yes," Rebecca replied as she touched up her makeup in front of a tiny mirror she had pulled out of her purse. "We are completely fine."

"Really?" Coco asked.

"Of course."

"Because that looked kind of serious."

"Oh, no, that was no big deal," Rebecca said. "Roberta just went to the ladies' room to powder her nose."

"Her nose was bleeding," Coco said.

"Exactly," she said.

"What were you two fighting about?"

"We weren't fighting," she said calmly.

"You weren't?"

"No, we were just discussing the merits and demerits of the transaction you proposed," she said.

"Discussing *my transaction?* That's what you were doing?" Coco asked incredulously.

"We were evaluating the pros and cons of the assets, the structure, and the leverage," she said. "It's the way we work. It's our process."

"But it looked like you were going to kill each other," Coco said.

"We are vigorous advocates for our clients and our own beliefs," she said. "In the end, we always support each other the same way all Chinese vessel leasing companies support each other."

"What did Roberta say?" Coco asked. "Does winning the fight mean you can do the deal?"

"Unfortunately not," she said. "Roberta rejected your loan request, which means I must also decline."

"How about the courtesy of a counteroffer?" Coco asked. "Can you at least give me that?"

"I'm afraid not," she said. "Roberta doesn't want to do the deal, and I must respect her wishes."

"But I really need this refinancing," Coco said. "Is there anything we can do here?"

"No," Rebecca said. "She won't let me finance your vessels unless I agree to let her do $2 billion worth of Mollusk Oil Aframax tankers at LIBOR plus dust."

"So do it, Rebecca!" Coco shouted. "For the love of God, just take the dust and let her finance Mollusk Oil so you can do my deal!"

"I don't think so."

"Nobody has ever gotten fired for financing Mollusk Oil!"

"Sorry, Coco," she said, jumping to her feet. "I need to go now."

"*What?!* Where are you going?"

"I have a meeting with Freddy Fingers at Chatham Bar," she said. "He wants *me* to charter his ships for ten years." She laughed. "Can you believe that? Freddy has $150 million of cash on his balance sheet, but he's desperate for some steady cash flow."

"Are you going to do it?" Coco asked.

"Probably," she said, winking a mascara-caked eye, "if Freddy gives us a profit share."

And just like that, Rebecca Chen, Coco's only real shot at refinancing his loan so that Athena could buy his fleet, vanished into the crowd of deal junkies.

Chapter 27

Immediately after Vinny had threatened Coco's life and booted him out of Elaine's little lunchroom, Camilla pulled the pocket doors closed. She turned around and walked silently over to the small table against the wall. Things were about to get ugly.

"Coffee?" she offered as she pushed down on the top of a silver urn causing a cascade of coffee to rush into a white paper cup.

Vinny didn't respond. He just closed his eyes, planted his elbows on the white tablecloth, and rubbed his temples with his bejeweled fingers. Then he removed a pair of AirPods from their small white case and inserted them into his clean-shaven ears.

He poked at his iTunes, and Camilla suddenly overheard the unmistakably menacing grind of AC/DC's "Back in Black" being pounded directly into his head. Vinny's eyes remained closed as he rocked his head back and forth to the savage guitar chords, slow-motion headbanging.

Camilla didn't make a move or say a word. She remained still and silent, as if being evaluated by a dangerous animal in the wild. As she observed her boss's haunting ritual, she could only imagine what thoughts were racing through his troubled mind.

Did he feel like a trapped animal ready to attack his attacker? Was he cooking up a gruesome way to end her life and Coco's life later that afternoon? Was he methodically devising some other way to get free from the terrible fact pattern he found himself in?

Was he thinking of where to find another $188 million to defend the $150 million investment in Scrubber Ships? Or was he in the process of rationalizing and capitulating?

What Camilla didn't know was this: that the most unique and powerful features of Vinny's personality were largely the same as Coco's. He was self-made, loyal, and motivated by more than money, and he never, *ever* gave up. In fact, Vinny's small but deeply devoted group of fans would remember him giving his *best* performances on the tennis court when he was at his most vulnerable.

"I thought you said he wasn't going to sell the ships," Vinny said in a calm voice as he stowed his AirPods back in their tiny white case. "You said he'd be crazy to sell the ships in this market."

"I guess I was wrong," Camilla said.

"Ya think?"

"And I had no idea RLB would sell the loan," she said.

"Haven't German banks been selling shipping loans for the past ten years?" Vinny asked.

"I should have known better," she admitted. "It certainly isn't surprising that LTO moved to immediately foreclose in light of the deteriorating market conditions."

"I don't know what they are up to, but those guys always have another agenda," Vinny said. "Another pain point."

"And I certainly never imagined that Coco's wife would restrict his access to the $175 million," she said. "That was a shocker."

"I thought she was your best friend in Miami?"

"She's my only friend in Miami," she replied.

"Do you think Coco is bluffing? You think he's trying to force *me* to pay the $188 million capital call, so he doesn't have to?"

"I don't think so," she said, shaking her head back and forth. "Successful tanker owners like Coco are like master chess players. They're always thinking a few moves ahead."

"We got hustled," Vinny said, exhaling loudly. "So what are our options now?"

Camilla couldn't help but feel a little bad for Vinny because she knew how desperately he needed the Scrubber Ships investment to work. Black Boulder had been underperforming its peers and all the relevant indices for three years running, and now even his most loyal investors were getting restless to get out.

They loved Vinny and appreciated all the cash he had made for them over the years, but that was history. Everyone knew Vinny was past his prime when it came to investing, and they had to get their capital into the hands of someone who could double their money every few years.

The problem was that most of his investors were contractually committed to keeping their money with Vinny for another two years. That was why they had made a compromise. As of January first, the limited partners of Black Boulder Asset Management agreed to forgive any catch-up provisions from Vinny's three years of producing underwater returns and reset his carried interest in exchange for Vinny agreeing to cut their lock-up period by half.

That meant Vinny would get twenty percent of whatever profits he could generate during that calendar year. No look-backs. No catch-ups. No setoffs. No whining. And no more spigot spewing management fees.

No matter how well he performed, Vinny had agreed to give them their money back on December 31. That meant right now was do-or-die for him. If he didn't generate juicy returns this year, he was heading for a major lifestyle downgrade and the stress that came with dramatically reducing the spending habits — and it wouldn't be easy to put that genie back into the bottle.

By the end of March, the year had been looking like a winner thanks to the $200 million gain on CheapSleeps, the roll-up of 140 roadside motels that he repurposed into homeless housing and subsequently leveraged up with non-recourse, socially responsible debt.

Had he been disciplined and stopped investing in March, Vinny would've had his best year in five and earned himself a $40 million carried interest. But when Camilla came back from Miami and shared the Scrubber Ships opportunity, his animal spirits were instantly aroused and he impulsively approved the investment.

"We have three options here," Camilla said. "We can ask our LPs to kick in another $188 million to support their investment. We can consent to Coco's fleet sale and put this nightmare behind us. Or we can do nothing."

"What happens if we do nothing?" Vinny asked.

"If we do nothing, and the tanker market doesn't improve quickly, LTO will probably arrest the vessels," she said.

"*Arrest?* That makes us sound as if we are criminals," Vinny declared self-righteously.

"It's nothing personal," Camilla consoled him. "It's a traditional maritime term. That's what it's called when a creditor gets permission from a court of law to detain a vessel at a port while the payment default is sorted out. If the creditor is successful, the court will give them the right to sell the ship at auction to get their money back or credit bid so they can take legal ownership of the vessel."

"Which ships would get arrested first?" Vinny asked.

In order to answer the question, Camilla opened her silver laptop and pulled up a file labeled *Voyages in Progress*. The Excel sheet was constantly fed with live data from the Automatic Identification System (AIS), so once she had logged onto the Montclair's Wi-Fi network she could see exactly where each ship was physically located at any given moment. Although some of the ships were sitting motionless in Chinese shipyards having their scrubbers installed, many of them were chugging along at sea.

"It looks like *Grandma Nona* will be the first to get nabbed," Camilla said once the data had loaded. "She stemmed two million barrels of crude oil in Saudi Arabia twenty-five days ago and is presently 125 nautical miles from LOOP off New Orleans. Ouch," Camilla added.

"Ouch?"

"*Grandma Nona* is only making $16,000 a day for this voyage," Camilla said. "That's about $9,000 below breakeven even *before* you consider the coupon on our preferred equity."

When Vinny first started showing the telltale signs of interest in making the investment in Scrubber Ships, Robert Fairchild had taken a page out of his own biography in order to make the kill;

Robert had promised that Vinny and his investors could name fifteen of the ships if they invested the money in the scrubbers. Vessel naming was a temptation few newbie investors could resist.

The term "passion investing" was generally reserved for acquiring beautiful things like paintings, objets d'art, sports cars, athletic teams, and trophy real estate, so it was puzzling to Vinny that a dangerous, tedious, gritty, and often unprofitable industrial grind could so effectively stir his loins. But stir his loins it did!

Vinny was instantly smitten by the idea of personally participating in the romance and centuries-old tradition of the shipping industry. He was also scintillated by the idea that the ship-naming parlor trick might distinguish him from the hundreds of other fund managers competing for the same LP dollars. He could even introduce himself to friends as a shipowner, which would be thrilling. He'd dethrone the Dos Equis guy as the Most Interesting Man in the World.

Before the week was over, fifteen of the thirty Scrubber Ships vessels had been renamed after wives, moms, daughters, grandmas, dead pets, and alma maters. There was even a ship surreptitiously named after a politician's paramour living sub rosa in a Park Slope condo: M/T *Airam*, Maria spelled backwards.

"*Grandma Nona?*" Vinny moaned. "Who named that one?"

Camilla ran her finger down the fleet list to find the particulars on the vessel. "Consolidated Septic Hauling."

"That's Bobby Buttaricci's grandmother," Vinny agonized.

"Correct," Camilla confirmed.

"But she's in the hospital now," Vinny said.

"I am sorry to hear that."

"Bobby is no stranger to arrest, but he ain't going to be happy if *Grandma Nona* the boat gets pinched while Grandma Nona the grandma is on her deathbed. He is a deeply superstitious man."

"I can understand that," Camilla agreed. "It adds insult to injury."

"Do you know which ship will be arrested after that?"

"Let's see," Camilla said as she looked at her Excel worksheet. "Once they nail *Grandma Nona*, the next ship to be nabbed will probably be *Love of Jesus*."

"Oh God!" Vinny shouted. "Who owns that boat?"

"The endowment of the archdiocese of River Falls," Camilla said after scanning the fleet list.

Vinny drummed his manicured fingernails on the table as he considered what a knucklehead he was. The data showed that ninety percent of wealthy families went from "rags to rags" in three generations. He was about to do it inside of one.

"What do you want to do here, Vinny?" Camilla asked. "Pay the $188 million, give Coco consent to sell the fleet, or take our chances with LTO?"

Vinny picked up a pen from the table and began to sketch a crude drawing on the notepad.

"Here is option number four," Vinny said as he pushed his drawing across the table so she could see it. It was a hangman's noose.

Chapter 28

After the last of the eightieth-birthday mint chip ice cream cake had been consumed, everyone in the Fairchild household reverted back into their natural state of existence.

Oscar fell asleep on the couch, his iPhone rising and falling on his snoring chest. Ollie went up to the thirty-second floor to play Xbox with his friend Homer. Grace started working through a towering pile of dishes, and Robert sat alone at the head of the dining room table contemplating what to do with the rest of his life.

It was a rare moment of quiet in the Fairchild family apartment. There were no doors slamming or alarm codes beeping or toilets flushing or radiators banging or televisions blaring or music playing or guns being fired on Fortnite. There was no talking or arguing or cursing or laughing or barking or belching or buzzing or farting.

Even the seemingly ceaseless din of honking car horns and wailing sirens had taken a break because of the storm and the shelter-in-place order. The only things Robert could hear were Oscar's snorkel-like breathing and the rushing hiss of Hurricane Harold spraying warm rain against the lead-paned windows.

While this rare absence of ambient noise, light, commerce, and chaos would have been peaceful for most people, the paralysis made Robert panic. It wasn't that he wanted to escape the city. In fact, he was a member of that rare species that might *never* leave the island of Manhattan save for the occasional sortie to the Caribbean, Martha's Vineyard, or Aspen.

But what unnerved him was knowing he *couldn't*. He had always enjoyed unfettered physical and socioeconomic mobility, but for the first time in his life he felt stuck. Claustrophobic. Trapped in his own home and post-professional life like a bird in a nicely decorated cage with gorgeous views, obscene real estate taxes, and outrageous maintenance fees. If he were still a shipping man, he would have plenty of legitimate reasons to plan a trip to Europe or Asia to see people and talk deals. But now he had none. He was stuck like a stick in the mud.

Robert couldn't stop replaying the day Coco fired him, three months earlier. Ironically, the terrible events were set in motion when the Norwegian wired him a $5 million bonus and invited him down to Churchill Cay to do some fishing and celebrate closing the financing with Black Boulder Asset Management.

After seven nauseating hours of stalking billfish in the rolling blue swells of the western Bahamas, the seasick American begged to call it quits.

"Now we will go to the Bimini Big Game Club!" Coco commanded. "For a big closing lunch of raw oysters and tequila!"

When Ziggy punched the throttles of the twin Yamaha 425 horsepower engines, Robert went tumbling into the stern of the thirty-two-foot Grady White center console. The sudden motion combined with the aroma of spent gasoline and rotting bait caused him to barf into the blueish-white bubbly prop wash.

"There's no need for more chumming!" Coco called out from the bow of the boat where he was standing. "We're done fishing for the day. Now it's time to party!"

Coco looked like he was riding a bronco. He had one hand hanging onto the bow line and the other waving through the air as the boat rose and crashed along the following sea. It had been a long time since Robert had seen him so excited. He had known Coco long enough to know that his Norwegian boss must have yet another transaction up his sleeve.

Robert's face was still green when he and Coco settled into an outdoor table next to the marina while Ziggy hosed down the boat on the far end of the dock.

"I want to thank you again for giving me the bonus," Robert said as he sipped ginger beer with a hint of black rum to calm his churning stomach.

"Don't mention it," Coco said, smiling as he went to work on his fifth beer. "Alex told me it's good luck for a winning gambler to tip the dealer."

The $5 million payment was partly a bonus for closing the $150 million Black Boulder deal, but it was mostly a five-years-overdue commission on the sale of Viking Gas, the fleet of partially constructed LNG ships Coco and Captain Bouboulina had sold to the People's Republic of China.

That transaction was the single most lucrative deal of Coco's career and the source of Thor and Olav's $175 million trust fund. Ordering new ships and flipping them for a profit before they were even finished or paid for was the Triple Lindy of speculative shipping investment; it rarely worked, but it was a thing of beauty to watch when it did.

"I really appreciate the money," Robert said.

"I'm lucky I found you," Coco said, expressing alarmingly more emotion than Robert had ever witnessed from him. The Norwegian sounded like he was dying.

"We were lucky to find each other," Robert said.

"Everyone deserves a great partner in life," Coco said. "You introduced me to my first one, Alex, and now I am going to try for two." He rubbed his hands together, with boyish excitement in his eyes.

"What do you mean?"

"Mr. Fairchild, I would hereby like to invite you to roll that $5 million back into my holding company and become a shareholder."

It was the first time since founding Viking Tankers, shortly after he completed his one-year stint chartering Hilmar's ships, that Coco had invited someone to become a partner in his holding company. Coco had had countless co-investors in special purpose companies that resided *below* his holding company, but he'd never had another shareholder in his holding company. The "HoldCo" was sacred.

"Interesting," Robert said. "What kind of equity valuation do you have in mind?"

"Excuse me?" Coco said. He was stunned by the vulgarity of the question.

"Well, you know, the Black Boulder deal took us to, like, ninety percent leverage, and the value of the fleet has fallen quite a bit since then, so I am just asking how much you think the company is worth and what percentage I would get for my five million," Robert explained.

"What are you saying?" Coco demanded.

"No, I'm just saying that Scrubber Ships doesn't have a very large equity valuation at the moment. This is just a guesstimate, but right now I reckon a $5 million investment in Scrubber Ships might equate to about one-third of the company, and I'm sure you wouldn't find that attractive."

"Are you saying my company is only worth $15 million?!" Coco shouted.

"Give or take."

"But I have a billion in assets."

"*Had*," Robert corrected. "Anyway, what valuation did you have in mind?"

"What I had in mind was that you would invest at the same price that *I* invested."

"You want me to come in at *book value?*" Robert choked. "Now?"

"That's what partnership is all about," Coco said. "Doing things on equal terms. No funny transfer pricing."

"Forget I mentioned it," Robert said. "The valuation doesn't even matter, Coco, because I've been thinking about retiring someday, and I don't think it would be prudent for me to put that money at risk," Robert said, to steer the subject away from the sensitive topic of valuation.

"Retiring?"

Coco was stunned by the words that had just left Robert's mouth. As he stared silently into the mound of shaved ice that cradled the forty-eight oysters, the Norwegian was enraged. Enraged that Robert had rejected his generous proposal. Enraged that his CFO had insulted him by saying his company was only worth $15 million. And enraged that he was threatening to retire.

"Here's the thing..." Robert closed his eyes and kept blabbering when Coco remained silent, his nausea causing him to miss Coco's social cues. "Ever since I first started working in finance, I told myself I would retire when I saved up $10 million. I figured I would simplify my lifestyle, lower my expenses, try to get healthy, maybe move somewhere cool, and use my skills to do something useful to the world."

When Robert opened his eyes, he was horrified to see that Coco's face had transformed from comic to tragic, like a Greek mask. That's when he knew he'd made a major miscalculation. He thought he'd crossed over the threshold from being Coco's CFO to being his friend.

That was why he openly shared his personal hopes and dreams. But in doing so he had unwittingly crossed over a different threshold, from ally to enemy. Friend to foe. Asset to liability. At that moment Robert knew it was over because Coco believed that if loyalty was lost it could never be restored.

"No, I just meant...I was only saying that I have...I..." Robert stammered.

"I sure as hell wish you had told me about your *retirement plans* before I gave you the five million bucks," Coco said.

"Why?"

"Because I thought you'd put that money back into the business and sit at the big boy table for once in your life. I didn't think a young guy like you would take the ball and go home! I thought I was making you my partner. I didn't think I was helping you retire!" Coco screamed, startling the other patrons.

"I probably won't retire now," Robert quickly backpedaled. "I just wanted to share how I have been feeling about my long-term plans."

"Let me tell you how I am *feeling*," Coco said diabolically. "I feel that our relationship is officially over!" He pressed his hands on the wobbly wooden table, took a few deep breaths, and then pushed himself to his feet.

"But —"

"Captain Ziggy, ready the vessel!" Coco shouted down the dock to his Rastafarian wingman. "There will be only two of us returning to Churchill Cay this afternoon." The Norwegian's voice vacillated between raging and weepy.

"*Irie*, Mister Coco," Ziggy agreed. "Fairchild no more."

"No, wait, Coco, *NOOOOO!*" Robert shrieked.

He was stunned by how quickly his life had unraveled. It was like he had committed an act of violence or infidelity; once it had happened, there was no way to take it back. Robert frantically trailed Coco like a dog as he walked out of the restaurant and toward the slip where the boat was tied up.

"Why are you doing this, Coco? *Why?*"

"I'll tell you why," Coco said, staring deep into Robert's eyes. "Because you and I were soldiers fighting alongside each other in the battle of shipping."

"Yes, of course," Robert said.

"But you just threatened to desert my platoon the very first chance you got," Coco said. "That means I cannot trust you anymore. And when trust is lost, all is lost."

"But —"

"Do you know how many times *I* could've cashed in my chips and left the casino?" Coco screamed, leaning in so close that their faces were almost touching. "Do you know how many times *I* could have played dead and scurried off the battlefield and faded into a life of comfortable mediocrity? Do you? *Do you?!*"

"A lot of times?" Robert said meekly.

"When I sold my first ship I had more money than both of my parents made in their entire lifetime," he said. "I could have returned to my old neighborhood in Nordnes and lived a happy, simple life."

"Why didn't you?" Robert asked.

"Because only cowards quit," Coco called out as the boat eased away from the dock and headed back into the deep blue Gulfstream water. "Cowards like you!"

Chapter 29

"Only cowards quit," Robert repeated the haunting words aloud as he sat at the head of the table in his Park Avenue apartment and listened to Oscar snoring on the couch. "Cowards like me."

If he had learned anything during his premature and forced retirement from shipping, it was how much the industry had become a part — in many ways the *best* part — of his life. Unlike most thankless jobs working for soulless companies in oppressive environments, performing meaningless tasks with annoying people, Robert's foray into shipping was the most fun he'd had with a suit on.

It was exhausting and nearly impossible to be consistently successful, but there was no commercial endeavor in the world that was more exciting, unpredictable, volatile, frustrating, engaging, and stimulating than ocean shipping; it was as delightfully difficult to master as golf.

During his decade in the business, Robert had come to realize that it was a privilege to work on the front line of international trade. It was an honor to be so personally and completely and constantly connected to global macro events on a daily basis. To have peers and colleagues in every part of the planet with whom he had so much in common.

Shipping gave him the gift of a wide world view and all the pleasure that came with it. But now all of that excitement and authenticity was quickly melting away. Before long he would be just another Upper East Side yuppie.

Ever since the moment Coco dumped him, Robert had begun to feel the walls of the world closing in around him. The decade he spent in shipping had given him a unique identity that he was proud of, but now it was disappearing.

Like many people who stopped working too early and for the wrong reasons, he was suffering the triple whammy of psychological, physical, and financial dissipation. He had initially enjoyed the freedom, but that thrill had worn off quickly. He already longed for action. Itched to be back in battle. Missed having fascinating conversations every day with interesting people all over the world.

For the first time in his life, he understood why some people died at their desks: because that was where they felt best. And that was the best exit strategy of all — to find something you enjoyed doing and then challenge yourself to keep evolving so that you never wanted to stop.

Compounding his agony was the fact that there were reminders of his ex-industry all over his home: The eight-foot-long model of a Samsung-built LNG carrier in his living room that Mr. Him had given him after Robert sold Coco's ships to the Chinese government. The small library of maritime titles on his shelf, including a signed copy of the shipping industry's Old Testament — *Maritime Economics* by Dr. Martin Stopford.

Even his home, a prewar classic-six co-op apartment on the twentieth floor of Eightieth and Park that Oscar had given them as a wedding present was inextricably linked with shipping, though that particular memory was not a pleasant one.

Robert had mortgaged the prime apartment without telling his wife and used the $5 million proceeds to buy an old French-built freighter from a Greek named Spyrolaki after getting drunk at an Astir Palace Posidonia party. Robert acquired the vessel purely so he could name it after his wife and brag to his classmates that he was a shipowner at an upcoming Harvard reunion.

"Bend over, Robert, so I can sign the MOA on your back," Spyrolaki had ordered that fateful night ten years earlier. Robert had complied. The rest was history.

He had loved shipping, but now he had lost shipping. Robert didn't yet know who had been trying so desperately to reach him on the phone during lunch since his wife had tossed his phone out the window, but he knew that it probably didn't matter.

He glanced down at his watch — 3 p.m. Marine Money Week was just about over for the year. He would have to take another trip around the sun before the ship finance carnival came back into town. Hurricane Harold was now in its final hours, and the MTA had announced that the travel ban would be lifted before the morning commute the following day.

Tomorrow the thousand-plus shipping dealmakers who had descended on the city of New York for three days would vanish like the storm itself, leaving behind happy memories and a trail of transaction origination as they disappeared to their favorite summer places — islands, lakes, yachts, mountains, and beaches.

Robert walked slowly down the parquet-floored hallway and turned left into the bathroom. He quietly closed the door behind him, mistakenly believing he had locked it. Before going about the business he was there to conduct, he took a moment to look at himself in the wall-mounted mirror inside an intricately carved gold frame.

He didn't like the man he'd become since he stopped working at Viking Tankers. He didn't look any older, but he recognized that he was at a tipping point when it came to his physical and mental health; everything could change in an instant if he didn't find some way to keep his mind, body, and spirit in good shape.

Robert dropped to his knees on the black-and-white tiled floor and pulled open the double doors of the wooden vanity. He lowered his shoulder into the carcass of the cabinet and slowly inserted his hand into the cluttered cavity beneath the white porcelain sink. He pushed aside the variety of debris found in the bathroom of families who have lived in the same abode for many years.

There was a plunger stuffed inside a plastic Duane Reade bag, tiny bottles of hair conditioner swiped from hotel rooms, half a dozen tampons, and a tube of gross toothpaste. His hand carefully cruised along a rugged terrain of rusty nail clippers, mildew-streaked bathtub alphabet letters, a shriveled cake of Ivory soap, an empty bottle of soft scrub, and assorted disposable razors that should've been disposed of long ago.

When Robert came upon the plastic Elmo step stool that Oliver had used to brush his teeth when he was too small to reach the sink, a tidal wave of memories was released. Maybe it was because he felt he'd lost his purpose in life; he no longer had a job, no longer spoke with Coco, and was apparently of little use to his wife and only child. The mere sight of the tiny step stool caused him to weep as a crudely spliced black-and-white film strip flashed the best and most intimate memories. The ride of his life wasn't over, but Robert couldn't help but wonder if the best parts were.

His emotional catharsis was cut short the moment his fingers felt the slender Q-Tips box in which he had stashed his backup iPhone. He spilled a bunch of old cotton swabs as he hastily dug the device out of the blue box and pressed the power button. The machine began to flash vital signs as it came to life.

He was surprised when it displayed a fully charged battery and five bars of turbo-charged 5G cellular connection. His stimulation swelled even further when he saw the unusually high volume of fresh messages in bold letters — tweets and texts, emails and missed phone calls. He was back! The tin man had been oiled!

Robert was just about to check the many messages that had downloaded onto his phone when his wife opened the unlocked door. She looked into the bathroom and saw her husband on all fours. His cheeks were wet with tears and his backup iPhone was clutched between his hands. It may not have been as sexually explicit as the Aristotle Incident, but it was equally pathetic.

"Grace, we need to talk," he said preemptively as he gazed up at her from his downward dog position.

"I'll say," she said, laughing. "But I think we might need to get a professional involved this time."

"I'm not doing so well," Robert admitted.

"I've noticed," Grace said. "Ever since Coco fired you —"

"I *retired*," Robert insisted.

"You told me he fired you," she said.

"Okay, yes, he did fire me," Robert admitted. "But he fired me because he got angry when I questioned the valuation of his company and I told him about my exit strategy."

"Watching 100 hours of Netflix every week in your sweatpants is not an acceptable exit strategy," she said.

"I know…"

"Ever since you stopped working for Coco, it's like you don't do anything anymore except look at that damned phone. I think you need to go back to work," Grace said. "You need to get back in a routine."

"What's that supposed to mean?" he asked defensively.

"Robert, the most excited I've seen you lately is when you dusted powdered cocoa on top of your banana bread the other day," she said.

It may not have provided the same rush as selling three billion dollars' worth of LNG carriers to the Chinese government or issuing $300 million of junk bonds, but Robert did recall feeling a flicker of excitement when he pulled that tray out of the oven and saw how the hand-shaved chocolate had melted into the shape of a daffodil over the top of the banana bread cupcakes.

"Come on, admit it, those were good," Robert said.

"They *were* good, honey," she said sympathetically. "I just don't like seeing you wearing my mother's apron. You were a lot hotter when you made a lot of money, traveled the world for Coco, and listened to Van Halen."

"So you're the kind of girl who likes…*runnin' with the Devil*," Robert sang.

"Definitely," she admitted. "You can go back to your phone now. I have kept you away from the true love of your life for long enough."

"How did you know I had a phone under here?" he asked.

"Who do you think keeps it charged for you?" she said, exiting the bathroom confessional.

Grace had taken just a few steps down the hallway toward the kitchen when she heard her husband scream. She ran back down the hall and into the bathroom.

"It was Coco!" Robert cried, his face glowing with excitement.

"On the banana bread?" she asked.

"No, Grace, Coco Jacobsen is the one who has been texting me and calling me for the last hour."

"*He's* been calling and texting *you?*"

"Twenty-seven times."

"Really?"

"Yes!"

"From the Bahamas?" she said, and covered her open mouth with her hand. "Are Alex and the twins okay on the yacht?"

"No, he's here in New York, at the Montclair Hotel," Robert said as he stared down at his phone. "He needs help," he added with excitement. "And he said I am the only person who can help him. He said he wants to put me back in the game to make an important play."

"Oh, honey, that's so exciting!" Grace said. "But why is he at the Montclair? I thought he wasn't allowed to travel to America until he clears up that issue with the nasty old guy from Texas."

"In two hours he is going to give the closing keynote address at the Marine Money Week conference," Robert said, looking at his watch.

"Too bad you can't go see him," she said.

"The hell I can't," he said.

"There's a hurricane raging outside, and the NYPD has issued a shelter-in-place order," she said. "You can't go outside. You might get hurt."

"A shipping man doesn't complain about foul weather," Robert said proudly. "I'm out of here."

Chapter 30

Robert Fairchild couldn't get to the Montclair Hotel fast enough. He dressed in haste. After struggling to pull on Oliver's blue rubber sailing boots, he grabbed his wife's yellow slicker from the wooden coat hook and ran out of the apartment, slamming the door behind him. He looked ridiculous, but he couldn't have cared less.

As he waited anxiously for the elevator to arrive, he scrolled manically on his phone to get up to speed on what the hell was going on. There were twenty-two text messages and five missed calls from Coco, which may not have been heavy traffic for his teenage son, but it was a lot for Robert. As the elevator descended, he scrolled up the ladder of gray text boxes and read them in the order Coco had sent them.

By the time the elevator arrived with a thud in the lobby of his building, Robert had at least some idea of the mess Coco had gotten himself into. It was classic Coco. Yet another one of his self-created financial fire drills that could be traced to his fundamental belief that delaying decisions until the last possible moment was a form of option value that he didn't have to pay for.

In this particular case, by waiting to refinance his maturing loan from Norway Bank and then insisting on refinancing an unfinanceable transaction, he had to give up his personal guarantee — a single stroke of the pen that had the power to undo his life's work and marriage. Now *that* was leverage — gone wrong.

Robert didn't know if he could save Coco, again, but he did know that if anyone in the world could do it, it was him. When it came to managing the complex social and financial elements of bailing Coco Jacobsen out of imminent financial ruin, there was no more experienced hand than Robert Fairchild.

Restless and impatient, Robert squeezed through the crack of the elevator doors the moment they began to open. As he sprinted past the wall of brass mailboxes and rounded the corner toward the exit onto Park Avenue, the gummy rubber soles of Oliver's sailing boots slipped on the wet red tile. Robert crashed to the ground and slid across the floor before slamming to a stop against the mahogany paneled wall.

"Um, everything okay, Mr. Fairchild?" the doorman, Rufus Murphy, asked with an Irish brogue as he observed the bizarre behavior and unusual outfit of the normally restrained resident of apartment 21A. "You have a couple glasses of wine with Mrs. Fairchild at Oscar's birthday party?"

"No," Robert said after he scrambled back to his feet.

"I'm sorry, sir," Rufus said, "but I can't let you leave."

"What?" Robert laughed.

"The NYPD implemented a shelter-in-place order that requires me to restrict our residents from leaving the building," Rufus said. "It is extremely dangerous to go outside right now. The wind is still gusting over 100 miles per hour."

"Then you better look the other way," Robert said. "Because my best friend needs my help, and there is no way you're stopping me, Rufus."

"I can't stop you if I never saw you." Rufus winked before concealing his face behind the *New York Post*.

Once he was outside, Robert turned right onto Park Avenue but was immediately blown to a complete stop by the hurricane winds. He lowered his head and began the trek, maneuvering around deep puddles and strewn garbage cans, errant umbrellas and toppled newspaper boxes. As he continued running against the wind, he spotted the glowing blue LED light on the roof of a police cruiser. As he expected, a patronizing voice came over the squad car's loudspeaker.

"Seek shelter immediately or you will be detained!"

Robert couldn't afford to lose time negotiating with the police officer, so he ducked into the Carlyle Hotel. He peered through the wet window until he watched the police cruiser drive out of sight. Once he was back outside, he continued to battle through the weather.

As he staggered down Madison Avenue, he may have looked like just another high-functioning but utterly stressed-out dude going to work in a hurricane. A desperate soul frantically hacking away in the goldmine of New York before all the goodies were gone. But that wasn't how he felt.

For the first time in a long time, he felt he had purpose. He felt needed. He felt that he possessed a special gift that could make a difference to another person. He felt that intangible and impossible-to-buy quality that miraculously allowed effort to eclipse talent — confidence.

He wasn't feeding the hungry or healing the sick, but Robert's unique ability to form capital around old oil tankers might actually be critical to saving the business and life of Coco Jacobsen, and that meant a lot.

Chapter 31

Once he was safely inside the Montclair Hotel, Robert dashed up the stairs and turned left toward the Marine Money conference registration desk located outside the grand ballroom. Just as he was passing by the unmanned cloakroom, he heard a voice whisper-scream his name.

"*Psst! Fairchild!*"

Robert stopped in his tracks. He slowly rotated his body 360 degrees, scanning the area to determine who was calling his name. There were dozens of people hanging around the registration desk and plenty more clustered at the entrance to the deal room, but there was no one in the hallway that connected those two areas. Robert was alone. Or so he thought.

"*In here!*"

When Robert peered into the cloakroom, he saw the whites of Coco Jacobsen's giant eyes popping out from his sun-charred face behind a wall of wet overcoats on hangers.

"Coco?" Robert said, confused. "Is that you?"

"*Shhh!*" the Norwegian hissed. "Get in here before someone sees you!"

"What the hell are you doing, Coco?" Robert asked as he slowly moved into the cloakroom.

"Close the damn door!"

"Okay," he said as he closed the door until it clicked.

"Welcome to my new office," Coco said.

"It's nice and spacious," Robert said as he looked around the dimly lit room. It was massive in size, which wasn't surprising considering that it served one of the largest ballrooms in New York City. "But would you care to tell me why you're hiding in a closet behind a bunch of wet coats?"

"Didn't you read the text messages I sent you?" Coco said.

"I sure did," Robert said.

"Vinny Vitale and his goons are going to *kill* me. Right here at Marine Money Week. *Today!* How could you have put me together in bed with that psychopath!"

"*Me?*" Robert recoiled.

"You were my CFO!"

"But Alex was the one who met Camilla at St. Lucy's Academy, and *you* are the one who ordered me to execute the deal!"

"Please don't use the word *execute!*" Coco whined.

"I don't even *believe* in scrubbers!" Robert said.

"Jah, but you're the one who forced me to change the name of the company from Viking Tankers to *Scrubbers Ships!*" Coco wailed but then lowered his head. "I'm so ashamed."

"I was in deal mode," Robert explained, invoking a term of art whose nuanced meaning was well understood by those in the deal business. Big transactions almost always got uncomfortably brutal at the end, but there was no turning back. Deals were like babies; they were conceived with passion and enthusiasm and born amid blood and screaming before being cleaned up for all the world to admire.

"But *Scrubber Ships?* Really?"

"That was Vinny's idea, and Vinny had the checkbook. You know as well as I do that when it's time to get a deal over the finish line, you do whatever it takes to get it done. If you have the right reasons for doing the deal in the first place, the last-minute concessions don't make any difference in the long term."

"None of that matters anymore," Coco said. "Right now we have some urgent things to discuss."

"In *here?*"

"It's one of the few private places at Marine Money Week. There are people *everywhere!* I discovered this cozy little place when Vinny assaulted me here an hour ago," Coco said as he wedged the top of a wooden chair beneath the brass doorknob to prevent someone from easily entering.

"You're the boss," Robert said.

"I'm so sorry," the giant Norwegian's voice cracked as he opened his arms and invited his estranged CFO in for a hug.

"Are you *crying?*" Robert asked.

"Allergies," Coco said, and smacked him.

"But you don't have allergies," Robert said.

"Shut up, Fairchild!" Coco said.

"Okay."

"I want to start by telling you that I'm sorry I called you a coward and I'm sorry I said you have no skills and I'm sorry I fired you and I'm sorry I marooned you on Bimini."

"Thanks, Coco," Robert replied. "I'm sorry too. I'm sorry I upset you by speaking so disrespectfully about the valuation of your business. I am also sorry I gave you the impression that I wanted to retire. I can totally see why that would have been irritating after all you have done for me. It was an act of disloyalty, and you were right to get angry."

"Jah, but I am just a big baby," Coco said. "I have been feeling very emotional lately. I think I must be going through manopause."

"I think you mean *menopause*," Robert said.

"Do I look like a woman to you?" Coco took a step closer to Robert and glared down at him.

"Your hair sure is long and pretty," Robert said with a chuckle. "Tell me what's going on."

After they sat down in the attendants' chairs, the Norwegian explained that RLB had entered into the Poseidon Principles and subsequently sold his loan at a ten percent discount to LTO Capital. He told him that LTO was run by Piper Pearl, who was fronting Rocky DuBois, who planned on stealing Coco's ships at the bottom of the market and then ripping him off a second time by going after his PG.

In addition to his financial problems, Coco said his wife and children were begging him to reduce his carbon footprint, so he had recruited Athena Bouboulina to help him do it. He had made a plan to sell the fleet to Athena, who would put ESDs on his ships, pay back LTO, and wipe out Vinny Vitale, but he had made two grave errors.

First off, Coco had promised Athena he would help her raise the $600 million of debt financing she needed, since she was working with $150 million of equity Henry Husk had given her. Secondly, Coco hadn't anticipated that Vinny Vitale would actually *kill* him if Black Boulder lost money. He was stuck.

"Now do you understand why I'm weeping behind a pile of wet coats?" Coco asked.

"So we have a $600 million hole that we need to fill. Is that right?"

"To pay off LTO at par, yes, but we to score another $150 million, plus interest, to pay back

Black Boulder if I'm ever going to see Alex and my three kids again."

"Okay, got it," Robert said. "And how much time do I have?"

"Until happy hour starts," Coco said after looking down at his watch.

"What? Are you insane?"

"Always have been," Coco said.

"That's ridiculous! How can you possibly expect me to pull together $750 million so quickly? A typical ship finance transaction takes at least two months — and this one is basically unfinanceable!"

"That's all the time we've got," Coco said. "After my speech everyone will go to the bar and then disappear for the summer. Plus, LTO is going to start moving against our ships in three days. Gerry Coyote told me that Piper's lawyers have already hired a new ship manager and drafted the paperwork to foreclose in twenty different jurisdictions. They are just waiting to press the button to activate the process."

"Why do you always parachute me in when everything is about to blow up?" Robert asked.

"Because that's when I need you most," Coco said sincerely.

"Thanks," he replied. "I guess."

"Can you do it?"

"Coco, what you are asking is *literally* impossible," Robert said.

"Everything good in life is impossible," Coco said. "Hell, life *itself* is impossible if you think about it, but here we are. So what do you say, amigo? Will you do it?"

"I'll try," Robert said, "but this one is going to cost you."

"What do you mean?"

"This is no ordinary refinancing."

"I'm about to die and you are worried about your fee?" Coco said. "I'll give you the standard one percent on whatever new money you can raise."

"Nope," Robert replied. "I want fifty percent."

"What the hell are you talking about?"

"This isn't a refinancing," he said again. "This is a maritime salvage operation, and I should get paid accordingly."

"I'm not following you," Coco said.

"Think about it. Scrubber Ships is sinking in debt, and I responded to your SOS to save whatever I can before everything is lost. This is just like when your VLCC saved my ship *Lady Grace* from those nasty Somali pirates. I should get paid according to the Lloyds Open Form rules," Robert said.

"The *LOF?*" Coco laughed. "For a simple financing?"

"You are in peril, and I am the salvor," Robert said. "This is a matter of life and death."

"Life and death?" Coco laughed.

"You said it yourself," Robert reminded him. "If I can't refinance your loan, Vinny will kill you."

"After all we've been through, are you actually going to hold me hostage in my hour of need?"

"Nah, I'm just messing you with, buddy!" Robert laughed as he put his arm around his friend's shoulders. "Of course I'll do whatever I can to help my best friend. No charge."

"Too bad," Coco said, smiling.

"Too bad?"

"Jah but I was finally starting to respect you, Fairchild, for recognizing your own value and sticking up for yourself."

"There is, however, one thing I need from you in order to proceed," Robert added.

"Everybody wants something from me. I am like the Giving Tree," Coco said, recalling another of the wonderful books he had read to Thor and Olav that made him cry.

"You have to let me do this alone," Robert said.

"What?"

"You have to give me full authority to negotiate on your behalf," Robert said. "This refinancing is going to be very difficult to execute, but if you try to give a counteroffer on everything, we will never get it done."

"Deal," Coco said. He wasn't comfortable giving Robert blank-check authority, but he figured he could always just reject whatever terms he didn't like.

"Not quite," Robert said.

"What *now?*"

"Whatever deal I come up with will not be subject to the 'approval of your board' or any other conditions precedent. You have to *agree to accept* whatever deal I tell you to accept. You need to trust me absolutely."

"But I don't trust anyone absolutely," Coco said. "Even myself."

"That's the only way I will even attempt this rescue," Robert said. "Otherwise I will be wasting everyone's time."

"But you could totally screw me."

"Why would I screw you?"

"For the same reason everyone screws everyone: because they can."

"I can't promise you won't get screwed," Robert extended his hand and held it a few inches away from Coco's, "but I can promise that I won't be the one doing the screwing. Do we have a deal?"

"Never say 'no' when you're in deal mode. A great CFO once told me that. Now let's see what you can do, kid," Coco said, and shook Robert's hand.

Chapter 32

Coco Jacobsen could feel his endorphins erupting as he began to make his way toward the grand ballroom to deliver what was sure to be a controversial keynote address.

He and Robert had spent the previous thirty minutes going through the eighteen-page list of the 1,200 attendees at Marine Money Week. They had circled in red ink the name of every person who might have some cash and some incentive to help fill the $750 million hole. Robert had then set up a refinancing "war room" in Coco's Presidential Suite and begun sending emails inviting each of the people on the list to come to the suite.

Before entering the conference, Coco collected a small white cup of black coffee and a huge chocolate chip cookie as he moved past the refreshment station. When he arrived at the entrance to the ballroom, he wrapped his hand around one of the ornate, baseball-sized bronze knobs of the double doors and pulled, prepared to receive a fanfare from the many people he had enriched over the years. But when he opened the door, nothing happened.

When Coco quietly slipped into the rear of the Montclair Hotel ballroom and squeezed through the standing-room-only crowd, he had a rare and disquieting sensation; for the first time in a long time, not a single one of the 1,200 people seemed to notice him. It reminded him of how he felt when he was in middle school in Norway — like just another face in the crowd.

Like any long-term celebrity, Coco had always imagined he would appreciate the opportunity to be anonymous in public, until it actually happened. Now his sudden translucence made him feel uneasy. It had been decades since a star like him had attended Marine Money Week and not been surrounded by a galaxy of service providers — lawyers, lenders, insurance brokers, and shipbrokers. Now he couldn't help but wonder if he'd been eclipsed. Was this yet more scientific evidence of climate change — that tanker kingpins like him were no longer celebrities at Marine Money Week?

As he slowly squeezed through the clogged artery of dark-suit-clad ship financiers with coffee cups in one hand and electronic devices in the other, he immediately recognized why they didn't recognize him: Their 2,400 eyeballs were glued to the young woman standing next to the dais at the far end of the room waiting to be introduced. Athena Bouboulina was about to take to the stage.

The stress of the Vinny Vitale disaster had distracted him from Operation Greta, but the moment he saw Athena next to the stage Coco felt his anxiety melt away and the excitement of the monumental plan come rushing back. It was showtime, and he loved showtime.

He veered left as he pushed deeper in the crowd and maneuvered around a makeshift encampment of audio-visual technicians working around heaps of equipment. Just seeing the troop of people dressed in black in the AV bunker, huddled around sound-boards and computer screens and monitors lit up like a Christmas village, brought back pleasant memories.

The scene reminded him of the early years of his own life spent hanging around the theater department of his middle school in Bergen with the other courageous kids who loved drama.

For all the personality and preparation, nature and nurture, innate intelligence and personal drive that were unique to each human being, Coco had come to believe that life's outcome depended on four things: whether you were lucky enough to stumble upon opportunity, adventurous enough to go with it, patient enough to develop the necessary skills to be good at it, and impartial enough to know when it was time to bail out — and that time for Coco was now.

Chapter 33

"There has never been a more remarkable time to be in the international ocean shipping business!" boomed Tim Torrance, the conference chairman and owner of Marine Money after he bounded up the stage, breathless with excitement.

Freshly tanned from an early summer weekend on Nantucket, Tim was dressed in the white linen suit that he and serial shipping executive Horton Farnsten always wore to the annual Marine Money Week event.

Since Tim had won the trade-publication and conference-organization company in a California card game thirty-five years earlier, he and his team had become the connective tissue of the ship finance community, helping to promote dramatic changes in the way vessels were financed. Along the way, Tim had become a trusted confessor to the biggest and most secretive shipowners and financiers in the world.

During Marine Money's three decades in business, the shipping industry had gone from being run like a collection of pizza parlors — highly fragmented, cash-only businesses that were privately owned by the same family members who made the meatballs — to having almost 100 publicly traded companies with professional management teams that obsessed over previously unheard of concepts like capital allocation, the return on risk adjusted equity, and maintaining liquidity in the global credit and equity markets.

The shipping industry hadn't finished the journey toward corporatization, and there was no telling whether its free spirit could ever be totally tamed, but it had definitely been housebroken.

"Capital sources are fragmenting," Tim proclaimed to the left side of the jam-packed ballroom. "Trade patterns are shifting," he said to the right side. Then he returned his gaze directly up the center aisle of the room and proclaimed, with both arms hoisted evangelically into the air: "And there is a towering tidal wave of ESG that will wash over this industry until it is carbon neutral!

"But now I need you to listen and listen carefully, ladies and gentlemen," Tim said as he lowered his voice and raised his hand to draw in the crowd. "I need you to *lean in* and feel the trillion-dollar opportunity. I'm talking about climate change, a challenge that the world's brightest minds have turned their talents toward solving. And we are very fortunate to have one of those bright minds with us today. It is my *personal pleasure* to introduce and interview one of today's most exciting maritime entrepreneurs. Please join me in welcoming the environmentalist, engineer, data scientist, freshly minted BIT graduate, and founder and CEO of Beta Ships — ladies and gentlemen, I present Athena Bouboulina!" Tim announced with a slow and sweeping flourish of his linen-lined left arm.

Athena was blushing from Tim's generous introduction as she began to make her way onto the stage. She had successfully navigated around a giant floor monitor when she stumbled over a cluster of AV wires that had been sloppily secured to the carpet with silver duct tape. After she had recovered and finally arrived on the dais, the blinding white spotlight illuminated a sartorial scene never before seen on the stage of Marine Money Week.

The smiling young Greek woman was wearing faded blue jeans, bright red espadrilles, and a sheer black blouse that covered most of her tattoos. Her dark hair had been freshly shaven whisker short, and she wore heavy black-framed Elvis Costello–style eyeglasses. The gold chain and anchor pendant around her neck, a gift from her grandmother on Chios, and the tiny diamond stud in her nose glittered in the blinding stage light.

"Hello, everyone," Athena said softly with the subtle accent she had picked up at a British boarding school. She waved sweetly as she tried to figure out where to clip on the lapel microphone that Tim had just handed her. "And thank you for that lovely introduction, Tim."

In decades past, most people in the audience of senior-level global ship financiers might have bolted for the Chatham Bar or the deal room when they saw the girl with the dragon tattoo take to the stage. They would have assumed she was the clove-smoking, possibly French-educated artist daughter of a shipping man who had turned up at the Montclair to see Daddy while he was in town for Marine Money Week.

But not anymore.

Nowadays it was the gray-haired men in the Savile Row suits whose economic and social utility was viewed with suspicion, while the good-intentioned, disheveled young women and men with degrees in data science from places like BIT had been transformed from cost centers into profit centers.

The old dudes were feared to be heavy overhead with outdated thinking, while the youngsters were revered for their potential to disrupt traditional industries long considered to have zero obsolescence risk — traditional industries like shipping.

"Athena," Tim said once they had both settled into the scallop-shaped white leather chairs, a design detail that attempted to create the ambiance of two people shooting the breeze in their midcentury-modern *Mad Men* living room. "Let me start by saying what a pleasure it is to have you with us. I want to thank you for coming down from Boston to be with us today."

"It is an honor to be here, Tim," Athena said with genuine humility. "I really appreciate the opportunity. It is very humbling to speak to such an impressive audience. I'm sure that most of you know a lot more about this industry than I do. I just hope I will be able to say something worthwhile. Something that gives you a new idea or inspires you or energizes you to look at things a little bit differently," Athena said.

"Now, Athena," Tim said as he looked down at his index cards of prepared questions. "People often say there are two ways to get into the shipping business: You are either born into it, or you get lucky and stumble into it. Which was it for you?"

"I've actually spent my entire life trying to *stay away* from the shipping industry," she said.

"And why is that?" Tim laughed along with the crowd.

"Because I am the fourth generation of a traditional Greek shipping family," she said. "Growing up in my house, ships were everywhere. We always celebrated the Greek Easter on a freighter. It was what my family talked about instead of sports or politics. It was where all my aunts and uncles and cousins and grandparents worked. It was everywhere, but I never felt I had much to contribute to make it better. That's why I figured I would choose a different profession."

"What changed your mind?" Tim asked.

"In Greek, we call it *pepromeno* — destiny," she said.

"Where did it find you?"

"In my senior year at BIT, I took a course called 'Creative Destruction' and each student had to analyze a traditional industry and then design a lab showing how it could be made friendlier to the environment and more profitable by using modern technology and data."

"And you picked shipping," Tim said.

"Actually, shipping picked me," she said. "We all pulled the names of different industries out of Red Sox cap, and I happened to pull a card that said *ocean shipping* on it. Can you believe it?"

"I bet your grandfather was excited," Tim said.

"He was so excited." Athena smiled. "And that made me very happy."

"He probably wasn't happy when he realized that you were developing technology that would disrupt the industry and put him out of business," Tim joked.

"Oh no, it is quite the opposite," she said. "I love my *papou*, and I couldn't have more respect for him and for what the shipping industry does for humanity. It is the most amazing business in the world and it operates very efficiently. Like all of you, I am very proud to be a small part of it. And what I realized from my studies at BIT is that I actually *can* make a contribution by using technology to reduce the industry's impact on climate change."

At the words *technology* and *modernize*, the huge room suddenly fell silent. Devices were flipped over,

Marine Money magazines were set down on tabletops, and small talk was temporarily suspended.

The long-anticipated disruption of the world's most traditional industry had seen many false starts since a bunch of prescient people launched LevelSeas during the dot-com boom. LevelSeas was twenty years before its time, but most people agreed that it was a question of when, not *if*, technology would change the shipping industry. Athena might just be the change that the industry had been waiting for.

"And how are you planning to modernize the industry?" Tim asked.

"Our goal is to reduce the environmental footprint of ships and make them more profitable at the same time," Athena said.

"Those are certainly two of the most beguiling challenges of our time," Tim said. "How are you going to do it? Are you going to order LNG-fueled vessels to replace older, inefficient ships?"

"Absolutely not," she said.

"No?"

"I have no doubt that dual-fuel ships will play an important transitional role, but they aren't for us. We think the total environmental impact of building new ships is significant, and we also believe that fueling preferences are likely to change in the medium term so that anyone who builds a new ship today might end up with an asset that is obsolete before the end of its useful life."

"So what *are* you doing?"

"Our focus is on improving the operational and environmental performance of the existing fleet. We think that's the smarter play for both climate and economic performance."

"If it's not just about fuel, what is it about?" Tim asked.

"It's about everything," Athena said. "We don't think it's about trying to find one silver bullet and everything else will simply continue as it is. For example, long-haul international ocean transportation is likely to be powered by fossil fuels for a long time because of the massive power requirement and the great distance from land, but short sea shipping is a different story."

"Athena, you mentioned to me earlier that you have recently purchased a fleet of ships," Tim said. "Can you tell us about that? What kind of ships did you buy?"

"VLCCs," Athena said. "A bunch of them."

Shipbroker Peder Hanssen suddenly woke from sleep. He was angry. If the young Greek woman had *bought* a bunch of VLCCs, that meant someone must have *sold* or ordered a bunch of new VLCCs. That meant he had missed out on a bunch of money — a one percent sale and purchase commission, to be precise. Adding insult to fiscal injury, he hadn't even *heard* the chatter through the London or Oslo broking fraternity. Information was a shipbroker's stock in trade. Once a broker was out of the loop, it wasn't long before they'd be out of the business altogether.

"Thank you, Athena. I have no doubt that there will be some questions from the audience, so let's do some Q&A before we run out of time."

Aside from the occasional academician or industry enthusiast, there were never many questions asked in a public forum at Marine Money Week. The most meaningful discourse went down in the more confidential and convivial confines of the deal room or the dozens of Manhattan rooftop bars and restaurants where the Marine Money deal junkies did nocturnal business. Aided by the lubricant of dim lights, fine wine, good fellowship, and potentially lethal doses of cholesterol, the questions were usually asked face to face.

When Tim's Marine Money colleague Ike plucked the wireless microphone off the metal stand in the middle of the central aisle and turned around, he expected to see the usual sea of lowered arms and averted eyeballs. What he saw instead were no fewer than twenty hands sticking up in the air. It looked like a giant classroom full of kindergarteners who couldn't wait to be called on. *Pick me!*

"Thank you for your very nice presentation," shipbroker Peder Hanssen said after snatching the microphone from Ike's hand. "I know the aggressive terms offered by Asian ship financing providers are tempting, but I sincerely hope you didn't order new ships. The last thing the shipping industry needs is a massive order of VLCCs that further oversupplies the market with tonnage."

"As I said earlier, we do not believe that building new ships is environmentally friendly or commercially rational. There is too much that goes into building new ships. Too much material. Too much human exposure. Too much energy. Not to mention the ESG issues around building unneeded ships and scrapping ships before it is absolutely necessary. We think the lifespan of ships should be maximized, not cut short."

"That makes sense," Tim said.

"We think ships, like everything else, should have the longest possible work life, as long as they are safe for the seafarers and the environmental impact is minimized through technology."

"So, Athena, to Peder's question, if you didn't order new ships, how old are the ships you bought?" Tim asked.

"We bought veterans," she said, smiling.

"Veterans?"

"I believe some of you refer to them as old ladies," she said. "All of the ships we bought are more than fifteen years old. We call them veterans because of the service they have given to the world."

"You bought a fleet of *old* VLCCs?" Peder asked, crestfallen.

Now he was *really* irritated! Buying and selling vintage VLCCs was his bread and butter, which meant Athena's transaction was hitting uncomfortably close to home. He didn't know who the seller was, but he felt the deep and depressing disappointment of learning that an existing client must have been unfaithful.

"That's right," she said.

"May I ask who you bought them from?" Peder asked, a crestfallen lover.

Apart from government-controlled national oil companies in places like China, Iran, and Saudi Arabia, there were only a handful of private owners who had "a bunch" of VLCCs on the water, and Peder had a direct and active relationship with every single one of them.

In addition to missing out on a commission and being the victim of sale and purchase infidelity, Peder knew that any one of them exiting the business had major implications; whenever a big, multigenerational owner with plenty of cash made a big move in or out of a market there was always a reason, and usually a pretty good one. Unless they were getting shaken down by their lender, the sale of a fleet also meant they were harvesting cash to make room on their balance sheet for new, presumably more exciting, investments.

"It's not polite to kiss and tell," Athena said. "I'll leave it to the seller to decide if they will make that information public."

"But *come on*, Athena, give me a break, if you are so concerned about the environment," pleaded a woman from the audience, "why did you buy a fleet of old VLCCs, which burn more than 100 tons of heavy fuel oil a day when operating at fourteen knots?"

"To prove our point," Athena said. "If we can significantly reduce the carbon emissions from those vessels, we can clean up anything. Plus, some of the improvements we will make are big, so we need a lot of physical space."

"What kind of improvements?"

"We have worked together with a leading classification society to make more than 100 modifications to modernize the vessels and improve their performance. We reckon we can make about $14,000 more per day on the ships and use one-third of the fuel."

"Are they commercial modifications or technical modifications?"

"Both."

"Can you give us some highlights?"

"We are still completing the tank testing at BIT, but we are focused on reducing fuel consumption by making improvements to vessel hydrodynamics and improving engine performance," she said. "We are also using a lot of cool digital technology to improve efficiency. We are using satellites to monitor the fuel consumption and operating performance and then automatically make adjustments in real time."

"Great stuff!" Tim said. "Athena, our audience is very involved with how ships are financed. Can you share with us where you got the capital to buy the VLCCs and make all of these improvements?"

"A gentleman named Henry Husk gave us our first $150 million." When Athena said the name, jaws dropped. If there was one person in the world whose unexpected entry in shipping could shatter the traditional way things were done, it was Henry Husk. His name was synonymous with disruption.

"*Henry Husk* invested $150 million in VLCCs?"

"When Henry learned that shipping generates more than twenty-five percent of transportation-related greenhouse gas emissions, he thought it made perfect sense to add marine into his portfolio of renewable energy companies. The good thing is, when you get money from someone like Henry, you automatically attract some of the most talented minds, which pretty much guarantees success."

"Okay, fine, but this is the pies in the sky," a burly Dutch ship manager with a deep voice and impossibly thick hair barked dubiously from the middle of the room. "How about the real work? Who is going to manage these ships day to day? Who is going to chip the paint and clean the slops?"

"Cassiopeia Shipping and Trading will perform the technical management for the vessels," Athena said. "That's my family's ship management company in Greece."

"Aha! That's a related party transaction! That's a conflict of interest!" the Dutchman declared. "That is not ESG!"

Related party transactions were an easy target for outsiders to vilify as being part and parcel of substandard corporate governance, but there was usually more to the story in the shipping industry. In many cases, related party transactions allowed a smaller company to access goods and services on better terms than they could get on their own. Whether it was finding cheaper debt or accessing better insurance, the biggest and best shipping companies in the world often helped out the smaller companies in which they had a financial interest.

"Actually, they are doing it for free," she replied.

"Nothing is free."

"They are also very committed to reducing the impact that shipping has on the climate, and this is their way of helping," she said. "Think of it as a philanthropic donation."

"Very kind of them," the ship manager mumbled as he sat down.

"Have you selected a commercial manager for the vessels?" asked the CEO of a crude tanker shipping pool, a commercial arrangement by which multiple shipowners pooled their vessels together and offered them to the market as if they were controlled by a single owner. "Who is going to charter the ships and generate the revenue?"

"Algos are doing that for us," Athena replied.

"Algos Shipping!" he protested. "The Spaniards? But they don't have enough market scale to have pricing power with the charterers. They don't even outperform the index!"

Without looking up from his keyboard, the reporter from *Ahoy Matey!* sitting in the second row blasted off an instantaneous Tweet: *Algo Snares Management of Husk Fleet.*

"I'm sorry, I guess I wasn't clear," she said. "When I said 'algos,' I was referring to algorithms. I have some friends in Boston who have built a machine that crunches millions of numbers every day. It looks at the current and future position of every ship in the world and then back tests it against every VLCC charter that's been concluded in the past twenty years. It's like playing chess against a computer.

After it runs all these calculations and determines the outcome probabilities, the machine sends a simple push notification to the Captain's phone and to the ship's weather routing service which tells them where to go next in the safest and most fuel-efficient manner. We estimate that this system alone will generate an additional $3,427 of incremental revenue per day."

"But how do you know all of your technical and commercial experiments will work?" Peder asked.

"We don't want them to work," Athena said, laughing, "at least not immediately."

"Excuse me?"

"Our strategy is to fail and fix," Athena said, describing the Silicon Valley tactic of bringing products to market and then improving them through trial and error. "That's the only way to make progress quickly. Innovation is a process not an event."

"But how do you make money?"

"So, I get that people in this industry measure success in dollars per day, because you have to, but we take a longer view. Technology businesses like ours are made great by failing and fixing. The faster we can try something that fails and then receive constructive user feedback, the faster we can fix it. The faster we can fix it, the faster we will have developed a product that actually works. The best companies are still failing and fixing. Every business that's any good should always be in beta."

"Hence the name Beta Ships," Tim said.

One thousand two hundred heads were silent as they processed Athena's theory, which was anathema to shipping, an industry in which a single mistake, such as paying too much for a ship or entering into a long-term charter with a company that would default, could sink a multigenerational shipping company in a matter of months; you had to move very carefully when standing on thin ice.

"Yes, fine, but how much will you charge for these *services?*" Peder asked, protective of his 1.25 percent commission.

"We aren't charging anything," Athena said. "We don't want to make *money.*"

"Then why are you doing it?" he asked with increasing frustration.

"Because we think that if we can build technology that makes the industry cleaner and more profitable, then the economics will take care of themselves."

"Now we are *really* out of time," Tim said to the stunned and silent room. "If you have any more questions for Athena, please ask Elaine for her email address."

"Thank you for having me, Tim. I would be very pleased to talk to anyone who is interested in learning more about what we are doing," Athena said. "All of our software is open-source, and we would be very happy to collaborate with anyone who has an idea."

Chapter 34

After Athena had finished inspiring, charming, and frightening the Marine Money Week audience, Ike quickly hustled her exit stage left and Tim Torrance instantly appeared behind the podium to introduce the much-hyped but still officially undisclosed closing keynote speaker.

Coco's presence at the event was supposed to have been quick and confidential. He had planned to come up to New York, execute Operation Greta, give his stunning remarks, and then hustle back to Teterboro, where the idling rental jet would be waiting to whisk him back to Churchill Cay. So far, every aspect of the plan had blown up in his face, and it appeared he was headed for disaster.

But as Coco was waiting to be introduced, the Norwegian was beginning to feel an emotion that was totally unexpected: relief. Although he had been terrified to empower Robert to make huge commitments on his behalf, decisions that might save or destroy his business and personal life, now he felt great. Relinquishing total control made him feel as though the weight of the world was off his shoulders. The heavy crown of sole decision-making was off his head. Coco had a feeling of lightness he hadn't experienced since he took control of his first ship.

Coco's style of shipowning wasn't a team sport, but he knew that he needed to change in a world in which technology had allowed collaboration to defeat competition. He also knew that in order for his friend Robert to reach his own potential, he would need to be given responsibilities, rewards, and consequences. Mostly, though, Coco had painted himself into a tight corner and had no choice but to give Robert control.

Tim cleared his throat to silence the room. He leaned toward the microphone and surveyed the swollen audience. There was nowhere to sit. There wasn't even anywhere to stand.

"Coco Jacobsen is one of the most exciting self-made shipowners in modern history," Tim said with deadly sincerity. "A man who is the epitome of what makes this industry unique and special. He gives our community energy, excitement, inspiration, and a lot of fees.

"In addition to being a pioneer as a shipowner, he has also been a pioneer in utilizing alternative forms of capital. His partnership with finance man Robert Fairchild has shown the power of combining shipping and Wall Street. Mr. Jacobsen, thank you for being with us today, and thank you for everything you have done for our industry. It is not an exaggeration when I say that without you this business would truly not be what it is today," Tim said before stepping down off the stage.

When Coco emerged from the shadows on the side of the stage, an excited murmur rose from the enormous crowd. Coco strode confidently onto the stage and positioned himself behind the wooden podium. He gripped both sides and breathed in through his nose as he scanned the room. The audience was silent, rapt with expectant attention as they waited patiently for the shipping industry's biggest and most mysterious magnate to speak publicly for the first time in his long and storied career.

Coco hated publicity. A legendary oil trader who had been one of Coco's early business partners had taught him the importance of information opacity when working in a commodity business. Whether it was the location of his vessels, the extent of his cargo book, or the identity of his key business partners, secrecy had value when everyone trafficked in goods distinguished only by price. But all that was changing now.

Even the most private owners were morphing from nocturnal to diurnal because the new generation of leaders was more comfortable with transparency than a lack of it. The digital information revolution that had taken place in the past fifteen years had also made it basically impossible to keep anything confidential. But perhaps more than anything else, private owners had been forced to step out of the shadows in order to gain access to the capital markets for growth and risk sharing.

Coco cleared his throat, leaned down to the microphone, and placed his hand over his forehead to block the glare from the bright spotlight. The crowd was hushed as he opened his mouth to share his wisdom.

"Can you guys turn off the searchlight?" Coco called to the AV technicians, who immediately dimmed the stage lights so much that Coco was almost invisible. "Thank you," he said.

With the glare gone, Coco could see the enormity of the crowd for the first time. It felt fantastic to be back on stage again, standing in front of a sea of faces. As a boy growing up in the countryside outside Bergen, an undiagnosed learning disability made school torture for Coco; the more demanding it got, the more unbearable it became. By the time he reached middle school, the only class Coco enjoyed was drama.

After watching a high school production of *Romeo and Juliet*, he began to fantasize about having a career in the theater just like the kraken named Lars that his dad described in his rollicking bedtime stories. He dreamed of an exciting life of costumes and makeup and curtain calls and the ability to escape into roles and accents and perspectives and imaginary places altogether different from his own. That was why Coco always brought an element of theater to his business dealings; it added some fun and excitement to an activity that was too tedious for his own natural tendencies.

As Coco was taking a deep breath to begin his address, he was distracted by a raucous group of people entering through the back doors of the ballroom. When he squinted his eyes to see what was going on, he was surprised to see the unlikely combination of people: Camilla Castro, Pratap Bhat, the Chen sisters, Gerhard Haffenreffer, Freddy Fingers, and Gerry Coyote. It was unusual that they were all together and unsettling that they seemed so damned *merry*. All Coco could figure was that they must have just finished their meeting with Robert. What the hell were they so happy about? Coco wondered. *What had Fairchild done to him?*

When Coco looked down and focused his eyes on the front row, he was stunned to see a hellish line-up of people: Rocky DuBois, Vinny Vitale, Piper Pearl, and Peder Hanssen. Rocky was holding up a small handwritten sign that read, *I just called the cops.*

"I am Coco Jacobsen," Coco finally grumbled. "And you are probably wondering why I am here today. I am also kind of wondering this too," he said, generating a laugh from the anxious audience. "These Marine Money people have invited me to speak at this event for twenty years, and I have never said yes before. But they never give up, and I have never given up before either. So I came here today to make a very important announcement.

"As some of you know, I have been at the shipping game for a quite a little while, ever since a very kind man named Hilmar Reksten gave me a chance to get into this business. But I came here today to tell you that now I am out. I am done. I've sold my fleet, and I just wanted to say goodbye. I also wanted to say thank you for being part of my wonderful life. I wish you all the best of luck," Coco said and began to walk off the stage.

Chapter 35

The packed grand ballroom of the Montclair Hotel fell silent as the crowd processed Coco's stunning, heart-breaking statement. It was impossible to imagine a global shipping industry without Coco Jacobsen. He was the sum total and symbol of everything beautiful and important and traditional and whacky that made the industry so special. After a period of solemn silence, Tim swallowed hard and broke the ice.

"Why now?" Tim asked, stopping Coco in his tracks. "Why did you decide to exit now?"

"Because a kind man once told me to always leave the party while I am still having fun, so I will always have good memories," Coco said as he reluctantly returned to the podium. "Memories don't cost anything, but they are worth a lot."

"Does today's weak market make you nervous?"

"Good markets are what make me nervous because that means people will order ships," Coco said. "A bad market just means a good market is coming," he added, and once again began to walk off the stage. "Thank you."

"Whoa! Not so fast!" Tim said as he jumped back up onto the stage and blocked the keynote speaker's premature exit. This was the Grand Finale, and Tim had to make sure it was a memorable one. "I think we have time for a few questions."

"You can ask me some questions if you want, but now I am going to smoke a cigarette," Coco said as he removed a red box of Marlboros from his pocket while he slowly walked back to the podium. "Raise your hand if you solemnly swear not to tell my wife about this."

Before Coco had even finished speaking the words, approximately 1,200 arms shot up toward the ceiling, giving the conference room the ambiance of a religious cult, which it basically was.

"If it's not the market that has you concerned, then why now?" Tim asked. "Why did you decide to exit now?"

"When it's time to sell, you sell," Coco said.

Coco thought about the evening when Alex gave him that advice, while they were sitting together on the top deck of *Kon Tiki*. It seemed like a million miles away and a million years ago. He wished he was back there with her at that moment. After spending forty years on the road, he was now homesick for the first time in his life.

"About ten years ago I got married and we had some babies, and now we live on my boat. My wife has taught me a lot of important things. One of the things she taught me is that true wealth is being able to control your own time. I have decided to adopt my niece, whose parents died, and she needs some extra help, and I have two small boys, and I want to see all of them grow up, but I am not so young or healthy anymore."

"But the market is very low," Tim said. "It is not a good time to sell. Why don't you just wait until the cycle turns up?"

"Because today makes tomorrow, Tim," Coco said, repeating the advice Thor and Olav had given him when they were in his office aboard *Kon Tiki*. "And today is tomorrow's yesterday," he added.

"I get it," Tim said, his eyes were closed and he was nodding thoughtfully. "You want tomorrow to start today."

"My wife told me there are three stages of life," Coco said. "During the first one, you depend on people like your parents and your teachers to help you learn things. The second stage is when you have knowledge, you start making decisions and people depend on you, like your kids and your employees. In the third stage, after your business can run without you, the best thing you can do is to help *other* people be their best."

"So I guess it's time for you to enter stage three," Tim said.

"Yes. And the other reason I'm quitting ship owning is because of people like the inspiring woman who spoke before me."

"Athena Bouboulina?"

"The world and the shipping industry are changing fast, and it is time for me to make room for the talented and energetic young women and men who are going to change it. So that's what I'm doing today."

"*Wait a minute!*" Peder shouted in a rage as he jumped to his feet, brutally breaking the solemnity of Coco's heartfelt confession. "If you *sold* a fleet of old VLCCs and Athena *bought* a fleet of VLCCs, that means..."

"That's right, Peder," Coco said, pointing at Athena, who was standing on the elevated gallery next to the stage and waving to the crowd. "Your new Shipping Woman is Athena Bouboulina."

At the precise moment when Coco spoke Athena's name, the Montclair Hotel lost power and the grand ballroom was suddenly plunged into darkness.

Then came a thundering metallic crash that rocked the room. It sounded like a car driving into a metal wall at high speed. When the hotel generator kicked on thirty seconds later, a frantic clamor erupted at the front of the room.

"Call *911!*" Tim shouted to Ike as he scrambled to the stage where Coco was lying lifeless on the floor. "Coco's down."

Chapter 36

Coco's still body ended up wedged between the two semicircular chairs where Tim had interviewed Athena. The one eye that was visible beneath the tangle of his grackle-black hair was closed. The Marlboro was still burning in his mouth, and the microphone was still clutched in his grip.

Tim plucked the cigarette out of Coco's mouth as hundreds of people rushed to the front of the room to see what the hell was going on. It looked like a tribal funeral ritual when they formed a tightly packed circle around the fallen shipping tycoon.

The most sanguine of the bunch assumed that the blackout had caused the mightiest of the mighty shipowners to simply trip and fall over the AV wires, as Athena had. But the ones who studied him more closely, or knew about his heart condition, feared for the worst.

Ike bolted up the stage and fell to his knees next to Tim. The blinking red digital clock that told speakers how much of their allotted time remained was still illuminated. It was casting an eerie red glow as it displayed the time remaining for Coco's remarks: 5:23, frozen in history.

With their knees on the golden carpet and their backs to the cheek-by-jowl mob of onlookers, Ike and Tim appeared to perform CPR on Coco. They constantly relieved each other from the exhausting task of compressing the shipowner's giant chest.

"I once performed CPR on a *huge* Bolivian bunker broker during a fuel oil conference in Coconut Grove," Tim panted heavily to Ike as he used every one of his 174 pounds to compress Coco's gigantic ribcage.

"I've heard those bunker brokers can really party," Ike said.

"They sure can," Tim huffed and puffed. "That poor hombre was in the middle of executing some beautiful salsa moves when he collapsed on the dance floor."

"Did you manage to save him?" Ike asked, his eyes following Tim as he moved up and down on top of Coco.

"Nah," Tim said, "but it was a hell of a way to go out. You wanna take over for a minute? I need to check my email."

After no more than five minutes of ostensibly unsuccessful CPR, a squad of ten officers in blue uniforms burst through the swinging kitchen doors. As if directed by a choreographer, the battalion of men filed into the grand ballroom and onto the dais. They knew exactly where to go. Within seconds they had huddled around Coco's body so that no one could see him anymore.

One of the officers removed a portable defibrillator from a yellow box that was slung over his shoulder. He removed the strap, placed the device on the floor, and fumbled with the paddles. Another officer appeared to be administering an injection with a harpoon-length syringe into Coco's limp arm.

The uniformed men looked at each other with grim faces and sad eyes. Coco Jacobsen was gone, and he wasn't coming back.

Chapter 37

Robert couldn't have been more enthusiastic or optimistic about what the future might hold when he woke up his sleeping iPhone to check the time. He was disappointed to have missed Coco's first ever keynote address, but excited that it must be just about over by now. A new chapter in both of their lives was about to start, and it was exciting.

Like a kid who couldn't wait to tell his parents about a high grade on a hard math test, Robert was counting the minutes until Coco returned to the suite. He was eager to share the news about what he'd accomplished. Against all odds, Robert had helped Coco, a person who had done so much for him. And helping a friend out of a jam was one of life's great pleasures.

Robert had filled the entire $750 million capital hole in less than ninety minutes. Not bad for an on-the-beach CFO armed with nothing but an over-leveraged fleet of old VLCCs, a Marine Money Week delegate list, and a phone.

He knew Coco might not be thrilled with all of the terms, but Robert was satisfied that he had done the best deal he could possibly do under the circum-stances. No matter how Coco reacted, Robert knew the Norwegian would honor the deal. He had always been a man of his word. It was the code by which he always said he lived and died.

As he waited for Coco to come home to the suite, Robert opened a can of Heineken from the minibar.

He knew it was bad luck to celebrate a deal before it closed, but he decided to tempt fate and do it anyway. He had taken off his rubber boots at the entrance of the sprawling hotel room and put his cashmere-covered feet up on the wooden desk.

He still had a bit of tidying up to do before Coco returned to the suite. He needed to put the finishing touches on the two summary documents, both of which were handwritten on a legal pad he had picked up from a table in the deal room.

The first document was the capitalization table, or cap table, in dealmaker slang, which showed the ownership percentage of each investor. It was pro forma for Operation Greta, which meant it reflected the ownership as if the transaction had already closed.

The second handwritten document was the sources and uses table, which summarized the various places where the money came from and what that money would be used for. Coco probably wouldn't like this part either.

In preparation for Coco's arrival, Robert began to tally up the sources and uses table. Like the two sides of a balance sheet, the two columns of a sources and uses table accounted for every dollar and had to add up; the amount of money coming in had to be at least as much as the money going out.

He had just totaled up the sources when his phone suddenly exploded with chirps and chimes as text messages and push notifications popped down from the top of the screen, obscuring the calculator on which he was doing his math. He swatted the first few notifications off the screen without even looking at them, but the one from *Ahoy Matey!* caught his eye.

The King Is Dead!

As Robert read the words, he felt a wave of nausea wash over him. He somehow knew what they meant even before he opened the message. With a blank expression on his face, he took his feet off the desk and planted them on the floor and gripped the armrests of his chair to prevent himself from falling onto the beige carpet. He went numb as he read the article.

Robert immediately concluded that Coco's death must have been the work of Vinny Vitale, which meant he was partly to blame. Robert hadn't known that Vinny was the Butcher of Bridgehampton when they did the $150 million preferred deal for the scrubbers, but his instincts had told him the transaction was a bad idea. A truly competent and confident CFO would have put his foot down and told his owner that the deal was a stupid idea. Robert didn't do that. He had just carried out the orders.

Robert suddenly had a burst of energy. He ran to the door, shoved his feet back into Oliver's soggy rubber sailing boots, bolted out of the room, and sprinted down the hallway. Unwilling to wait for the arrival of the Montclair elevators, one of the last attended lifts in New York City, he spotted the door that led to the stairwell. He bounded down the steps, rubber boots squeaking on the painted concrete floor.

As he pushed through the double doors of the grand ballroom, he was expecting to see a large crowd of people, press, and police, but the place was hauntingly empty. The only individuals in the ballroom were a dozen grim-faced men in uniforms standing on the stage looking down at a shape that Robert instantly recognized as Coco's barrel chest —

covered by a white tablecloth. A tuft of his long black hair was lying across the crimson carpet.

Robert was unable to take another step. He turned around, exited the grand ballroom, and walked toward Elaine Marstons, who was meticulously packing hundreds of name badges into a cardboard box.

"Excuse me…" Robert said.

"I'm sorry, but badges are no longer available," Elaine said without looking up. "The conference ended a little early this year. Our next event is Marine Money Week Asia in Singapore in September. I hope to see you there. Have a nice summer."

"I'm not here for a badge, Elaine," Robert said. "I am here to find out what *the hell* happened to my best friend…Coco Jacobsen. I'm here for answers."

Elaine suddenly looked up when she recognized the voice. "Oh, Robert, I am so sorry for your loss."

"What happened?"

"I don't know all the details," she said, fighting back tears. "You'd better ask Tim. He was right there when it happened."

"Where is he now?" Robert asked.

"I think he's in the deal room," Elaine said, and lowered her head as she went back to her task.

Chapter 38

When Robert entered the deal room, the solemn atmosphere and haunting silence broke his heart. All eyes were on him, but no one knew what to say. He felt as though he was seriously ill or bankrupt or had been charged with a heinous crime or unknowingly captured on film doing something embarrassing. It was awkward.

Everyone in the market knew that Coco and Robert had broken up, which meant they also knew Robert was probably grieving in the same melancholy and unsatisfying way one might grieve the passing of a former lover. With the regret of thinking about what might have been had different decisions been taken, patience been exercised, the pause button pressed on personal wants and needs.

Robert finally located Tim tucked away in the far corner of the deal room, whispering with his hand over his telephone. When Tim spotted Robert, he hastily shut off his call, stuffed the phone into the jacket pocket of his white linen suit, and approached Robert.

"Thanks for coming over, Robert," Tim said. "You're great to be here. Shall we go for a drink?" Tim suggested. "A nice bottle of Pinot Noir? Perhaps something from the Willamette or Russian River valley?"

"I wish I could, Tim, but I have a very difficult phone call to make in a few minutes."

"The wife?"

"The widow," Robert said. "Alex is going to ask me a lot of questions, and I need some answers."

"I'll tell you everything I know," Tim said. "But I'm afraid it isn't much."

"Thanks," Robert replied.

"Coco had just finished giving a very emotional keynote address when the hotel lost power. Just after the lights went out, there was an unbelievable crashing sound. By the time the emergency lights came on, Coco was on the floor. Ike and I tried to give Coco CPR, but it was no use. He was already gone. The police are still waiting for the city medical examiner to arrive, I guess she's busy with hurricane-related deaths, but the EMTs are writing it up as a massive heart attack based on his medical history."

"Let me ask you something, Tim."

"Sure."

"Do you happen to know a guy named Vinny Vitale?"

"As a matter of fact, I just met him for the first time today," Tim said. "He's quite an unusual character."

"Did you happen to see him during Coco's speech?"

"Of course," Tim said. "He was sitting in the front row."

"That's what I was afraid of," Robert replied, bitterly shaking his head back and forth. "Bastard."

"What are you saying?" Tim asked.

Robert looked around the room to make sure no one was close enough to overhear their conversation.

"What I'm saying, Tim, is that Coco made some enemies over years."

"Hold on, wait a minute, you think Coco Jacobsen might have been *murdered* at Marine Money Week?" Tim gasped.

"Yes," Robert said, nodding. "I want you to text me when the medical examiner arrives. I just want to have a word with her and make sure she knows to look for evidence of foul play."

As Robert was handing Tim his former Scrubber Ships business card, he spotted Rocky DuBois sitting on the bench behind a black grand piano in the opposite corner of the deal room. He immediately felt his anger rise.

"Excuse me, Tim," Robert said. "I need to have a word with Mr. DuBois before he disappears."

As Robert approached Rocky, he heard a soft melody and saw that the old cowboy's head was down, suggesting he was the one playing the Andy Williams song "Feelings."

Robert smacked his open hand down violently on the lid of the piano. Rocky looked up, startled. The nearly ninety-year-old oil man instinctively raised both hands into the air as if in surrender, but the sappy song kept playing on the mechanical piano.

"You scared the socks off me," Rocky said when he saw Robert.

"Why so jumpy?" Robert asked. "Got something on your mind?"

"I'm so very sorry for your loss, Robert." The big man rose from the piano bench and opened his arms for an embrace.

Robert felt like he was being welcomed into the arms of Satan — the lord of darkness dressed in a perfectly tailored, chalk-striped gray J. Press suit, starched white shirt, and red power tie, with salt-and-pepper hair as buttery thick and well-groomed as Robert Mueller's. A touch taller than six feet, the geologist turned oil man had alligator-thick skin from spending decades in the sun.

"I knew Coco's heart disease was serious, and that he refused to get it fixed, but I didn't know just how serious it was," Rocky said. He looked at Robert with his deep-set brown eyes.

"I don't know if that's what killed him, but I do know that you were one of the causes of his heart disease," Robert said.

"Me?" Rocky gasped. "How dare you?"

"Cut the crap, Rocky. You spent the last thirty years beating the snot out of Coco Jacobsen," Robert blurted out, taking a step closer to the Texan. "If you weren't almost ninety-years-old, I would kick your ass."

"What did I do?"

"Everyone in the entire shipping industry knows that you hated Coco. You hated him for making you look like a fool."

"No, I hated him for frothing the bunker tanks like a venti latte and stealing my bunkers. That's how he really got the equity to grow his fleet. And what does he do? He turns around and screws me by squeezing the market," Rocky fumed. "You think that sounds fair?"

"Well you shouldn't have put his ship off hire on that bullshit *force majeure* claim in Nigeria just to save a few bucks," Robert said.

"Yes, okay, we had a sporting rivalry, but that's healthy in shipping. Shipowners and charterers have a natural conflict of interest; owners want day rates to be higher and charterers want day rates to be lower. We play a zero-sum game."

"Charterers like you don't want shipowners to make enough money to pay their crew and maintain their vessels," Robert said. "That's not a zero-sum game. That's just plain wrong."

"No, what's wrong, son, is that when the tanker market gets tight, shipowners like Coco try to squeeze every last drop of blood out of us. Guys like Coco don't give a damn about what high charter rates do to *my* business. That's why we have to take advantage of them when we can. It's the law of the jungle."

"That's because shipowners like Coco are always trying to play catch-up with the lousy rates you pay them when the market is weak. You guys did nothing but antagonize each other."

"Shipping is no different from football," Rocky said. "Players hit each other on the field, but when the game is over, we all get together in the steam room and snap towels."

"That's a truly revolting image," Robert said, and began to walk away.

"Hey, it's not my fault I won the final match," Rocky snickered. "Oh, and one more thing, Robert."

"What's that?" Robert asked.

"As you may know, LTO has agreed to sell me Coco's fleet once they foreclose and take title."

"How much are you paying for our ships?"

"Same deal I made when I approached LTO," Rocky said. "I will pay LTO what they paid for the loan, and they get to keep whatever they collect from the personal guarantee."

"That's dirty," Robert said.

"Making big money often is," Rocky replied, starting to laugh. "For what it's worth, I can't believe you let Coco put a personal guarantee on the loan. What kind of shit-ball CFO are you, anyway?"

"You're an asshole," Robert seethed.

"I do have some good news," Rocky said.

"What's that?"

"My lawyers and ship managers tell me it may be a month or two before I can actually take possession of Coco's ships, so if you would like to charter them to me in the meantime, I would be willing to do that. That would allow me to get my crew members on board to get familiar with the vessels. And you can spend your summer relaxing on Martha's Vineyard with Grace and Oliver."

"Go to hell, Rocky," Robert said. "I won't be doing any relaxing until I figure out what happened to Coco, and something tells me your hands are dirty."

Chapter 39

By the time Robert had walked back into the rotunda of the Montclair Hotel, his anger had eclipsed his sorrow. The whimsical round room adorned with trompe l'oeil frescoes of clouds drifting across the sky-blue ceiling had been a magical place when it was filled with chatty dealmakers a couple of hours earlier.

But now it was deserted. The whimsy had turned haunting, and the artwork suddenly seemed macabre. Robert figured the deal junkies had probably adjourned to Chatham Bar next to the Montclair's main entrance on Sixty-First Street, where they would grieve with heavy hearts and full glasses, just as Coco would have wanted it.

He had tried to reach Camilla countless times since he first learned about Coco's death, but she had gone dark. He was disturbed and confused by the fact she hadn't answered any of his calls or texts. It was very unlike her under any circumstances, but especially now.

He and Camilla had spent nearly an hour together in the Presidential Suite, quickly building the new financial model in Excel and structuring a recapitalization plan for Scrubber Ships that might actually work. He couldn't have done it without her, but now she had vanished. Something didn't add up.

Had the New York area airports not been officially closed, he would have suspected that she was on a southbound airplane executing her own exit strategy

— but now he wondered if she too might be dead. Yet another victim of the Scrubber Ships financial fiasco.

Robert knew he had to tell Alex what had happened, but he also knew that she would demand answers and he needed to have some. He had to gather more information before he made the call.

As Alex had astutely observed, no one knew everything about Coco's business dealings, but Gerry Coyote knew more than anyone else. He had been the Norwegian's almost exclusive lawyer, unofficial rabbi, and chargé d'affaires ever since Coco's first money hunting safari to New York thirty years earlier.

Robert sat down on a green bench just out of earshot of an NYPD officer and his German shepherd wingman standing inside the hotel's Fifth Avenue entrance. He jabbed his index finger against the screen of his phone until he located Gerry phone's number on his contact list. Then he pressed the green circle and took a deep breath.

"Hello, Robert," Gerry said softly. "This is a sad day."

"I know," Robert said as he stared down in defeat at the hotel's marble floor, shaking his head back and forth. "And we were so close to a solution."

"I'm sure you did everything you could," Gerry said.

The soothing sound of Gerry's voice immediately brought Robert to tears. He hit the mute button and sobbed into the elbow of his green cashmere sweater.

Robert couldn't help but feel partially responsible for setting in motion the events that had resulted in Coco's death. In addition to the feeling of profound loss, Robert was also shocked and confused. He thought he had come to a peaceful resolution with

Vinny when he convinced him to participate in the recapitalization arrangement just one hour earlier.

Vinny had agreed to play ball, albeit in a very unorthodox, if potentially criminal, manner. Now Robert wondered if it was all a charade. Maybe he had given Vinny an alibi. Or maybe Vinny's willingness to make a deal was just a red herring used to throw Robert off the scent while Vinny's assassins practiced their craft in the grand ballroom of Marine Money Week.

"Robert, we need to talk," Gerry said.

"We are talking."

"Face-to-face," Gerry said. "Can you come up to room 801? I have something that Coco wanted me to give you."

"It's a little late for a black eye," Robert said.

"No, Robert, this is something very special."

"Special?"

"Something you'll be quite interested in," Gerry said.

Chapter 40

When Gerry opened the door to room 801, Robert proceeded directly to the pale blue couch positioned against the windows and collapsed into the soft cushions.

"May I offer you a drink?" Gerry asked.

"Two Heinekens please," Robert said.

"Coco would have wanted it that way," Gerry said.

As Gerry bent over and rummaged around in the minibar, Robert looked around the hotel room. On the table across from the bed was a giant television screen broadcasting a message, *Welcome Mr. Coyote. The weather today is: TROPICAL STORM HAROLD.*

Robert didn't see a suitcase or clothes or any evidence that Gerry was actually residing in the room. There were piles of paper on every flat surface. A blizzard of clip-bound documents covered the bureau, the nightstands, the tiny desk, and the bed. It looked like a transaction closing and ship registration were underway.

"I guess the hurricane was downgraded," Robert said with a laugh, pointing toward the screen. "Maybe that means you will be able to get out of this hotel tomorrow."

"I hope not," Gerry said. "I like it here."

"I guess there are worse places to get stuck," Robert said.

"Here you go," Gerry said as he handed him the pair of frosted silver-and-green cans, one in each hand. "I know how difficult this must be on you."

"It's pretty bad," Robert admitted.

"Coco told me that you guys had an argument down in the Bahamas," Gerry said. "I want you to know that he regretted that very much."

"Did he tell you the story?"

"Not really."

"He fired me because I didn't want to invest every cent I have in Scrubber Ships at his book value when the company had almost zero net asset value," Robert said. "He said I was being disloyal and he called me a coward, but the company blew up a couple months later."

"Coco was a wonderful man, but he could be very black-and-white when it came to things like loyalty and valuation," Gerry said. "I hope you can forgive him for that."

"Yeah, I forgive him," Robert said. "No one defended Coco like you did. You were always so good to him."

"*Me* good to *him?*" Gerry laughed. "It was quite the opposite, Robert. Without Coco Jacobsen, my life and career would look a lot different."

"I think a lot of people in the shipping industry could say that," Robert agreed. "Coco didn't finish the eighth grade, but he sure did put a lot of kids through university."

"I don't think he set out to do it, and I don't think it's why he did it, but he changed a lot of lives for the better, especially mine," Gerry added.

For better or worse, a single relationship often determined the outcome of lives and careers — and such was the case with Gerry and Coco. Their serendipitous symbiosis had been sparked nearly forty years earlier after Gerry passed the bar and started working at a generalist commercial litigation law firm in Battery Park.

Late one sweltering Friday afternoon in July, a towering man who resembled a rock star had wandered into the office clutching a crumpled scrap of paper he'd torn from a yellow pages directory he'd found in a Battery Park phone booth.

The mysterious man explained to the puzzled receptionist, who understood only about one in every five of the Norwegian's words, that he had convinced someone in New York to give him $86,000 to buy bunkers for a Panamax tanker he wanted to charter from a Swiss bank that had arrested the ship in Lake Maracaibo. "Now I just need someone to make the papers," he said.

Coco's curious case was assigned to David Jones, a senior partner who was deemed to have maritime experience because he wore topsiders and owned a twenty-seven-foot sailboat that he kept on a rented mooring in Shelter Island.

Attorney Jones had just begun to feel his way through the complicated international documentation when his head plunked down on the desk. After his body was removed and his office was sanitized and lightly deodorized, Gerry was installed as the firm's maritime expert because all the other lawyers had already left for the weekend. The king was dead, long live the king.

Coco's deal in Venezuela proved to be a winner, and there was no better way to accelerate a new business relationship than when everyone made some fast money. Gerry and Coco formed a bond that would last a lifetime.

Before long, Gerry became known around the firm as "the shipping man," a mostly misunderstood moniker that resulted in him undertaking all matters maritime — in addition to having packages requiring postage left on his desk whenever he wasn't around.

Between loan agreements, capital markets transactions, cargo claims, insurance issues, collisions, and civil and criminal litigation as both plaintiff and defendant, Gerry learned that even a single ship produced a never-ending stream of work for a lawyer. From the moment the new building contract was drafted and reviewed to the day a cash buyer like Pratap Bhat bought the ship and dismantled it, ships were machines that carried cargo and produced legal work.

And when an independent owner like Coco had thirty ships, a need for secrecy, and no in-house counsel, the legal workflow was unimaginable. Their professional relationship had even expanded to include estate planning after Alex found the default notice from LTO and made herself sole trustee of Thor and Olav's $175 million trust.

"We have all been fortunate to work for Coco," Robert said as he pulled open the heavy yellow brocade curtains with both hands and gazed onto dark and stormy Central Park. "It's difficult to imagine this industry without him. I don't know what the future holds, but I do know it won't be as much fun."

"The shipping industry is changing," Gerry said solemnly. "And we all need to help prevent it from becoming a beautiful industrial ruin."

"Coco certainly did his part," Robert said. "He helped save shipping from becoming just another boring corporate industry." Robert raised his can and offered a phantom toast. "Skal."

"He kept the passion alive in the shipping business," Gerry said.

"If you had asked me one hour ago what I'd be doing right now, I would have told you I'd be in the Presidential Suite celebrating with Coco," Robert said. "But here we are mourning his death."

"What were you planning to celebrate?" Gerry asked.

"The fact that I pulled off the deal of the century," Robert said. "Almost."

"What do you mean?"

"Didn't he tell you? I somehow managed to cobble together a $750 million refinancing for the Scrubber Ships fleet in ninety minutes," Robert replied.

"What? That's amazing," Gerry said slowly.

"Maybe, but the deal is dead on arrival because Coco isn't around to actually close it," Robert said. "I should probably give you the details because I'm sure Alex will need your help in sorting through everything once LTO commences litigation."

"Okay," Gerry said. He grabbed a yellow legal pad so he could take notes.

"As you probably know, Coco came to Marine Money Week with a plan to get himself out of trouble."

"That plan really backfired," Gerry said.

"He had agreed to sell his fleet to Beta Ships, which is owned by Athena Bouboulina, Henry Husk, and a group of investors in California, for $750 million. He needed to sell the fleet so he could pay off LTO Capital and cancel the PG that Alex was so upset about."

"I counseled him against giving that PG in the first place," Gerry said. "I almost refused to document the transaction because I was so uncomfortable with that, but he insisted."

"Me too," Robert said. "I was actually with Gerhard in Hamburg when we did that deal and I can assure you that Coco didn't have a choice. Anyway, the fatal flaw with Coco's plan was that he would have to wipe out Vinny Vitale's $150 million investment because there wasn't enough money to go around."

"I get it," Gerry said. "Cram down."

"But he didn't realize how Vinny was going to react."

"What do you mean?" Gerry asked.

"When Coco came to New York, he figured Black Boulder could easily take a $150 million hit like some of the mega funds that lost money in shipping. He didn't realize the loss would blow up Black Boulder, or that Vinny was the kind of person who would have Coco killed if he didn't pay him back, with interest."

"That was a major miscalculation," Gerry said.

"Coco's other big mistake was in assuming that the Chen sisters would provide the $600 million debt facility that Athena and her investors needed to complete the purchase."

"They didn't want to?"

"Of course not," Robert said. "Roberta Chen refused to do it."

"Strike two for Coco," Gerry said.

"That's when Coco called me and asked if I could put together a bailout deal for him," Robert said.

"Again," Gerry said.

"Again," Robert agreed.

"That sounds just like Coco," Gerry said with a laugh. "So how did you put together a refinancing when no one wanted to do a deal?"

Robert explained that he had convinced Pratap to put up $50 million of equity in exchange for getting a share of ownership plus the right to buy the ships for scrap at a discounted price of $150 per ton when their useful life concluded. He had also enticed Freddy Fingers into investing $50 million in exchange for Scrubber Ships taking ten of Justice Shipping's VLCCs on charter for three years at $35,000 per day — enough so that Freddy didn't have to cut his dividend and destroy the valuation of his shares.

"But that's only $100 million," Gerry said.

"Plus the $150 million from Henry Husk."

"But you said you needed $750 million, so where did the other $500 million come from?"

"The Chen sisters and Gerhard Haffenreffer agreed to advance us $450 million as a first preferred ship mortgage loan secured by the fleet."

"I thought they said no."

"I was able to convince the Chens to comingle the loan to Beta Ships with a loan Roberta wanted to provide to Mollusk Oil," Robert said. "By combining the cash flow and the collateral of the two fleets, I was able to create a synthetic borrower that was acceptable to both Rebecca and Roberta."

"Brilliant," Gerry said. "Like a mini collateralized loan obligation."

"Exactly."

"How about Gerhard? I thought it was his bank that sold Coco's loan to LTO and started this entire mess."

"It was, but when I told Gerhard that Athena was planning to retrofit Coco's vessels with technology to significantly reduce carbon emissions, he actually begged me to let him in on the deal."

"Funny."

"Apparently Germany has a new program where the government will guarantee loans made to companies that make existing assets more environmentally efficient. The bank wanted to show their shareholders they are taking action against climate change."

"Ironic," Gerry said. "But you are still missing $50 million. Where did you get that?"

"From Alex," Robert said.

"But I thought she refused to let Coco use the trust fund for this? That's what he told me."

"She refused to give the trust fund money to Coco," Robert said with a sly smile. "But she was happy to give it to St. Lucy's Academy, where Maisy goes to school."

"I'm not following you," Gerry said.

"I told Alex that if she gave me $50 million to complete the refinancing, the income from Coco's shares in Scrubber Ships would be assigned to St. Lucy's Academy, which is apparently having some cash flow challenges."

"And she said yes?"

"Yup. Her one and only condition was that we give LTO an $8 million haircut on the loan to make up for the $8 million bonus that Piper stole from her when he fired her."

"Now that's justice," Gerry said. "But I highly doubt that Coco would have agreed to give his cash flow to St. Lucy's Academy."

"That's why I insisted that Coco give me the full authority to negotiate whatever deal I felt was best," Robert said. "And he agreed to accept it as is."

"Hold on, are you saying a special needs school in Florida owns the income from a fleet of supertankers?" Gerry beamed. "How cool is that?"

"It would have been very cool if Coco was still around to complete the transaction," Robert said. "The arrangement would have produced enough cash flow to keep the school afloat even in an average VLCC market. But I don't know what's going to happen now."

"What about Vinny?" Gerry said. "You're still short the $150 million of preferred equity that Coco owed Black Boulder Asset Management."

"I think I resolved that too," Robert said.

"How?"

"Vinny made a deal with his investors. They were eager to get out of his fund before their lock-up expired, and he agreed to give them back 100 percent of the principal without a return. He had made a large profit on the sale of a company called CheapSleeps, which made up for the loss on Scrubber Ships."

"What does Vinny get?"

"I agreed to put a twenty percent stake of Scrubber Ships in his personal account in exchange for him writing off the $150 of preferred equity."

"What about Athena?" Gerry asked. "I thought she wanted to control all the equity in the ships."

"She and her investors never even wanted hard assets," Robert said. "The only reason she agreed to buy the ships was so she could beta test all of her carbon-reducing technologies."

"Wow," Gerry said.

The veteran lawyer was visibly stunned by what Robert had accomplished. He had been executing shipping deals for decades, but he'd never seen anyone so skillfully construct a capital structure of fellow travelers — a tribe of people who banded together to share risk, enjoy incentives, and contribute different talents to the venture. It was a collab.

"It was a cool deal, but it's all worthless now that Coco is gone," Robert said as he finished his first beer and put the empty keg can on the wooden end table next to the couch.

"I think I am going to go home now," Robert said. "Did you say that you have something Coco wanted me to have?"

"Oh, yes, thanks for reminding me," Gerry said, walking over to the small desk.

Gerry laid his old-fashioned leather briefcase on the bed and went to work dialing the four-digit combination into the locks. Once he had cracked the code, he opened the latches, lifted the lid, and removed a letter-sized envelope from the inside pocket.

"Here," Gerry said, handing the envelope to Robert. "Coco wanted you to have this."

"What is it?"

"It's his letter of final wishes," Gerry said.

"His what?"

"His final wishes. He wanted you to have it in case something happened to him during his trip to New York," Gerry said.

"He must've had a bad feeling," Robert said as he began to open the crème-colored envelope.

"*Stop!*" Gerry said in a tone more forceful than Robert had ever heard from him.

"What?"

"You can't open it now."

"Why not? He's dead."

"Because Coco specifically directed me to have you open this in front of the audience."

"What audience?"

"He wanted you to read it in front of all the shipping men and women who were attending Marine Money Week."

"You mean like reading a last will and testament in front of the potential beneficiaries?" Robert asked.

"I suppose that's right," Gerry said.

"But you can't be serious," Robert said. "Coco didn't even know most of the people here today."

"We are not the arbiter of his intentions," Gerry said. "I implore you to honor Coco's wishes. It's the least you can do for him after everything he did for you."

Chapter 41

"May I have your attention, please," Elaine Marstons' distinctive voice came over the scratchy emergency PA system of the Montclair Hotel. "I have a special announcement."

After Gerry gave him his instructions, Robert told Elaine about the letter of final wishes and Coco's request that Robert share its contents in front of all the Marine Money conference delegates. Without any hesitation, Elaine agreed to pull together one last, impromptu session of the three-day event.

"In ten minutes, we will begin a very special encore session of Marine Money Week in the grand ballroom," Elaine's voice continued to come out of the PA system. "This bonus session will feature the former CFO of Viking Tankers, Mr. Robert Fairchild, sharing the details of the letter of final wishes drafted by Mr. Coco Jacobsen shortly before his death. Mr. Jacobsen asked that the letter be read aloud for the first time to all Marine Money delegates. This is a session you will not want to miss."

In addition to making the announcement verbally, Elaine sent the identical information via email, text, Twitter, Instagram, and LinkedIn to everyone who was registered for Marine Money Week. The deal junkies were scattered all about the hotel. Some were in their rooms, working, chilling, napping, or talking on the phone. A few were outside smoking beneath the marquee. Others were chatting in small groups in the deal room. But most were still huddled over drinks in the various hotel bars.

No matter where they were located or what they were doing, within a matter of seconds each and every one of the constant checkers had received, read, and forwarded Elaine's message to even the farthest corners of the globe. And their reaction was universal; they were aching with excitement to find out what their supreme spiritual shipping shaman, Coco Jacobsen, wanted them to know upon his death. They longed to learn the recipe for Coco's secret sauce.

Once the grand ballroom was jam-packed with people and pin-drop quiet, Robert walked onto the stage and wrapped both hands around the sides of the wooden podium. He had butterflies in his stomach thinking about what incriminating and brutal and embarrassing truth might be contained in the letter, but he owed it to Coco to share it with the world. It was the least he could do.

Robert cleared his throat as he removed the crème-colored envelope from the inside pocket of his wife's yellow rain slicker. He took the letter out of the envelope, unfolded it, and smoothed it out on the slanted surface of the rostrum.

"Good afternoon, ladies and gentlemen. My name is Robert Fairchild. I want to thank you for being here. Coco Jacobsen instructed his personal and corporate attorney, Gerry Coyote, to have me read his letter of final wishes in the presence of all of you. No one, besides Coco and Gerry, has seen this letter. I was not even aware of its existence until Gerry gave it to me half an hour ago, along with Coco's request that it be read aloud to all of you.

"I would like to start by displaying the document," Robert said, holding it high in the air for all the delegates to see. "I can report that it is handwritten and printed on the letterhead of an establishment called Nancy's Bar & Grill on the island of Eleuthera in the Bahamas. It is dated June eighth and was officially witnessed by a gentleman named Mr. Ziggy Madsen, who was Coco's friend and personal fishing guide. Now, without any further delay, here is what Coco wanted to say," Robert announced, taking a deep breath.

"Dear Shipping Friends, if you are reading this letter, I am gone, which is okay. The only things I regret are things I didn't do. I have never asked anything of anyone and especially from other shipowners, but if you would like to honor my life as a shipping man, I have one simple request: Please slow down for 60 days. Love, Coco.

"Thank you," Robert announced as he folded up the letter and placed it back into the envelope. "Safe travels home. Have a nice summer."

Have a nice summer? What the hell? The audience let out a powerful and collective sigh of extreme disappointment. *That was it?* Talk about an anti-climax; they expected a lot more from the legendary Coco Jacobsen than just another bullshit cliché about slowing down and being present and having purpose and appreciating the little things in life. What a hunk of Hallmark card crap!

The dumbfounded silence was broken when Rocky DuBois stood up and began to slowly clap and told Ike with a nod that he wanted a microphone.

"Our fallen brother Coco is right," Rocky proclaimed, stroking his cleft chin ponderously as he paced the front of the room like a preacher. "Coco and

I didn't always get along when we were playing the chartering game, but we always respected each other back in the clubhouse."

"Coco hated your guts," Robert scoffed under his breath, unaware that his mic was still hot. The crowd laughed uncomfortably.

"Now, to honor our lost friend," Rocky continued, "and to respect these final wishes that Mr. Fairchild just graciously shared with us, we must slow down to enjoy the small moments in life. Friendship is one of the things we must appreciate and enjoy. Therefore, I would like to invite everyone to the bar, where the first round of drinks is on American Refining Corporation," he said as he began to exit the ballroom. "We will toast the remarkable life of Mr. Coco Jacobsen."

Just as 1,000-plus disappointed, and always thirsty, delegates rose from their seats and began to head for the bar, Gerry Coyote raised his arms into the air and cried out from the back of the ballroom.

"That's wrong!"

Every person in the room immediately froze in their tracks, turned around, and looked at Gerry.

"What is it?" Tim Torrance asked. "Do you have something to say, Gerry?"

"That's wrong!" Gerry cried out again with uncharacteristic intensity as he slowly walked up the center aisle and approached the stage, the eyes of the delegates closely watching him.

"Yes sir, it *is* wrong," Rocky agreed. "It is sick and sad and wrong that a man like Coco Jacobsen, a man in full, could be *cut down* so young."

"No! What Rocky said a few minutes ago is wrong," Gerry said as he stood behind the podium and spoke into the microphone. "That's not what

Coco meant at all. Please, take your seats again. I will explain the true intent of Coco's letter of final wishes."

"Whoa, now, partner," Rocky said as the crowd settled back into their chairs. "I do not think it is appropriate for us to take liberties when interpreting Mr. Jacobsen's very clear and unambiguous final wishes."

"Sit down and shut up, Rocky," Robert said. "Carry on, Gerry."

"I was on the phone with Coco the morning he drafted this document a few weeks ago," Gerry said into the reverberating microphone. "Except for a minor beer buzz, I can attest to the fact that Coco was of sound mind and body. And I know his intent with absolute certainty," Gerry said.

"And what was his intent, Gerry?" Robert asked. "Please tell us his intent."

"Coco's intent was for all the VLCC owners in the world to honor him by reducing the speed of their vessels by at least four knots," Gerry said. "He wanted them to slow down, literally, not metaphorically."

"Huh?" Rocky grunted, visibly stunned by Gerry's words.

The ballroom began to stir as the delegates looked at each other and smiled. This sounded more like the flair for the dramatic for which Coco Jacobsen was world famous.

"He wanted the shipowners to come together, if only for a little while, to understand that if they work together they have the power to change the world. Coco didn't want a funeral, he wanted a two-month tanker party!"

"Hot damn!" Peder Hanssen slapped both thighs with eager excitement as he leaned back in his chair to watch the drama unfold. "That sounds more like my Coco."

Gerry continued. "Coco knew that slowing down would reduce carbon emissions and increase charter rates at the same time. He knew that shipowners had never been able to come together on this topic, but he hoped that his brothers and sisters in the VLCC market would use his death as an opportunity to do good for the earth, which was his wife's personal cause, and to squeeze the nuts of the charterers until they sang in falsetto, which was his personal cause."

"Ha...ha...ha!" A slow and steady laugh emerged from the back of the room.

All heads turned around to see Freddy Fingers in the far left corner of the back row, smoking a cigarette as he leaned back in his chair with his shoes off and his pink socks on the headrest of the unoccupied chair in front of him.

"Bravo, Coco!" Freddy said as he raised his Marlboro into the air, the blue smoke brightly illuminated as it floated through the beam of a ceiling-mounted spotlight. "Even in death you continue to give this industry life," he said with a chuckle, looking up toward the ceiling and folding his hands together in prayer.

Just then, a tall man with a lion-thick mane of wavy red hair and penny-round glasses slowly rose above the sea of faces in the middle of the ballroom. Once he was standing, he pointed his right index finger toward the sky as he thoughtfully stroked his chin with his left hand and began to speak.

"I would like to empirically confirm that this is a scientific fact!" he said. "Mr. Jacobsen was correct."

"It sounds like Einstein has a theory," Freddy said. "Speak up, mate."

As the only known shipowner with a Ph.D. from Harvard in experimental high-energy physics, the man nicknamed Einstein brought a different kind of analysis to an industry dominated by gut instincts and contrarian investment behavior. He brought rigorous math and data-driven science.

"According my calculations, if you run a ship from point A to point B at a speed that is x percent of the normal speed, then fuel consumption will be $(x/100)^2*100\%$ of normal consumption."

"What does that mean?" Freddy asked.

"It means that, roughly speaking, if the ship goes ten percent slower, she will consume twenty percent less fuel, represented as $(0.9^2 \sim 0.8)$. Here's where it gets *really* sexy," Einstein said with a naughty giggle. "If this ship were to go twenty percent slower, as Coco apparently suggested, then she would burn approximately thirty-six percent less fuel, which equates to $(0.8^2 = 0.64)$."

"*No!*" Rocky cried out as his reality suddenly came into focus.

"Take a seat, Rocky," Robert said.

"But this is junk science!" Rocky continued. "Slow steaming would actually cause *more* carbon emissions. If ships slow down, we will need to build more ships to carry the same volume of cargo over the same distance. This will be less efficient and cause more environmental damage. It may create a short-term increase in charter rates, yes, but it will make the long-term problem even worse just as we are trying to fix it!"

"Tanker party...tanker party...tanker party." Freddy started the tribal chanting softly, melodically, to himself in the back of the room. Only the people sitting in his immediate vicinity could hear him.

"The concept of slow steaming might make some sense for the huge container ships that travel at twenty-five knots," Rocky continued, "but not for tankers. Slowing down tankers will disincentivize owners from building the kind of new ships that will make this industry more efficient."

"Tanker party! Tanker party! Tanker party!" the English oil tanker owner continued as he rose from his chair.

Freddy increased the volume of his chant and repeatedly lifted his open hands to encourage his fellow Marine Money Week delegates to join him by standing up and chanting along with him. Before long, the low murmur had exploded into a thundering call to action that rocked the Montclair Hotel.

"TANKER PARTY! TANKER PARTY! TANKER PARTY!" the delegates cried, stomping their feet on the ground and pounding the tables in front of them.

"But slow steaming is absolute nonsense!" Rocky insisted.

Without even lifting his head, the *Ahoy Matey!* reporter in the front row pecked a story into his tiny laptop. Seconds later the headline had instantly spread to shipping women and men ashore and at sea all over the world: *Freddy Throws Tanker Party for Best Friend Coco!*

"On behalf of Justice Shipping Limited," Freddy said, "and to honor and respect the wishes of my dear friend Coco, I will hereby order every one of my VLCCs to reduce speed by four knots. Furthermore, I will instruct our attorneys to amend the terms of all charter parties to state that our ships will not exceed twelve knots. And I will ask my lawyers to explore drafting legislation and regulations to impose ceilings and floors when it comes to vessel speed. I propose that this modification be called" — he paused while he inhaled deeply though his nose and stared up at the ceiling — "*The Coco Clause!*" he announced, raising his fist into the air. "We will be Coco Strong!"

The clattering chatter was silenced when a Japanese man rose from his chair in the middle of the crowded room. "I only have eight VLCCs, but I too will reduce the speed by four knots," he said in earnest. "And I will adopt the Coco Clause in our future time charters. I loved that man. He earned our respect."

"*Vi vil også seile sakte,*" an impeccably dressed Norwegian CEO said after standing up and adjusting his horn-rimmed eyeglasses. "We will slow down because that is the proper thing to do."

"*Φυσικά και θα τιμήσουμε την επιθυμία του Coco να μειώσουμε την ταχύτητα των βαποριών,*" said one of the world's most successful self-made Greek shipping magnates after smoothing her short hair.

"My family is from a small island in the deep blue Aegean Sea, where life has always been slow, so the Coco Clause will be a natural atmosphere for us," a Greek scion said after he stood up on the opposite side of the room. "We prefer to go slow. It is nice."

"We will move fast when it comes to slowing down our ships," said an American tanker CEO as she simultaneously composed a text message on her phone.

"You bet we'll do that," concurred her affable CFO, who was standing proudly at her side smiling. "It's the right thing to do!"

Then a towering Belgian oil tanker owner stood up near the front of the room. "We will of course take the Coco Clause because Coco was one of the last shipowners with a big set of —"

"*Guts!*" his younger brother interjected after elbowing his big brother hard in the ribs. "Coco had a big set of *guts!* We admired his *guts!*"

"*Ausgezeichnete Idee, Dr. Einstein!*" a German KG manager announced boldly. "Technically speaking, the VLCCs in my fleet are owned by a syndicate of Bavarian doctors and dentists, but if Dr. Einstein's calculations can be independently verified by no fewer than three experts with appropriate credentials, we might consider making a formal proposal to the board of directors to form a committee to review the procedures required to evaluate a reduction in vessel speed."

"This is so gnarly, dudes!" a Cayman Islands–based dry cargo owner from Korea agreed. "I don't even own VLCCs, but I am totally into this!"

"*Moi aussi,*" said a stylish Parisian shipowner with a heavy accent. "Even my President Macron has considered making a mandatory speed limit, although, okay, I consider this to be the *responsibilité* of the IMO. I just hope no bulk carrier owner, especially *moi*, has to die on a stage at Marine Money in order for the dry cargo ships to slow down."

The initial international commitments to reduce vessel speed were followed by a standing proclamation delivered by half a dozen other VLCC owners who publicly pledged to reduce the speed of their vessels to honor their fallen friend, reduce carbon emissions, and jack up charter rates before the summer slowdown. In an unprecedented act of solidarity, shipowners controlling more than half the world's fleet of 797 supertankers had just agreed to slow down their ships.

"Aw shit," Rocky said slowly as he realized he'd been caught with his Brooks Brothers boxer shorts around his ankles.

If the VLCC owners followed through on their pledge to honor Coco's crazy posthumous plea, the Coco Clause, Rocky was totally and utterly screwed. He was eleven months pregnant with crude oil; he had more than twenty-five cargoes to move in the next sixty days, and he hadn't chartered in a single ship. He had remained dangerously short on tanker tonnage because he had been planning on doing the same sportif thing he always did around this time each year — tempting anxious shipowners with a slightly profitable rate before they left for summer holidays.

The Texan started pecking a message to his chartering desk back in Houston instructing them to immediately start chartering-in ships from the market, but it was too late. Charter rates immediately went up like the business end of a hockey stick as soon as shipowners realized they had just taken control. If supertanker chartering was like a game of tug-of-war, the owners had just pulled the charterers into the mud.

By the time the delegates had started charging hundreds of costly cocktails to Rocky's room, the Tankers International (TI) app began spewing a flurry of push notifications onto tens of thousands of iPhones around the world. More than thirty VLCCs were being negotiated for charter.

It was a bloodbath for the charterers and a rare and badly needed bonanza for the owners. American Refining Corporation had agreed to charter in the 2011-built vessel *Kid Money* from the Arabian Gulf to Singapore, loading July 1 to July 4, at a rate of $85,000 per day. The next fixture involved American Refining Corporation taking the VLCC *Lopart Express* on time charter from West Africa to China at a rate of $110,000 per day.

By the time Rocky's panic-fueled short-covering orgy was over and the TI app finally stopped emitting notifications of "fully fixed" supertankers, American Refining Corporation had taken fifteen ships on charter, squeezing rates to an eye-popping final fixture of $212,000 per day for the ninety-day voyage of a 2005-built VLCC named *Grandma Nona* — $19,000,000 of freight income for a vessel that was worth about $22,000,000.

And that was the beauty of shipping — when operational leverage combined with financial leverage, the creation and destruction of wealth could be more extreme than in any other business in the world. It could be agony or ecstasy when it came to the calculation of personal net worth.

"The faster we can repossess Coco's boats," Rocky DuBois texted Piper Pearl, "the sooner I will be paying myself those hefty charter rates and the sooner we can go after the PG secured by his family's assets."

Chapter 42

As the carnival atmosphere died down and the crowd thinned, Robert found himself sitting alone at the far end of the counter at the Chatham Bar. He had participated in a momentous, history-making event that would cause Coco to not soon be forgotten. And Coco had given a generous gift back to the industry that had given him so much; he had aligned shipowners and thereby given the industry an inspirational reminder of the strength that could be created when they collaborated instead of competed.

But despite all the excitement, the depressing reality was that Coco was gone and the shipping industry would never be the same. An important and exciting era had just come to an end. The industry had lost its pacesetter.

Robert wasn't sure exactly what would happen to Coco's fleet, but he assumed Athena would be unable to complete her purchase and LTO would foreclose. Black Boulder would get wiped out, Rocky would walk away with a massive fortune, and Piper Pearl would shake down Alex and the twins to collect on Coco's personal guarantee.

Robert knew it was time to call Alex and tell her what had happened. She would be shocked and confused. When Robert had spoken to her before Coco died, they had both been jubilant and excited that he had managed to put together a bailout refinancing that would eliminate the PG, reduce the environmental impact of Coco's ships, and create a long-term dividend stream that would keep St. Lucy's Academy afloat forever. It was far and away the most exciting transaction he had ever even heard of.

But that dream had died along with Coco.

Now Robert would have to tell Alex that her husband was dead and she should expect to be served a flurry of papers from the legal and forensic accounting team representing Piper Pearl and LTO Capital. They would make an endless number of demands, from document production to depositions from her and the two "independent directors," Thor and Olav. They would immediately secure the judgement and court orders needed to begin arresting Coco's ships in ports all around the world.

It was exactly the kind of time-consuming and psychologically painful mess Alex didn't want to spend her life cleaning up, but now she would have no choice. Alex had correctly encouraged Coco to get his affairs in order, and Coco had reluctantly agreed, but he started the process too late. An exit strategy had to be put in place long before the exit itself.

Robert drained his beer, took a deep breath, and prepared to call Alex's number. He was going to tell her what had happened, and what would probably happen next. But before he had a chance to dial, an incoming call appeared on the screen of his phone. Camilla Castro Mobile.

"*Camilla?*" he said quietly with his hand cupped over his phone.

"*Hola, Roberto,*" Camilla Castro said in her unmistakable Cuban accent. "*Como estas?*"

"Where are you? You disappeared."

"It was me," she said.

"What was you?"

"I am the one who killed Coco," she said. "I did it."

"What!"

"But there is more to the story, Robert," she said.

"Why are you telling me this?"

"Because I'm going to prison for a long time and there is something I need to tell you," she said.

"Tell me now," Robert said. "I'm listening."

"I need you to come up to Coco's room right now," Camilla said. "I will tell you everything when you get here. I am going to take a shower now," she said. "The door will be open. Please come in."

Chapter 43

When Robert returned to the Presidential Suite, the heavy, white wooden door was cracked open, just as Camilla had promised it would be. The cautious part of him considered going back downstairs and telling one of the NYPD officers everything he knew. But the shipping man in him decided to take his chances.

"Camilla?" he called out through the crack in the door. "Are you in there?"

He waited for her reply, but there was no answer. As Robert listened in the silence, he could hear water running in the shower and a soft murmur in the distance. He couldn't tell if the hushed voices were coming from within the suite itself or from a neighboring room.

After knocking softly, he pushed open the heavy door and tentatively stepped into the darkness. The entrance hallway of the massive suite was at least fifty feet long and covered with white woolen carpet. It was also pitch black. Robert knew that Camilla and Alex had become friends while volunteering at St. Lucy's Academy in Key Biscayne, but he couldn't imagine how a heartwarmingly benign relationship could have possibly resulted in her desire to assassinate Coco in cold blood. It didn't make any sense.

Vinny was a different case altogether. He had 150 million reasons, plus interest, to kill Coco. He also had a reputation for violence when it came to punishing people for financial underperformance.

Robert cautiously baby-stepped down the long, dark hallway. His heart was pounding as he approached the bathroom about midway down. As he got closer, the bathroom door suddenly slammed shut in his face. That was when Robert realized he had probably walked into some kind of a trap. Maybe he was about to be ambushed by Vinny's goons — the ones who had presumably iced Coco during his keynote address.

Despite his fears, Robert soldiered on. It was better to die with honor than live in shame, Coco had once told him. He continued to move slowly down the hallway, passing a series of expressionist paintings as he moved deeper and deeper into the hotel suite. If someone attacked him from the living room or the entrance, Robert wouldn't be able to make it out alive. There was no turning back now.

Chapter 44

When Robert Fairchild reached the end of the hallway and rounded the corner, he struggled to process what he saw. The room in which he had spent the previous two hours had been totally transformed.

The dozens of pieces of furniture previously located all over the enormous suite had been consolidated and rearranged into a summer camp-style semicircle — and relaxing on the daffodil-yellow couch in the center was Coco Jacobsen sipping from a flute full of champagne.

The scene was silent, momentarily frozen in time. Without moving an inch or saying a word, Robert studied the Norwegian's deeply tanned face smiling back at him. Before he took a breath, blinked his eyes, or altered his facial expression, Robert's mind began cycling through a series of emotions like a rebooting computer.

He was shocked that Coco wasn't dead. Relieved that Alex and the boys would still have him in their lives. Angry that Coco had tricked him. And hurt that he was, once again, on the outside of whatever scam Coco was running. But most of all, he was happy. Happy that they would have the opportunity to do more together. Happy that they were getting a second chance — and second chances were a gift.

"I thought you were dead," Robert said.

"Not yet," Coco replied with a laugh. "But I'm definitely getting closer after this trip."

Robert couldn't help but smile when he saw a vitality in the Norwegian's eyes. There was a brightness he had only seen a few times since they met: when he first saw Alex on the video conference call, when he became a father, when he and Robert bought back the bonds at a discount with the bondholder's own money, when he chartered in every available VLCC and squeezed the market so high that Rocky bought him a $150 million yacht. Those had been the most joyous moments in Coco's life. And Robert was witnessing another one. He just didn't yet know exactly why.

"We all thought he was dead," Freddy Fingers said as he slowly stepped out of the bedroom. "Coco's middle school acting career continues to serve him well."

Shortly after Freddy had arrived in the living room, a single-file parade of people emerged from the shadows: Vinny, Gerry, Camilla, Athena, the Chen sisters, Pratap, Gerhard, and the Marine Money crew of Elaine, Tim, and Ike. All the people Robert had arranged to invest in the recapitalization of Scrubber Ships were present. It was like a curtain call.

Robert watched the Norwegian beam with unbridled excitement as the new entrants took seats all around him.

"What's going on here?" Robert asked.

"We're having a closing party," Coco boomed, throwing his arms into the air. "And you are the guest of honor."

"What are we closing?" Robert asked. "Your company?"

"We are closing on the sale of our fleet to Athena — which was made possible by your brilliant refinancing!" Coco announced.

"How did you even know about that deal?" Robert asked.

"Gerry called and told me about it," Coco said, looking over at Gerry, who shrugged his shoulders. "So I suggested that we invite everyone up here for a closing party. I already told Tim that I'm nominating you for Marine Money's 'CFO of the Year' award."

"I don't understand," Robert said. "What the hell is going on here?"

"That was brilliant the way you pried $50 million out of my wife by telling her the money would be donated to St. Lucy's Academy for Maisy's benefit. You're a smarter man than I am."

"You aren't upset about that?" Robert asked.

"Upset? Hell no! You set me free!" Coco exclaimed. "Don't you see? I have finally entered Stage Three — thanks to you Fairchild! It's like Alex told me: When you do a deal for the right reasons, it hardly matters what the terms are."

"But what's he doing here?" Robert pleaded, looking at Vinny. "I thought he was the one who killed you! He *kills* management teams who lose his money!"

"Fake news!" Coco said, exploding with laughter.

"What do you mean *'fake news'?*" Robert asked. "You said it's all over the internet."

"Tell him, Vinny," Coco said, hardly able to hold back his giggling.

"It's all bullshit, Fairchild!" Vinny interjected. "Complete and utter bullshit."

"But..."

"Okay, here's what happened," he said. "A couple years ago, my daughter Theresa wrote a fictional story about me being a psychopath on her Instagram after I refused to buy her a white Range Rover for her sixteenth birthday," Vinny said, chuckling.

"I don't understand."

"Within a couple hours, that fictional story of hers had gone viral."

"Are you kidding?" Robert asked.

"I haven't even told you the funny part yet," he said. "After it happened, I told my PR advisor about it, you know, because I figured we were going to have to launch a campaign to restore my reputation, but they loved it!"

"The PR people loved it?" Robert said.

"That is so lovely and so unexpected!" Freddy howled.

"Yeah, they liked the idea of me having a bad-boy reputation. They thought it would be a good way to distinguish me and Black Boulder from all the other asset managers. They also thought management teams at our portfolio companies might work a little harder and be a bit more realistic if they thought I was going to kill them." He laughed.

"It sure worked on me!" Coco said.

"Before long, the PR firm started making up all kinds of other crazy stories about me and putting them on social media. Pretty soon, people were posting their *own* fake stories. And I loved acting out the part. It became like my alter ego."

"Sounds like Vinny enjoys acting as much as Coco," Gerhard said.

"We're all acting, all the time," Freddy said. "Life is one big act. We each pick the role we want to play and then get into it."

"But what about all the private families and churches who invest in your funds?"

"That part is true," Vinny said. "My wife, Mary, and I are very large donors to the Catholic church. We are deeply religious people, and the archdioceses all over the East Coast use our firm to help them manage their money."

"Now that we've cleared up that little matter, let's all have a drink," Athena said as she pulled a bottle of Dom Perignon from one of the six silver ice buckets that were positioned around the massive suite. "There is a time to work and a time to celebrate," she said, "and you must do both to truly enjoy life."

"Did you arrange this entire charade?" Robert turned to Elaine.

"Oh yes," Elaine smiled. "It was a benefit of Coco's Gold Level corporate sponsorship of Marine Money Week," she added, looking over at Tim and Ike with pride.

"How about the police?" Robert asked.

"They were hotel waiters," Elaine said with a giggle. "A delightful bunch of gentlemen."

"Coco managed to track down the uniforms from a costume shop on Broadway," Ike added.

As Coco beamed at Robert, he took a huge bite of the avocado toast sitting on a plate in front of him, leaving a pale green mustache around his mouth.

"Athena made me try this," Coco said, holding up the trendy toast. "For a plant, it's pretty good. These millennials aren't so bad after all."

"How about the VLCC owners who agreed to slow down?" Robert asked. "Were they in on the charade?"

"You mean the Coco Clause?" Freddy asked, chuckling. "We were in the dark just like you were."

"Don't be angry with me, Robert," Coco said. "There was just no other way to do it."

"Do what?"

"Execute Operation Greta," Coco said. "Do you remember when we were in the cloakroom and I told you I'd come to Marine Money Week to announce that I'd sold my fleet to Athena and tell everyone that I was exiting shipping forever?" Coco asked.

"Yes," Robert said.

"There was something I didn't tell you."

"What's that?"

"When I was a boy working at the gas station in Bergen after my dad died, Hilmar Reksten told me something I never forgot."

"What?"

"He told me that I should try to bring shipowners together in one room and show them that if they work together, they possess the power to change the world."

"And goosing the charter rates didn't come at a bad time for you, either," Freddy chimed in. "We all needed a bit of free cash flow."

"But when did you come up with this plan?" Robert asked.

"A few weeks ago," Coco said. "It all started when Alex wanted me to get rid of the personal guarantee before LTO came after me. I called Athena to see if she could help me get my hands on some ESG money to refinance LTO. One thing led to another and we hatched Operation Greta to help the shipping industry be part of the solution to climate change."

"And then I explained to Coco that there's more money in *solving* the climate problem than there is in continuing to *cause* it," Athena said.

"I hope you are right, Athena, but for now we are doing it because it's the right thing to do," Coco said.

"Just so I am clear, you faked your own death in order to complete a transaction?" Robert asked.

"It was the only way I could think of to get other shipowners to slow down," Coco said. "Plus, I love theater and I thought it would be fun to play the role of an assassinated shipowner and give the delegates at Marine Money Week a show they would never forget."

"It was one of our more unusual final sessions," Tim said.

"I know I'll never forget my first Marine Money Week," Vinny said. "That was quite a performance."

"And there was another reason I did it," Coco said. "A more selfish and immature reason."

"What's that?" Robert asked.

"I wanted to end my career by showing Rocky DuBois that I could still stick it to him one last time, so I will always have nice memories," Coco said.

"What do you mean *'one last time'*?"

"After today, I will no longer be actively involved in the commercial operation of the vessels," Coco said, laughing.

"But you still own a substantial portion of the equity," Robert said. "I pledged the *income* from your shares to St. Lucy's Academy. I didn't actually give them your shares."

"We might as well give them the shares too," Coco said.

"Really?"

"Look, Robert, there comes a time when giving money to people who need it is more fun than just amassing more of it," Coco said. "Besides, everyone in this room agreed to change the name of the company from Scrubber Ships to St. Lucy's Shipping, SLS, so it's only right that the school owns the shares. Gerry, can you take care of that share transfer please?"

"Will do," Gerry said, jotting down some notes on a yellow legal pad.

"But you love chartering ships more than anything," Robert said. "How can you give that up?"

"Because Athena has a bunch of computer scientist friends in Boston who will be using artificial intelligence to charter the vessels from now on," Coco said.

"But you still need a CEO to run the day-to-day business," Robert said. "You will still do that, right?"

"Actually, that's where you come in," Athena said. "All the stakeholders have agreed on that." She looked at Pratap, Rebecca, Roberta, Freddy, Camilla, Vinny, and Gerhard, who were all nodding in enthusiastic agreement. "We think you would be a great CEO."

"*Me?*" Robert gasped. "You want *me* to be the CEO?"

"You're the best, Fairchild," Coco said. "Clearly a lot better than me."

"I'll need to ask Grace if she's okay with that," Robert said.

"Don't worry, she's more than okay with that," Coco said with a laugh. "I called her while you were reading my final wishes. She's definitely ready for you to put on the big-boy pants and get out of the house to go to work every day."

"She said that?"

"What do you say, Fairchild?" Coco asked as he filled Robert's champagne glass. "Are you ready to become a co-CEO? Are you ready to get back on the battlefield?"

"*Co*-CEO?" Robert said. "Does that mean we will do it together again?"

"I'm afraid not," Coco replied. "It's time for this old shipping man to step aside. I'm going to get a long overdue valve job on my heart, and then I am going to take some time off. When I'm ready to get back into action, I'm going to do something that has more incremental utility to me than buying more ships."

"Did you just say *incremental utility?*" Robert repeated.

"Alex taught me this term," Coco said.

"Hold on, are you saying that *I* am *your* exit strategy?"

"Yup," Coco said by way of a sharp inhale.

"Mine too," Vinny said. "I'm shutting down Black Boulder Asset Management and moving to Palm Beach so I can improve my tan while lowering my tax bill."

"As soon as Rocky finds out I'm alive he's going to call the police and tell them to come get me," Coco said. "That's why Vinny and I are actually going to head down to Florida tonight in his weird bus. Ziggy is going to meet me in Miami in the Grady to take me back to Churchill Cay."

"I will also look to recycle fewer vessels and spend more time at my house in Florida," Pratap said. "I will meet the fellows down there next week."

"And as it turns out, Coco, Pratap, and I all play tennis," Vinny said. "We are looking for a fourth for a weekly doubles match. What do you say, Fairchild?"

"It would be a long commute," Robert said. "I don't live in Florida."

"Not yet," Coco said, smiling. "But Grace said she'd be happy to move there. She's already looking for a nice house by the sea, and we are going to open an office."

"But if you're not my co-CEO," Robert said to Coco, "then who is? And *don't* tell me it's Spyrolaki."

"Spyrolaki has become a monk on Mt. Athos!" Coco exploded.

"*Buenos tardes, amigo,*" Camilla said, raising her hand and smiling widely at Robert. "It is me."

Coco rose to his feet and raised his glass of champagne high into the air with one hand and motioned for everyone else to join him with the other hand.

"In Norway, it is customary for the guests to make a nice toast," he added, looking around the group. "Who would like to start?"

"I will," Vinny said, raising his glass. "I want to thank all of you for giving me the opportunity to be part of your family. Shipping isn't easy, but it's the most amazing and authentic industry in the world. Challenges create opportunity for change and all of you are the change I needed in my life."

"Here's to us working together to reduce the CO_2 emissions of the global seagoing fleet," Athena said, raising her glass. "One ship and one ton at a time."

"I want to sincerely thank each of you for supporting St. Lucy's Academy and the work they do helping kids who were dealt a tough hand but never complain about it," Camilla said.

"Here's to ships lifting another billion people out of poverty!" Freddy said, raising his glass.

"Ships change the world," Gerhard agreed. "They always have, and they always will."

"And here's to working as a team," Pratap said, turning to the smiling Chen sisters, who enthusiastically slapped a high-five.

"We are stronger together," Coco said.

"Together," each of them said as they touched glasses.

"Now let's all head downstairs to the tanker party," Coco said, chuckling. "I want to have a word with Rocky DuBois before Vinny and I hit the road."

"Are you going to rub his nose in his failure once again?"

"There's no more time for that kind of thing," Coco said, shaking his head back and forth. "I want to thank him for his generous support of St. Lucy's Academy and invite him to join us on our new adventure."

The End.

MARINE MONEY, INC.